THE JOURNEY PRIZE

STORIES

WINNERS OF THE $10,000 JOURNEY PRIZE

1989: Holley Rubinsky for "Rapid Transits"

1990: Cynthia Flood for "My Father Took a Cake to France"

1991: Yann Martel for "The Facts Behind the Helsinki Roccamatios"

1992: Rozena Maart for "No Rosa, No District Six"

1993: Gayla Reid for "Sister Doyle's Men"

1994: Melissa Hardy for "Long Man the River"

1995: Kathryn Woodward for "Of Marranos and Gilded Angels"

1996: Elyse Gasco for "Can You Wave Bye Bye, Baby?"

1997 (shared): Gabriella Goliger for "Maladies of the Inner Ear"
          Anne Simpson for "Dreaming Snow"

1998: John Brooke for "The Finer Points of Apples"

1999: Alissa York for "The Back of the Bear's Mouth"

2000: Timothy Taylor for "Doves of Townsend"

2001: Kevin Armstrong for "The Cane Field"

2002: Jocelyn Brown for "Miss Canada"

2003: Jessica Grant for "My Husband's Jump"

2004: Devin Krukoff for "The Last Spark"

2005: Matt Shaw for "Matchbook for a Mother's Hair"

2006: Heather Birrell for "BriannaSusannaAlana"

2007: Craig Boyko for "OZY"

2008: Saleema Nawaz for "My Three Girls"

2009: Yasuko Thanh for "Floating Like the Dead"

2010: Devon Code for "Uncle Oscar"

2011: Miranda Hill for "Petitions to Saint Chronic"

2012: Alex Pugsley for "Crisis on Earth-X"

2013: Naben Ruthnum for "Cinema Rex"

2014: Tyler Keevil for "Sealskin"

The BEST of CANADA'S NEW WRITERS

THE JOURNEY PRIZE

STORIES

SELECTED BY
ANTHONY DE SA
TANIS RIDEOUT
CARRIE SNYDER

McCLELLAND & STEWART

ABOUT THE JOURNEY PRIZE STORIES

The $10,000 Journey Prize is awarded annually to an emerging writer of distinction. This award, now in its twenty-seventh year, and given for the fifteenth time in association with the Writers' Trust of Canada as the Writers' Trust of Canada/McClelland & Stewart Journey Prize, is made possible by James A. Michener's generous donation of his Canadian royalty earnings from his novel *Journey*, published by McClelland & Stewart in 1988. The Journey Prize itself is the most significant monetary award given in Canada to a developing writer for a short story or excerpt from a fiction work in progress. The winner of this year's Journey Prize will be selected from among the twelve stories in this book.

The Journey Prize Stories has established itself as the most prestigious annual fiction anthology in the country, introducing readers to the finest new literary writers from coast to coast for more than two decades. It has become a who's who of up-and-coming writers, and many of the authors who have appeared in the anthology's pages have gone on to distinguish themselves with short story collections, novels, and literary awards. The anthology comprises a selection from submissions made by the editors of literary journals from across the country, who have chosen what, in their view, is the most exciting writing in English that they have published in the previous year. In recognition of the vital role journals play in fostering literary voices, McClelland & Stewart makes its own award of $2,000 to the journal that originally published and submitted the winning entry.

This year the selection jury comprised three acclaimed writers:

Anthony De Sa is the author of the fiction collection *Barnacle Love*, a finalist for the Scotiabank Giller Prize and the Toronto Book Award, and the novel *Kicking the Sky*. He attended the Humber School for Writers and Ryerson University. He lives in Toronto with his wife and three children.

Tanis Rideout is the author of the novel *Above All Things* and the poetry collection *Arguments with the Lake*. Her work has been shortlisted for several prizes, including the Bronwen Wallace Memorial Award for Emerging Writers and the CBC Literary Awards. She has an M.F.A. from the University of Guelph. She lives in Toronto, Ontario.

Carrie Snyder is the author of the novel *Girl Runner*, which was a finalist for the Rogers Writers' Trust Fiction Prize, as well as two books of short fiction: *Hair Hat*, a finalist for the Danuta Gleed Award for Short Fiction, and *The Juliet Stories*, a finalist for the Governor General's Literary Award. She lives in Waterloo, Ontario.

The jury read a total of ninety-six submissions without knowing the names of the authors or those of the journals in which the stories originally appeared. McClelland & Stewart would like to thank the jury for their efforts in selecting this year's anthology and, ultimately, the winner of this year's Journey Prize.

McClelland & Stewart would also like to acknowledge the continuing enthusiastic support of writers, literary journal editors, and the public in the common celebration of new voices in Canadian fiction.

For more information about *The Journey Prize Stories*, please visit www.facebook.com/TheJourneyPrize.

CONTENTS

INTRODUCTION

When you're handed ninety-six short stories—a record number of submissions for the Journey Prize—and given a limited amount of time to read, ponder, and form opinions about them, it's hard not to feel overwhelmed and underqualified.

So as jury members we each came up with a plan of attack. We made schedules and swore to read two short stories every morning in order to meet the deadline. We sat down with twenty, thirty, forty pages and several cups of coffee and tried to put everything out of our heads: what our fellow jury members would think of a certain story, what they'd think of any one of us for saying we liked it; what should a Canadian short story look like; what are the criteria for good, for better, for best.

We read and we read and we read.

We slipped into the stories themselves and started to think about what themes, what places, what ideas are preoccupying Canadian writers. Sure, there are lakes and cabins, but there's also the apocalypse and politics with both capital and small *P*'s. There are strange characters and seemingly ordinary ones. There are wrestlers and ghosts—sometimes together in the same story.

Eventually, even those thoughts went away; once we were sucked into a story, all those questions and concerns simply evaporated. It was when we found ourselves longing to talk about a character, or a moment, or a scene, or thinking about a story or a setting while washing the dishes, that it became clear: we'd found it. We found what makes good, better, best—and we hoped the other jury members did too.

But we knew our individual experiences of a story wouldn't necessarily be corroborated by another's experience of the same story. So we were sweating (just a bit) the face-to-face meeting with our fellow jurors, where we'd be obliged to defend our personal favourites. Coming together as a jury forced us to formulate criteria with which to evaluate our choices—forced us, too, to question our assumptions about what ingredients make for a good story. How important, for example, is polish and technical skill? Of course, structural integrity should never be discounted; and yet, and yet. What about the rough stone that knocks a hole in your chest? What about the piece that rambles but pleases the senses?

Does the size of the story matter? Does the depth and ambition of the story matter? Does originality trump a classically elegant construction?

Well.

There's no telling where emotion comes from, but there were times when we read a story and we just knew: this is really fucking good.

What we were looking for underwent subtle changes during our conversation. If a story had a voice we couldn't get enough of; if our curiosity was piqued; if we laughed; if an ending gave us chills—maybe the rawness didn't matter quite so much. How to quantify the mystery, the magic of a smashingly good read?

In the end, we embraced the simple pleasure of discovery.

We wanted, as readers, to encounter stories that were not all the same. Some stories in this anthology challenge, and others charm; some play with language, and others cleave to form; some are raw, some more polished. This collection is proof that a story well-told comes in a variety of shapes, sizes, voices, and forms.

The one thing we wanted most, and that unified us in our discussion, was the element of surprise in discovery. Good fiction should surprise, should be something you cannot turn away from. The twelve stories we've selected for this anthology are full of surprises. These writers surprised us with language and structure, they experimented with voice and dazzled us with the unexpected.

Perhaps the greatest surprise can be found in how these stories affected us. Some of the stories grabbed us from the very beginning, while others rippled out like water disturbed by a pebble. Regardless of how they took hold, they all engaged us with their richness—the layered and nuanced telling of that story. The more we discussed their individual merits, the more we appreciated how beautiful or smart or gritty these pieces were.

The stories we've chosen are all well-crafted pieces that tantalized us, made us question what we think we know, and provoked us with unfamiliar worlds. The sheer diversity of styles and the breadth and depth of subject matter showed us that literary journals and magazines in this country play an extraordinary role in shaping Canadian literature.

This whole process has confirmed for us that the short story form is flourishing.

Expect pleasure. Expect delight. Expect surprise. Expect these twelve writers to emerge as some of this country's most interesting voices.

Anthony De Sa
Tanis Rideout
Carrie Snyder
April 2015

LORI McNULTY

FINGERNECKLACE

Peppermint saliva lips, two numb bums. Lick, stamp, stick around the salvaged oak table in the common room where Joe and Gus compete on Fish Friday. First one to lick and label five hundred envelopes gets his pick of the fresh cod Mrs. B will serve tonight with garlicky roasted red peppers.

"All good, my jumblies?" Mrs. B scans the mail metropolis forming at Gus's elbows. "Break for fresh air?"

Joe stomps his feet. Gus pinches a perfect three-fold letter, head low. "Suit yourselves."

Mrs. B has been group home supervisor since her husband accidentally shot himself eight years ago. Now she pitches life-buoys in a sinking, four-storey heritage house in Greektown that Gus calls the HMS Shitstorm. Tomorrow, when she's flat-lining on the couch with a migraine, he'll try to kiss her on the lips.

Joe flicks the long braid that dangles down his back like a fat black squirrel tail. Whenever he squirms, Gus feels the rodent claw up his own spine.

"Don't steal my Cheerios," Gus howls, slapping Joe's hand away from the cereal bowl between them. Gus pulls the mournful face that makes him look like a plumpish fifty-plus, though he's only thirty-six.

"You chew like an Indian," Gus shouts.

"You stink like catfish," Joe replies, stomping his lizard-skin boots. His face is braided with sun and age, soft as kid leather.

Marlee enters, slumps down next to Gus, who is quietly nibbling at the edge of an O. She and Gus grew up on the wrong side of sane so they're next-door neighbours. Nuthouse Knobs. Crackpot Criminals. *The Deranged.* Marlee came in off the streets, the thing men fucked behind dumpsters. Now, she's on low-grade watch at the home. Not that she'd ever go through with it, but one rainy afternoon she swallowed a jar of paint thinner just to wash the stench from her throat. The last time Gus acted out—packed his life in a duffel and hitched the Don Valley to his brother's place—Donny sent him back on the Greyhound from Peterborough, pronto. That was two summers ago. He's been good all year.

Mrs. B returns, pointing to her watch. Gus plucks two skinny whites from his silver pillbox. He'll be slow-mo soon, bleary by dinner.

The rice is one item on the plate. The rice is yellow and smells like buttered bones. The red peppers curl, sodden and sad in their oily, garlic swim. At the dinner table, Gus pokes at his rumpled fish, feeling his organs flip.

"Last time," Mrs. B says, rising from the table. She fixes Gus a peanut butter sandwich she glues together with clover honey. With a quick flash of her blade, she splits the sandwich four ways. Dropping the plate before Gus, she taps the table.

Gus is squeezing his head. He can see his mother's ash fingers tap-tap the ashtray. She is butting the stub out, covering her ears. Can't stop the blue-splitting shrieks.

"Come on, Gus," Mrs. B taps again. He shakes his head, tries sorting patterns on his mother's peeling yellow linoleum.

"You need your energy. Donny's coming tomorrow," she adds.

Donny's greasy jeans are tucked into oil-stained work boots in the living room of the care home. He checks his watch, pacing. Crew's on site. Fuck. Shit. Piss. He's got the engineer's change orders. Cost overruns. Goddamn job is killing him. Looking up he sees Gus lumbering down the stairs still wrapped in his white terry cloth robe. Big as a hollowed oak, premature belly spread. Donny shakes a full prescription bottle at him.

"Don't skip out on me, Gus. You know what happens."

Donny watches his younger brother's eyes dart around the room, taking inventory. He sees Gus freeze at the sight of his work boots.

Gus bunches the terry cloth belt in his palms, squeezes, lets the fuzzy ball drop to the floor. He yanks it back up like a fishing line, absently lets it drop. Donny pats the couch cushion, coaxing his brother over.

"Look, Gus, we can't do our usual pizza run this aft. Got a date with a wrecking ball."

Gus bunches the belt in his lap, blinks wet, wandering tears. Donny wraps his arms around his big old stump of a baby brother, tries to hold the roots down, keep the disease from spreading. Root rot. Runs in the family.

Gus sobs into his brother's neck. "I want to come home."

Donny holds him close, tries to stop twenty years of trembling. Five years, six major episodes, a thousand pills and private dreams between them.

He can see it in his brother's puffy eyelids, the grey, candle-drip skin. New meds are doing a number. He looks more like her now. Same mess of auburn hair, same staple-sized crease below his lip. Donny pictures his mother seated on the stairs, the dim glow of her after-dinner cigarette, eyes going in all directions. And Gus at nine years old, past the biting and moodiness, withdrawing into his mumble mouth, doing after-dinner dishes in the pyjamas he's worn all day. While Donny fucks off to his buddy Cheevie's house for double dessert. Cheevie has Nintendo on the set, a mother who never once tried to pry open their bedroom door with a chef's knife. Smooth exit, just like the old man.

Donny loosens the belt around his brother's waist. "Gus, you can't come home. You know Pinky's happy as horses with the house all quiet."

"Fuck Pinky," Gus says, turning away abruptly.

What's he supposed to do? Gus left them broke, wandering for days then begging for money on their doorstep, sending his wife for depression pills. Pinky won't let any more of his bad blood in. Last time they took Gus back, he sold Pinky on the internet. Amazing how many men will drop the price of a used car on a mail-order Chinese bride. Gus posted her picture on a dodgy-looking website advertising Exotic Lucky Asian Brides. Pinky was wrapped in white-and-pink wedding chiffon, a purplish-pink orchid in her hair, something bite-sized dangling on the end of a shrimp fork. Gus wrote that she was petite, submissive, ornamental. Some old goat paid Gus $1,400 cash on a subway to share his life with "Pinky Cameroon Sparkle."

Cheap Chinese takeout, Gus said to Donny, winking, flashing his wild smile, as he handed over a wad of hundred dollar bills in the hallway. Donny could tell Gus was on a mounting high, heading from glue-headed to God in a few hours. Meds were sparks going off, Gus had told Donny. Light screaming through his skull, flash fireworks, followed by the inevitable hours of blind panic. Gus said he was only trying to pitch in. Pinky was ready to move out.

Gus pulls his belt from his housecoat, tying it like a tourniquet across his bicep. The familiar phrase rattling in Donny's skull. Think you can save your brother? You can't even save your marriage, useless fuck.

"Pinky will come around," Donny says, trying hard not to look restless. "Her dad's covering my new equipment loan."

Gus starts to flap his arms, a whooping crane in a stiff wind. Donny holds his brother's arms down. Gus wrenches away, rising to his feet.

"Pinky's got a face like the back of a shovel."

"Gus," Donny orders, trying to wrap his arms around his brother's aches, hold his burden tight.

Gus steps away, shouting in a faux-Asian accent. "Twyme, twyme, me, moneybackgawantee." He flaps and turns away again. "Fuck Pinky."

Donny met Pinky in one of those mahogany-and-brass steakhouses with the deer antlers mounted above the bar. She was serving rib-eye steaks to men who chewed the fat over real estate deals. Turns out her dad owned the place. Owned three apartment complexes and a dry-cleaning franchise. Her family was an empire. His was a broken tenement. She danced through the room, pale blue moons dusting her eyelids, still as a watercolour. He knew he wouldn't be worthy but he asked her out anyway, tumbling over his syllables. On their fifth date, he made a nest of his long arms, cupped her bird bones inside, called her My Lily Hands.

Donny pulls Gus's hand away from his dismal face, turns to see Joe pound down the stairs toward them.

"Get away Tomahawk Chuck," Gus shouts, seeing Joe approach.

Joe grabs Gus firmly by the terry cloth shoulder—"Smoke break. It's noon polar bear. Let's migrate"—leading him toward the front door.

Donny moves in to help, but Joe raises a dismissive hand, motioning for him to stay put. Gus is led to the front door. Donny hurries to stuff an envelope filled with pizza money inside Gus's housecoat. Joe shoots him a puzzled look, stomping his feet.

Native guys float, they had told Donny. Mohawk or Cree, toeing twenty-storey beams, steady rivet gun in their hands. It was all bullshit. Joe preferred doing the ground metal framing but left to repair a support brace on the third floor. Crew said he must've had a rubber backbone the way he bounced down in one piece. Whatever was on his mind back then never came back. Joe was on his own so Donny found him a place with Mrs. B. Once Joe settled in, Donny figured it would be good enough for family so he dropped Gus off with two green garbage bags and a blue duffel bag, two days after his brother had set fire to their shower curtain. Abandon ship! Blame Pinky? Sure. He was fucking free.

On site two hours later, the front-load driver shouts down to Donny: Okay to take another run? Donny nods, directing traffic. Raising its toothy bucket, the driver steers the front loader through wet mud, shattering glass on a downward strike. Whining like a beaten dog, the low-rise splits in half. Burying his toe in sharp debris, Donny thinks—this is the job. Build an extension off the house to give Gus his own entrance. Donny returns to his truck, roughs up his estimate pad, knowing the numbers won't add up. Pinky will never go for it. Her parents would pull the loan. He's nothing but a low-level contractor. Pinky's mother is a princess. Her tiara's halfway up my ass, he thinks. Fuck it. He'll find the money. Set Gus up in some studio apartment close by. Take him out twice a week, get his meds on track.

Donny knows the drill. Pour concrete slab, pound the building out, pad an invoice or two. Take his commission off the top. Throw me an extra buck, he'll tell the subs, I'll throw in the townhouse complex too.

Things Gus will do for a dollar:
Clean the kitchen floor with a soapy grey mop.
Commit to Cheerios in the morning and finish them.
Buy Marlee and himself cigarettes when she gets her Thursday cheque.

Gus pulls two turtle blues from his pillbox when Donny leaves, his arms heavy rubber fins. He lumbers to the bus stop, watches the number 12 roll up. He stubs out his cigarette and climbs the stairs. Staring down at the fare box, he watches the coins tickle the steel throat, then spit out a paper tongue at him.

"Alberto's Pizza," Gus slurs like a drunk directing a cab.

Brusquely, the driver motions him to the back of the bus. Gus sits in the last row, opens his pillbox, swallows another. Blearily, he watches Bookbag get on. She sits up front with a friend but waves back. Gus can't lift his sweaty hand. They rumble on for ten minutes until Alberto's red neon lights up. He yanks the cord.

At Alberto's, an alert hostess ushers Gus to a back table. He's blinking fast. Skipping ropes and twigs start to stretch and snap in his head. Flat bottom spinning between the temples, Gus stabs a fork into his leg so he's clear enough to order his usual Hawaiian Special. When the silver tray arrives, a large pie, thick crust smeared with pineapple and ham, he dips a wedge into his Coke. He orders another coffee, adds six sugars, then pockets the spoon. The table is pivoting, but he needs to piss.

Along the corridor in the restaurant, Gus counts gold diamonds fringing the emerald carpet all the way to the men's room. He teeters before the urinal next to a bank of stainless-steel sinks. The burly man next to him bounces on his toes. Watching him, Gus bounces too. The man zips. Gus pulls slowly at his fly. The man calls him something Gus can't grasp. Gus grabs his own crotch, fumbling furiously.

"Pull that faggot shit on me again, you're dead." The stout man drops his shoulder and drives Gus hard into the mirror before walking out the door.

"Don't you cry," Gus says, pounding his thigh on the bathroom floor. "Don't."

He weeps silently, then rising, pictures himself racing up the stairs of his mother's house, hands locked around a pair of scissors. He digs his keys into his thighs.

Gus enters the middle stall, unfolds the tabloid paper left behind on the floor, and drapes it across his lap. When he's through emptying his loose bowels, he scoops out his own feces with the newspaper.

"There's stuff in here that could bring me down," he mumbles, folding the mess up on his way back to the table.

When he returns, the manager is waiting to escort him out. Rain flooding the streets is gunfire in his head. He slaps at his skull while he waits for an overcrowded bus to stop.

Donny thwacks his muddy work boots against his truck. His cell is ringing the special tone. He holds up a finger to the impatient engineer.

Gus has left his shit (Mrs. B says "excrement") on the table at Alberto's Pizza. Donny listens, but the phone cuts out so he asks her to repeat it. She does. "I can't just leave," he shouts at the phone. "I'm the fucking guy in charge," he says, instantly regretting his tone. He punches the truck door, feels acid backing up in his throat. Donny digs his boots into the muck. Mud sucks his ankles until his boots disappear to the top red stripe of his wool socks.

Beetles storming his lids, something loose crawling. Riding back to the HMS Shitstorm from Alberto's Pizza, Gus paws his eye socket, fist deep, until he sees lime-coloured streaks. He slides the bus window open and breathes, the stench of sweaty fish seat making his stomach churn.

At the next stop, the bus door opens with a shudder. Bookbag waves from the aisle, then sits down next to him.

She's dressed in black, wishbone thin, prickly teenaged forehead. Gus watches her smooth back her raven hair, bunch a ponytail she never fastens. Her fingertips sift and sort, thunderbolts, won't stop moving light around.

Gus pockets his balled fist. He tries to focus on the brittle slogans screaming across her tits: *No blood for oil. Draft beer, not war. Fuck yoga.* Seeing the bulge in her breast pocket, he taps two fingers to his lips. She slides out a Player's Light and hands it to him.

"You okay, Gus?"

Gus drives his palm heel into his cornea. Her voice, too shrill. He closes his droopy lids, makes a wish, opens—she's still there. Emma twisting the curling iron at her cheek. An orange ball bursts from the rod, ashes dusting her gingham blouse. A mouth opens—a thousand night birds shrieking.

Gus pulls out the spoon he's stolen from the restaurant, licks the metal, and sticks it to his chin.

"That's cool," Bookbag says, "like a shiny goatee." She rakes her fingers through her tangled hair.

Gus can't stop the screams, sees all the bones in Emma's cheek shattered. "Savemesavemesavememoneybackguarantee." Gus's mouth begins running on bus rhythm.

Bookbag pulls Gus's hand from his face, gently turns it over. His whole body vibrates while she smoothes the padded skin. After a while, Gus's baggy body slumps down in its seat. Together they look out the rain-spattered window, watch the hanging duck breasts glimmer along the gluey sidewalks of Chinatown's Dim-Sum Drive.

"This is me," Bookbag says, rising uncertainly. "Gonna be all right?"

Gus hauls her back down. She stiffens when he slaps something into her hand. A wad of bills crackles in her palm. Gus is rocking in his seat again.

"Okay, okay, I'll keep this safe for you," she says uncertainly. "Four more stops then pull the cord. See you tomorrow?"

Gus watches Bookbag climb down the stairs, light up, blow a silver plume through the open doors. He fans the sulphur sting, feeling sharp metal boxes clang and clip the corners of his skin.

Mrs. B is waiting for Gus in the doorway, knowing better than to make him talk. She leads him back to his room and settles him down on the bed.

"Trouble comes," she says, patting his hand, then pulling a tight arm around his torso. "Blame genes, or blame Jesus, just don't let it get you down." She rises to fetch water for his pills. "Better tomorrow."

Gus lies with his back against the wall, watches the floor beams split, the light shattering him into a thousand pieces.

Two heel-clicks, three stomps down the hall before lights out. When Joe knocks on his door, Gus doesn't answer. Gus swallows two white pills, letting the night swarm slowly under his chin. Metal flies and bounces from the top of his skull. Knife-prick fingertips until his hands go numb.

By 3 a.m., he is still wide awake. His knocking head won't quiet. He decides to slip downstairs to the kitchen, grabs his favourite apple-green cereal bowl from the cupboard. Mrs. B is lying on the living room couch, a wet facecloth across her forehead. Gus fills his bowl with Cheerios, tucking the box under his arm. Creeping past Mrs. B, he sees her hand jerk on her belly. He bends over, kissing her lightly on the lips. Her eyelids flutter but she hardly moves. Padding back up to the third floor, he pushes on to the end of the hall, closing the bathroom door behind him.

From the back of the toilet tank, he removes the pills he's been collecting all year. He drains the last of the Cheerios box, mixes the blue turtles and O's with water, watches the candies sink and toss in their oat sea. He tosses in another few. He pulls the restaurant spoon from his khakis' pocket and stirs the mess before shovelling it into his mouth, craving a long, cement-headed sleep.

Mrs. B is clutching the cordless when Donny arrives. The ambulance attendants are balancing Gus on the stretcher as they descend the stairs, Joe yelling at them to hurry.

Donny orders them to put his brother down in the living room. Reluctantly, they set their burden down. With all his force, he lifts his brother's torso from the stretcher, works his way down the arms, torso, feels for the broken soul bones.

Sirens silent, he watches the ambulance roll down the street.

Donny motions he'll be right back, needs to get the cell from his truck to call his wife. He closes the front door, making sure he hears the solid click.

In the truck, he steers straight for an after-hours bar. Head swimming in booze, he drives until he remembers.

On his way home from his buddy Cheevie's house, pie-stuffed and pleased with himself after winning drunken Pong on Nintendo. Light on in his sister's room above the garage. When the acrid stench reaches him in the hallway, he mounts the stairs two by two.

From the doorway, Donny sees Emma on her knees, hair locked in a curling iron set flat against her skull. Smoke streams from the brittle strands of Emma's hair. Everyone is screaming. Lying next to his sister, Gus is face down, his right hand closed around a pair of scissors to set Emma free.

Head swimming with Cheevie's dad's cheap rye, he watches Emma punch out weakly with her left arm. His mother is giving Emma the old Fingernecklace from behind, her hands locked around his sister's fragile windpipe. Donny touches his throat. So drunk he can hardly move.

It won't stop.

Not when Emma falls forward, face striking the bed stand.

Not when his mother tears the electric cord from the wall, lifts the ceramic lamp overhead.

Parked on the demolition site, Donny sucks in a chestful of diesel. The smell comforts him, in a quiet way, as dawn breaks between glass and steel, bathing Yonge Street in fractured yellow hues. He bends to tighten his bootlaces, then rising, deliberately smashes his face against the side-view mirror.

Gus and Mom and he and Gus and Pinky and Joe and the sharp, bottomless world tucks a rusty hook in his mouth, hoisting him over the city twenty storeys. His swooning face a wrecking ball, Donny cracks a fat-lipped grin, the momentum in him growing, knowing now he'll never be able to avoid the crash.

K'ARI FISHER

MERCY BEATRICE WRESTLES THE NOOSE

G host-Mom has been hanging around me all evening, smoking her cigarette. When she was alive she always had a pack of her *fer shit sake sticks* nearby in case of an emergency. Now that she's dead, a machine-rolled Du Maurier hangs endlessly from her lips. She sucks on it pathologically. In the last few months, I've yet to see her need to light a new one.

"Why are you *here*, Mercy Beatrice?" she says. Her see-through body bristles up like a used scrub brush. "I told you to stay away from this place."

Here is Bodie, British Columbia. Bodie used to be a self-sufficient whistle-stop along the Canadian Pacific Railway during the lure of Gold Mountain. When the rush was over, they flooded 920 hectares of forest to power the twin turbines running the aluminum smelter on the other side of the cordillera. Now all that remains is my father, his junkyard that operates off scrap brought in on the train, and Pauley.

I know she isn't really angry because I'm in Bodie; she just wants to know why I'm hanging around my father. My mother's ghost is a bit like the ones in those Biblical bully-fests she used to read to me at bedtime. Her voice comes from a bottomless pit, and there's a warning in it, like she's asking for some sort of repentance, but I don't know what for. What does she expect me to do? Air-grip her legs and squirt tears of supplication out of my eyes? She's on repeat: Why are you *here*? I told you to stay away from *this place* . . . over and over. When she sucks in, the fiery cherry burns off her fog-body and evaporates her mouth.

The first time I saw her here, wind was tearing through the rusted carcasses in the junkyard, gathering speed off the reservoir. It was a few days after I'd arrived and she surfaced suddenly, as if she had always been there, but the wind took away the haze, leaving behind only the stubborn: the rocks, the trees, my mom. Immediately, cold goosebumps prickled up along my arms, but when I went toward her, there was nothing—no smell of her tar soap or trace of acrid cabbage soup on her breath. I cautiously waved my hand through her torso. She just stared and drained her cigarette like she always did when she thought I was being theatrical.

I have to admit, Ghost-Mom looks amazingly accurate, even down to the wiry dark hairs on her forearms, the muscular face, and the thin lipless dash of her mouth. She's always dressed in her professional wrestling costume, the one she wore when she performed as "The Polish Poo-Bah," with the blue tights and a flowing shirt with a wide red belt cinched around her diaphragm where her breasts should be. Her cape, with its carefully embroidered gold crucifix, falls flat against her back and its stiff collar rises behind her head like an old carapace. All I had when I got to Bodie was my suitcase and my dad's old trading card, fished out of the garbage from one of Mom's tossed cigarette packs years ago. The picture was taken around the time my parents met during a mixed tag-team event, when he was one of the world's most feared heavy-weights. He had just won the 1940 Midwestern title. His name, "Little Lew," sashays across the stiff paper and under-neath my father looks out like an Adonis.

When I handed over the money I got from Mom to buy the train ticket, I slipped Dad's card into her empty cold-cream tin to take with me and held tight. All I knew of him was what was found on the back of that card: 6 feet 2 inches tall; 140 consecutive wins; 350 pounds, plus an anecdote describing how he once jumped off a balcony with a noose tied around his neck while he whistled "Yankee Doodle"—and lived due to the impressive strength of his 22-inch neck.

I stepped off the train and waltzed up to the junkyard with a dry knot stuck like a hairball in the heart. I couldn't believe that I was about to finally meet my long-lost father. That I had made it here on my own. Most of all, I was relieved to have finally escaped the confines of the Old Ursine School for Orphans, its endless laundry chain, and the nuns with their arthritic charity. Even Mom in her last days of fighting TB was more chipper than Sister Patricia.

My father, it turns out, is pink-jowled and hog-necked. His pants are usually held up with twine suspenders tied with multiple knots because he doesn't bother to undo when he goes to bed at night; he just cuts his way out with a knife. Pauley told me soon after I arrived that my father downs a daily spoonful of brandy mixed with strychnine, his old manager Blumenkranz's prescription for broken collarbones and bent knuckles.

That first time we met he looked at me through milky eyes, perplexed, his forehead wrinkles lapping the shore of his balding head. He smelled like old Mr. Armchair Antoni from the front lobby of our last apartment. And he must have seen it in my face—the sheer disappointment. I tried, unsuccessfully, to mask its presentation. Oh great, I thought. Then again, who did I think would ever marry The Poo-Bah?

"It's your long-lost daughter," I chirped, spreading my arms.

"Daughter?" he grunted, stroking his chin with knuckleless fingers.

I grinned, but even to me my smile felt rubbery and huge and my eyes red. Despite my efforts, I could feel one eye twitching wildly under the weight of his stare. There I was, one tiny moment away from jelly-lipped. I grinned a little harder.

"What's wrong with your face, kid?"

I get the feeling that there aren't many moments in life where what you think is going to happen works out exactly like how you'd plan it. That by the time you comprehend the sinkhole reality of it, it's generally too late. It wasn't like I thought my father would appear in a golden glow and sweep me into his arms. But I didn't think the first thing he'd do after he met me was reach down and grab a 200-pound yard sow snuffling around his feet like a puppy, and then, in some sort of potential display of mentorship, jack it over his head.

"This pig's been here since she was just a two-pound runt," he slurred. Underneath the mass of his brow, his eyes looked small and sad. He did a slow, shaky turn and, as if to affirm that doggedness is the main key to worldly success, said, "I've just made it a habit of lifting her a little *every day*."

And then there's that devastating moment when you see that you may have based a choice on shaky foundations.

Pauley and I live a life of routine. We slop the hogs, meet the weekly train, separate scrap, and every night after dinner, warm in the heat of the potbelly stove, we practise wrestling. My father is astonished Mom never taught me the trade. He tells me about when they used to wrestle in theatres and how, afterwards, men in lapels lingered about in lobbies, twisting their moustaches about the most recent article in the *New York Times* Sports section.

"It's a shame and a pity," he says, "that wrestling has become about gimmicks: the mud, the rings full of fish."

"Wrestling is the oldest sport in the world."

"Did you know that Abraham Lincoln was once a pro wrestler?"

My father's erratic.

He'll spend a full day teaching Pauley and me how to do a flying mare and then the rest of the week out in the wallow by the tire pile, checking his precious pigs for drooling ear, snot balls, and hoof sunburn. He teeters in late for dinner, knocking over cutlery with his elbows.

And it's true Mom rarely let me watch her wrestle. Instead, I'd spend the entire time down in the dressing room, where I could prance around some made-up ring in a spangled outfit with knee-high slipper boots. Mom used to say I had a rich fantasy life.

My father tells me wrestling is more than carnival enter-tainment, or even good versus evil, or Chief Chewchiki versus Cowboy Bill, or the Red Skulls versus the Flying Frenchmen, or Clops Cannibal versus the Alaskan Strongman. There's no limit, my father insists, to physical development. Pauley slurps up this information like it's sweetened cornwater.

Daily exercise, he says, should be as regular as eating. A high degree of physical development can lead to a real pleasure in the mere act of living. He appears to be completely blind to the spectacle of his own strength; the tricks and shows of grandeur he submits Pauley and me to on a regular basis. "Look at me tear this deck of cards in half." "Look at me scis-sor this bag of grain in half with my thighs." "Look at me drive this iron spike into a railway tie with the sole of my foot." Yet, I admit, there is something wondrous about learning to leverage my weight, and my muscles, I can tell, are sticking firmer to my bones than ever before. Wrestling might be in my blood, but there's still a lot to perfect. I have my mother's small compact body, which my father says may have once won her the Women's Championship, but only because of her savage temperament.

Pauley, I am told, was abandoned on the hood of a gutted Model A parked by the lean-to off the kitchen. My father said Pauley's parents must have seen the cross-like gold-mining derrick, thought the lean-to was a church, and left him think-ing that nuns would flock out and coo over a baby. Right. I guess he hasn't noticed that the yard is the only place for miles with electricity. The derrick is clotted with creatures my father welded together during some sort of artistic flare-up.

There's a half-horse with radiator ribs and a monkey with flat-tened bean-can feet. Years ago he found a hubcap with a face-like rust pattern so he made a crankshaft body, stuck the hub on, and pulled his "dazzling masterpiece" up the rotting 100-foot-tall derrick using nothing but a pulley and the strength of his 26-inch biceps. Now it dangles from the boom chains in the middle. Pauley says it looks a bit like a bearded Jesus; I think it looks more like Abdullah the Turk. But it does tower like a beacon over the pines that grow on anything not water-swamped around here.

Pauley's one of those quiet types who is always angry. He does jackrabbit jumps to conclusions. The minute I mention anything about Chicago, he says, "If you hate it here so much, why don't you just leave?" I'm pretty sure that by living with my father, Pauley has been home-schooled in nothing but everlasting solitude. I can't even imagine what it was like around here when he was a baby and my *father* had to look after *him*.

And he's wrong. I actually like it here. Sure, the town is boarded-up storefronts with dandelions growing out of con-crete cracks. When it rains, discharge from a nearby flume runs down Main Street, creating a muddy stream that Pauley calls "The Gran' Canal." But behind the junkyard is a forest with sunny patches of billowing trees and bushes of ripe ber-ries. The morning air is thick with mist and if I walk close to the flood-line below Sandy Mountain, chunks of shoreline break off and sink slowly into the water where it melts into a sugary cloud. A few weeks after I arrived, I took the rowboat out and looked down into the reservoir. I expected a grave-yard of dead trees, with stuff bubbling at the top like on the

Chicago River below our old airtight apartment behind the meat-packing plant. But the water was clear and the submerged trees green, their branches waving with the lapping of the lake as if in a breeze. I cupped my hands for a drink: pine perfume! That night I stayed awake until I heard the morning chatter of palm-sized chipmunks.

On windy nights, the breeze comes in off the lake, howls through the junkyard, and starts my father's Jesus rocking against its chains like it's trying to get bucked off. Pauley and I train, but it's hard not to get distracted. Ghost-Mom's hanging out in the corner, oblivious to the grunting aspects of Pauley's internal massage exercises, swaying to the screeching effigy as if it's music. Pauley's got his mouth cinched tight, his puny fists are balled up, and he's trying to force a big breath of air out of his abdomen while resisting at the same time. Around the time his face turns red and his eyeballs pop out, he starts rubbing and squeezing his stomach muscles with both hands.

"This is the key to controlling the internal organs," my father told us during our lesson last week. "The best way to train for a punch to the stomach."

I generally don't look forward to one-on-one matches against Pauley. Even though we are about the same age and he's smaller than me, he thrashes like an animal afraid of water, and he's hard to pin down. Plus, last night I told him about Ghost-Mom. Now, every time I look at him he pretends he's rubbing a lamp, then purses his lips, lets out a poof like a dry fart, and his eyes get all big and round like there's a genie bobbing in the air somewhere in front of him. I guess what can you expect from someone whose own mother left him on the hood of a Model A? It's the most common car in the yard; my father once told me it was possibly the biggest junker of all time.

"Seen anything phantam*tastic* today?" Pauley grins, his face still flushed from the exercises.

"You're going to regret that."

Halfway through, Pauley's almost got me into a Lesson 4: a Beell's Waist Hold. I'm on my hands and knees and he's behind me with both arms wrapped around my middle. I can feel his scrawny ribcage pressed against my lower back—he's too far forward. Then my father lurches in and starts clapping from the sidelines. He stomps his feet on the floor and slurs, "Mercy! Get up and fight."

I back up and grasp Pauley's foot, pulling it forward even more. My father's leaning in expectantly, his stomach straining desperately against his twine suspenders. It's difficult to believe that his signature Little Lew Double Leg Takedown once pinned the best heavyweights in the territories. He was once an undefeated champion! He had a Triple-A card!

And then somewhere deep inside of me, I sense a cache of strength, wiggling and faint. I grab Pauley's wrist and raise his foot at the same time; he pitches ahead and lands face down on the dirt floor. A classic roundabout! I throw my head into his armpit and secure him in a half nelson. With one hand wrapped under his arm and the other around his neck from behind, I can feel his shaky intake of breath. He's started crying. Pauley's snot-whistling into the ground, his back quivering. I ease up and he jumps free and runs out of the room.

—

It's about a half-hour walk up to the powerhouse chamber that controls the water flow into the turbines and Ghost-Mom is trailing me the entire time, puffing through the trees and picking up speed like a steam engine. The chamber was blasted into the heart of Boer Mountain. It takes a moment for my eyes to adjust so I can make out the engraved aluminum plate screwed just inside the entrance: *110 ft. long, 80 ft. wide, 118 ft. high parabolic arch. A wonder of modern engineering.* It's generally empty except for a couple of times a year when workers from Smeltersite come to Bodie for an inspection. Pauley always comes here when he wants to be alone. Ghost-Mom never ventures past the chamber mouth; she must know what's going on downstream. I think ghosts are like tiny drops of water clinging to a riverbank, waiting for gravity to push them in. She must sense the penstocks, the 900-metre vertical drop, and the dark 16-kilometre tunnel out to the wide-open ocean on the other side.

I walk in and spot Pauley lying on his back in the dirt, staring up at the smooth ceiling covered in spiderweb veins of dusty quartz. The wind is dead in here, with a cotton-ball silence, an airtight egg-ness like an ear-change in pressure.

"Your dad says your mom thought her shit smelled like roses," he says, sitting up. His voice is tough, but it's hard not to notice there's envy in it too.

Ever since I got here, Pauley's been telling me variations on the same theme. I'm pretty sure he has some sort of care-meter going on in his mind and that I'm coming out on top. And I just haven't got around to explaining to him that I already know all about my mom, that it's impossible to be with someone your entire life and not be cognizant of every tiny thing—like how Mom hated umbrellas and always said "No" when she actually meant, "It's all right."

When Mom used to catch me sneaking out, she'd make me stand with her hardcover Bible held out in front of me, the one with at least four thousand extra Polish verses, until my arms fell off. I think she thought that just by holding it I'd catch something, like the bums who skimmed the river by our apartment for lard floaters. She'd slap at it with her calloused palm so I'd almost drop it. "Dis," she would say. "Dis is love letter. To you, from Him." Then she would motion up with her cigarette butt to somewhere beyond the yellowed ceiling, the knocking water pipes, and the thousands of pigeons that spent their day crap-shellacking the roof of our complex, where the wild blue yonder was. Mom did everything with a purpose that reeked of faith. And she made it her job that I should never stop knowing the sacrifices she made for me. She didn't seem to notice that I was just a kid and I was always rushing to keep up.

"Father says Blumenkranz is coming in tomorrow," I say to Pauley.

"I know. I can already smell his breath."

The air in the chamber smells a lot like Blumenkranz's halitosis. Years ago, Mom told me how he left Europe by hiding in the boiler room of a theatre-company ship heading to the U.S. Then he used his contacts to deliver the greatest wrestling villain of all time, the Russian Ogre.

"THE UGLIEST WRESTLER IN THE WORLD! WOMEN FAINT! MEN SHOUT! CHILDREN CRY!" Pauley yells into the chamber like he's reading my thoughts.

"What are you doing here, anyway?" he says.

"Fresh air."

Pauley snorts and we both laugh.

I put my arm around Pauley and squeeze. He freezes, his breathing stops like he's so confused his only response is to play dead. I squeeze harder, but there's nothing worse than trying to hug someone who is trying to tell you with every muscle to bug off.

"Pauley," I croon into the empty chamber. "You unfortunate child."

The minute I say it, I know that I'm mimicking the Old Ursine nuns. And I realize that Pauley's following my father's ideas about fundamental defense. You never know, he says, when you might take a chair to the back of the head. Suddenly Pauley's at me, pinning me to the ground. I tap out but he ignores it and presses me harder against one of the rock walls. I know I could flip him over and pin him in a clutch, but I just let him hold me there until he quits doing noodle-arm swings at my body, lets out a big rough wad of air, and stomps out of the chamber. My teeth are coated in dust. I can hear the skeletal clack of bare aspen branches outside the entrance. I roll toward it and above the purple mountain ridges spot the full moon, its surface bare like a calloused palm. I think about the stories Mom used to tell me. Like the one about Jacob staying up all night to wrestle the angel and how all he wanted was for the angel to tell him that it was okay, that everything was going to be all right.

Blumenkranz is outrageously glamorous. He dresses like an opera singer and when he makes an exceptional point, he snaps the elastic bands that hold his ruffled shirt cuffs at the wrists.

"Wrestling has chutzpah," he says. "It'll never die." Snap!

My father's eyes sparkle in agreement. For the first time since I met him, he looks almost alert.

About halfway through the night they start hatching a tag-team father-daughter duo. But first, Blumenkranz says, he needs to see me in the ring. The closest place is in Smeltersite and there's only one woman on the bill: Paula Pocahontas. My father says they're a bunch of barn gladiators, and he and Blumenkranz start arguing about it.

Blumenkranz's hands in their dirty white gloves flutter around like doves, stopping mid-flight only to snap at his wrist-elastics. They remind me of the songbirds that used to drop dead after running into the fresh scrubbed windowpanes at Old Ursine.

It seems to me that this is another one of those moments: those sinkhole realities. And even though I can see the noose, the possibility of a noose and the shaky foundation, it doesn't help. I look over at my father, he's wildly reminiscing, torturing his chair.

Ghost-Mom puffs through the pantry wall.

I decide to wrestle Pocahontas.

Blumenkranz's gold bodysuit is too big in the top and it's hard not to notice the sweat stains under the armpits. He says that I'm supposed to pretend that I'm rich and snooty: a sure way to get the workers at Smeltersite to turn against me. "It's the heels that are the moneymakers," he tells me. "People bet far more *against* the people they hate than *for* the people they love."

Pauley's acting strange. He sulks around my father while we practise, pretending to comb the pigs for hock mites. He eyes me sideways in my golden suit and flushes. He sits on the tracks waiting for hours for the train to come in, with this look that I recognize from my final days at the orphanage. But I can't help but think he has nowhere to run to.

It's a full house at the Smeltersite Pub. A bare light bulb sheds its light on the ring: a thick strand of hairy rope strung between posts stuck into floorboards sprinkled with beer-soaked sawdust. Ghost-Mom's by the referee and then over by Blumenkranz and then back to my father. She's a dark shadow except for the red glow of her cigarette, which jitters about the crowd, fidgeting through men's chests at lightning speed.

I step through the ropes and Pocahontas starts circling the ring, blowing fat kisses at the crowd. People are whistling and clinking their glasses together. Hooting wildly, they chant her name. Blumenkranz said I should pretend like I don't care, I should check my nails or something. Maybe roll my eyes. But I feel like I'm deep in the powerhouse-chamber egg. Somehow, its cotton-ball silence has returned like a case of swimmer's ear, a muffled silence that's strangely comforting. My feet are wadded up in yoke and I can't move. Somewhere by the counter, Blumenkranz starts taking bets.

Pocahontas comes at me. She's a horror of wild hair, black eyes, and feathers. My heart's hammering and there's nothing, nothing in the world except this giant of a woman and her flaming red lips. Until Mom. Ghost-Mom throws her *fer shit sake stick* on the floor, flows right through Pocahontas and like water down a drain, twirls down my throat, legs kicking. I feel the back of my neck rise, an old carapace lifting plates of fossilized armour. I can hear the crowd cheer as I take the first punch, the sound of fist on bone so much louder inside my own body than hearing one land long ago, the dull thud of the fight through the dressing-room wall, when my mother was in the ring. I can tell that the match will be nothing but a series of drop kicks and heart punches, and try as I might I will walk into a fist, probably over and over. I search the crowd for my father but he's gone, I can't see the living for the dead.

CHARLOTTE BONDY

RENAUDE

Mischa and I met on the second day of grade nine when our French teacher mistook him for a girl because of his long dark hair and cheekbones like Kate Moss. Everyone giggled and Mischa flushed red down to his shirt collar. After class I found him in the hall and told him I was jealous of his curls. I also told him this story about when I was twelve and had a terrible mushroom cut. My mom took me to the Gap to buy a pair of velvet pants. The salesperson kept trying to steer us to the men's section, away from all the leggings, until my frazzled mother eventually pointed at me and yelled, "She's a *girl!*" After I told him this, Mischa gave me his special look, the one where his eyes squeeze shut like a smiling Buddha. Then he asked if I wanted to eat lunch with him and that was that.

Mischa and his mum live on the second floor of an old row house on Parliament. When I'm over there everything feels exotic. The smell of Mischa's mother's cigarettes sits heavily in the air. There are built-in bookshelves and coloured glass bottles of foreign liquor. Mischa's mother sometimes speaks to him in Russian and her words sound livid and impassioned. When I ask him to translate afterwards, it's usually something mundane, like asking him to take out the recycling or clean out the litter box. I love the way she pronounces my name. *Claw-ra*, drawing it out like it's something important and precious.

The two of them moved here from Moscow when Mischa was nine, and she is working on her doctoral dissertation, something complicated to do with physics. His dad was a radical Russian poet and left when Mischa was still a baby. His mum hasn't dated anyone since. She's always in the lab, working. When she's out, Mischa and I pretend that the apartment is our own. We make fancy devilled eggs and drink loose-leaf tea in china cups. Or we put on a classical record and waltz around the tiny kitchen, taking turns to lead. Occasionally at night when we're bored or stoned we watch porn on the laptop in Mischa's bedroom. Mischa watches porn the same way he watches nature documentaries, his head angled to the side, a mixture of confusion and fascination settling over his face.

Luckily, my parents let us have sleepovers a lot. We like to stay up until the sun rises, playing Do, Marry, Die and dreaming about running away to Amsterdam to live on a houseboat. Mischa has just discovered French cinema, as he calls it. He watches *Breathless* basically on a loop. He says it makes him nostalgic for something he's never experienced. He's always saying that kind of stuff and I'm always rolling my eyes at him. Mischa's mother says he's an old soul. Sometimes, in the mornings, she makes us coffee in her French press, pushing the top down slowly with the flat of her palm.

My seventeenth birthday falls on the weekend before we start our last year of high school. It's the end of a summer in which basically nothing has happened. Mischa and I started hanging out at this 24-hour Lebanese diner called The Lip. It's actually called the Tulip but the *t* and the *u* have been burnt out for as long as I remember. If you order cold tea, they bring you a giant white teapot filled with Labatt 50. The owners have a son named Carl who works the night shift and silk screens his own T-shirts that say lewd things in Arabic. Carl's a bodybuilder and he's always sitting in a booth, loudly eating a cut of red meat, with his girlfriend, who wears white denim and has nodes on her vocal cords. Carl loves Mischa and me. Calls us his young thugs and even gave us one of his T-shirts for free. It was purple with gold writing that apparently spelled out the words *Bitch-Tit*.

For my birthday, Mischa takes me to a gay bar on Church Street with the fake IDs we had made in a basement downtown which say we're twenty-year-olds from Michigan. But when we get to the door I'm too nervous, so instead we go sit on the swings at Riverdale Park. You can see the whole skyline spread out in front of you and pretend you're sitting in a diorama of a city. The grid of condos and office buildings look like you could pluck them up and put them in your mouth. We decide to eat some mushrooms that Mischa bought from a white guy with dreadlocks at school, but nothing happens except stomach cramps.

"The CN Tower looks like a dick," Mischa concludes, and we hop off the swings onto the grass below, rolling down the hill. Mischa does a cartwheel at the bottom and his shirt rides up, exposing a chest that's so skinny it looks concave.

"Eat a fucking cheeseburger, Misch," I call out to him. And he comes over to tackle me on the grass. Pretends to take a bite out of my forearm. He walks me home and, standing on my front porch, he digs around in his pocket and produces a flat rock. I look at it closer and it's a fossil, the shape of a small butterfly encrusted on the cool stone.

"It's a trilobite," Mischa says. "I found it when Mum and I went up to the Bruce Peninsula last month." He brushes the face of the rock with his thumb. "It's Paleozoic. Old school. Happy birthday, Clara."

I hold him tightly for a long time, listening to the cicadas pulse underneath the porch light.

On Monday, the first day of school, a girl shows up twenty minutes late to our Canadian history homeroom. Dark bangs in her eyes. Wearing a baseball shirt and Doc Martens, a black bear tattooed on her forearm. Mischa and I exchange a significant glance as the teacher explains that she's a transfer student from Montreal. Her name is Renaude. The teacher mispronounces it, and Renaude softly corrects her, then shrugs. At lunch we go to the usual spot by the park. I pick up two cans of club soda from the Korean grocer and we sit on top of the picnic table, drinking them while Mischa rolls a joint. I curl one of his brown locks around my index finger and then let it go, watching it re-coil itself. We pretend to make fun of Renaude.

"She's trying too hard," I say, and Mischa nods with his eyes closed, sparking the joint.

He exhales and takes a sip from the can. "This stuff tastes like static-y sweaters," he says. "And yeah. Maybe she's just like, a pure aesthetic object."

I laugh, but I can tell that we're both already a little bit in love with her.

It only takes two days of thoughtful observation before we figure out how to intercept Renaude at lunch. She goes to a deli down the road from school. We wait for a few minutes before walking in one lunch hour to find her sitting in one of the cracked vinyl booths, drinking coffee and reading *Lolita*. I raise my eyebrows at Mischa and he smiles.

We ask if we can sit with her, and she nods and gestures toward the other side of the booth. We sidle in and order grilled cheese sandwiches. Renaude gets a side order of kosher dills, and we ask her questions about her life. She speaks in this frank, unapologetic way, gesturing a lot with her hands. Between her raspy smoker's voice and Québécois accent, all her words have this fiery quality, curling at the ends like slow-burning paper. She tells us about how her mother died six months ago. Afterwards, her father needed to get away. He got a job here and sold their house in Mile End.

"And he's already dating someone new. A Japanese painter with tiny tits." She bites the skin around her thumbnail.

We ask her if she likes it here, and she looks up at the ceiling for a few minutes. "No."

Before class we go behind the diner to smoke. Afterwards, Renaude re-applies her red lipstick in a way that makes my lower intestines quiver. She looks up at us.

"So. Are you guys together or what?" Mischa and I look at each other.

"Well, Clara likes girls," he says, pointing a thumb in my direction.

"And Mischa likes girls," I say, pointing a thumb at him.

Renaude smiles at this and nods, twisting the lipstick back into its tube.

That night I go over to Mischa's. After watching *Fight Club* for like the sixth time, he throws a sock at my head and says: "Okay. You gotta fuck one, marry one, kill one: Tyler Durden, Taylor Swift, and Renaude."

"I'd fuck Renaude, marry Tyler Durden, and kill Taylor Swift. Easy."

Mischa looks at me and curls a strand of hair behind his ear. "I love you, Clara."

I give his clammy hand a squeeze.

On Friday night, Renaude invites us over to her father's house. He and his girlfriend are supposedly out at a dinner party. They live in an old chewing gum factory that's been converted into lofts. It's a cavernous, raw space. A lot of stuff is still in boxes and a gigantic projector screen takes up an entire wall. Renaude's bed is separated from the rest of the room by one of those flimsy Japanese dividers. She's wearing a flapper dress and a porkpie hat and cracks open a bottle of her dad's Prosecco as soon as we walk in the door. I feel immediately homesick for the soft domestic clutter of my own home, where my mum and dad chop onions for soup while listening to the CBC.

After the Prosecco, Renaude pours us fingers of vodka from a bottle in the freezer and starts sifting through some records that are stacked in a milk crate beside a turntable in the corner. She pulls out a copy of *Histoire de Melody Nelson*.

"I love Serge Gainsbourg. He's so sexy." She droops her eyelids and puffs out her bottom lip, pulling a cigarette out of her pack.

"*Tu t'appelles comment?*" she whispers huskily, brushing the edge of my jaw with her fingers. Then she laughs and carefully lowers the record onto the turntable. She does a strange-looking interpretive dance to the music as Mischa and I hover clumsily around her.

We smoke cigarettes on the fire escape, their lit tips dangling between the wrought iron rails. Renaude sits in the middle of us. An arm slung across each of our shoulders. There's a moon and I'm about to ask whether anyone knows if it's waxing or waning when I hear the sound of the front door being unlocked.

It must be Renaude's dad and his girlfriend, home early. Their voices are raucous, speaking half in French and half in English. Suddenly, Renaude's dad calls out her name and she puts her finger to her lips, glaring at Mischa and me as though she thought we were about to give her away. We hear her dad's girlfriend say, "Thank God" loudly, and then the sound of the freezer being opened, ice clinking into glasses. High-pitched laughter and singing and then the soft, wet sound of two people kissing. I look over at Renaude with alarm, hoping she will offer some kind of way out, but her face is stoic. At one point her dad says, "We have to hurry, I don't know when she's coming home." It's the first time I've heard people have sex in real life and it doesn't sound nearly as loud or as showy as it does in the porn that Mischa and I watch. In fact, there are a lot of uncomfortable sounds, like boxers during a particularly brutal round. At the very end, Renaude's dad sounds almost whimpery and I hunch my shoulders up around my ears, but then all of a sudden it's over.

When I look over at Renaude, she has this creepy half-smile on her face, her fists clenched into white knuckle balls. The alcohol has burned through me and I'm left with a dull throbbing in my left temple. I want to go home to bed. Renaude suddenly points down, to where a long black ladder unhooks and connects the fire escape to the ground below. Mischa and I look at each other, and nod. He begins shimmying down the side of the ladder, and I wonder whether Renaude is going to follow us, but when I look back to the grated platform she's still sitting there, knees pulled into her chest, tapping a cigarette out of her pack.

We catch the Dundas streetcar and walk the four blocks to my house. My mum is waiting up for me. I can see her reading the paper on the living room couch, with Oscar curled up on her stomach. When we walk through the door she stands up to give us both a big hug and I squeeze her back for much longer than usual. She's wearing a nightgown with a pattern of moose wearing cross-country skis trotting across it.

"How was the movie?" she asks, stroking my hair. Mischa shrugs. "Not great."

We make hot chocolate and take it downstairs to the basement, where we lie side by side on the futon. Mischa flicks on the television. A re-run of *Trading Spaces*. He lies back down, and I curl my body around the soft parabola of his spine, thinking of how few ways there are for bodies to fit together.

GEORGIA WILDER

COCOA DIVINE AND
THE LIGHTNING POLICE

t is 1979 and the silkscreen letters on my *DISCO SUCKS* T-shirt are all cracked and falling off, so it just says *I CO UCK*. Better not be too much of a butch rocker chick here anyhow with those girly het-girls in strappy sandals and spandex dresses and everyone a little on edge from doing poppers all night. Cocoa Cherry Divine, aka *Mon Cherie*, the Divine Cocoa Puff, steps off the stage and begins to circulate through the crowd. She hugs Billy from behind, shedding glitter on his sweaty black satin shirt. "You be wantin' a cock up yo' ass and tits aflappin' on yo' back, honey." Her long green nails caress his hair. Billy's wasted: "You need permission from my girl-friend here first," he says to Cocoa, winking at me. Katrina's is a mixed bar—a lot of David Bowie groupies with bi-curious chic: Toronto's provincial outpost of the Studio 54 avant-garde. I'm sipping a tequila sunrise, chewing the ice cubes to stave off drunkenness. I look into the glass as the coloured layers dance into one orangish liquid cloud. Staring beyond the bevelled edge of the tumbler, I can see the reflection of my eye swimming toward the half-submerged cherry garnish. Alcohol tastes like shit but ordering ginger ale is the damn stupidest way for a juvie to get blown off the scene. You've got to tip well but not so much as to seem like a bribe. Better to be really nonchalant, like you've got some citified *ennui*.

Jacques weaves through the crowded dance floor hefting a tray of drinks over his head. He works out at Gold's Gym on Yonge; he keeps his arm slightly bent under the weight of the tray to show off his muscles. Even his forearms have little bulges, like Popeye's. Angelo swaggers over, gold chains snaking through his bushy chest hair. His shirt is unbuttoned to the waist. "My girlfriend thinks you're cute," he slurs, handing a fiver to Jacques. "*Merci, merci beaucoup, ooohlala,*" says Jacques, sizing up the breeder and pretending not to speak English. Jacques tucks the fin into his jock strap and blows Angelo a kiss. He smacks Cocoa's ass on his way back to the bar. "*Cochon!*" she exclaims in mock outrage.

Angelo sulks back to his girly-girl with the Farrah Fawcett hairdo; her kohl eyeliner has smudged into a bruised boxer kind of look. Jacques winks back at Cocoa, his *amour.* Angelo and boxer girl start necking to give them a show. He pulls her onto the dance floor and feels her up to the music; then he stops suddenly and points to the ceiling. I look up to see what he's pointing at and the mirror ball makes me dizzy. Then I realize he's trying to strike that John Travolta pose and the Bee Gees are singing "Night Fever," their creepy falsetto voices whining mosquito-like against the pneumatic backbeat. I hate the Bee Gees. I hate their saccharine harmonies and their blow-dried hair and their pretence of wholesomeness: the Brothers Glib. Give me synthesizers that pound like electronic jackhammers, not polyester snare drums. It's the deceit that gets to me.

I stare up at Cocoa just trying to look bored. "Billy is an asshole, saying I'm his girl," I say. I reach over to her shimmering fingers, where her cigarette is idle. I bring her hand to my lips and I take a long haul off her smoke before I say anything. "Fuck him, Cocoa. I'm nobody's girlfriend and I would pay you to screw him up the ass." She looks down at me with a raised eyebrow. I realize that she must be nearly as old as my mom: thirty-five, at least—she's the mom and dad I really want, all rolled into one tall, black drag queen with a penetrating eye. She snaps out of her vernacular: "I am not some common whore, you know!" I've fucked it up. She gazes down into my pupils and takes back the last drag of her smoke. She says something about being a true libertine, like it's got to have rules. I'll think about it later. I'm too fuzzy now. I suck in my cheeks and bite down on the insides of my mouth. I taste a little blood, but I have to bite harder to feel any pain, trying to find a way to shake off this tequila buzz. "Coffee," I think, and the next thing I know I'm at work.

I'm training Stacey-Jane. "Just be sure there's a new paper filter in there before you open the bag. Just dump it in—that's right, the whole bag. Remember, if you push the button without putting in coffee, you just get a pot of hot water. If you don't put in the paper filter, the grinds clog the hole and boiling water spills all over—like that mess we just cleaned up." We scalded our fingers trying to stanch the flow of boiling water and coffee grinds that flooded the counter, and we've dumped a pot that looked like a giant's urine sample because Stacey-Jane pressed the hot water button without changing the used filter. Cocoa has dropped by for a coffee. I can feel her waiting for her caffeine fix, captive attendant to the slowly brewing pot. I gently touch Stacey-Jane on the shoulder: a reassuring pat, a tiny feel of her soft arm. I go a little further, Cocoa's gaze daring me from behind. I give Stacey-Jane a pals-y shoulder squeeze, brushing my fingers through her hair as if by accident.

Stacey-Jane is a Roman Catholic girl from Saskatoon. She's sweet and pure and perky and so supremely gullible that even the concept of religious hypocrisy is far beyond her grasp. Her honey-brown hair curls a bit at the shoulders. She has big brown eyes and full lips and a slight gap between her front teeth. I love saying "Stacey-Jane"—the long assonant *A*'s feel delicious in my mouth. Whenever I suspect that someone might suss me out as a naive country girl, I just sidle up to Stacey-Jane's farm-fresh face and feel like a kick-ass urban butch intellectual. She makes me feel canny: not just by comparison, but there's something genuine about her aura that helps me think before I open my mouth. She is so completely without artifice that she's sexy, and the air kind of tingles around her.

We have two head waiters, John and Steve. They both have wispy blond hair, little moustaches, and rectangular chrome-framed glasses. John moves like a *premier danseur* from the Bolshoi, while Steve walks like he has a pickle up his ass. The problem with Steve is that he is a born-again sanctimonious asshole who just can't leave shit alone. "Bronwyn," he says, "check the table bottoms for chewing gum. Kitchen will give you a putty knife to scrape it off." For an extra twenty cents an hour, Steve takes the head waiter thing pretty seriously. He's gunning for the title of evening shift manager. He probably has wet dreams about getting it embossed on his plastic name tag, like getting a medal pinned on his chest. Lots of folk have a narrow compass, see only the part of the world that fits between horse blinders; but Steve's gaze rules a microcosm that contracts into the crosshairs of a rifle sight: pop-gun tyrant of serviette dispensers, invigilator of the extra creams. We're all just moving targets. He is a cardboard parody of the dinner table dictator who I tried to leave behind. It's been over two weeks since I got the hell out of there, but my brain still drags some luggage along. The filial Sunday dinner switches on in my head.

Dad sounds like he's loud, but he's not. He's just got righteous intensity. That's a different thing, he says, than those neurotics, always flying off the handle. "Ed Sullivan should be shot for what he did," says Dad, staring me down like it is news, like I've done something wrong. "Take your elbows off the table, Bronwyn. Bringing the Beatles to America; what insanity he let loose on this generation of heathens." I just keep eating. Beatles got their place in history but I'm not old enough to remember them as a band, and Ed Sullivan is dead. My music is Poly Styrene, Lou Reed, Bowie, Queen, Joan Jett, Sex Pistols, Siouxsie Sioux: no point in saying so.

Dad complains that Diefenbaker scrapped the Arrow and that Trudeau, French and effete, joined Ed Sullivan's conspiracy. "Beatle-mania, Trudeau-mania. Mob psychology," he says. "All those kids screaming like rabid animals. No discipline. Is that roasted chicken? Damn that rock and roll and those crazy hippies. What we need is another war. Pass the green beans. Please! What do *you* think about this women's lib malarkey, Bronwyn?" It's not a question. It is a test for The Amazing Kreskin. He wants me to read the secret answer in his head, not tell him what I really think.

I dress like a boy because girls can't do shit if they dress like girls, and what I really think is that Dad can take a great word like *liberation* and make it sound like a bad taste in your mouth, like something loud and fat and embarrassing: *lip* or *lipid* or *libido*. I haven't heard the term *hippie* since grade five, and Trudeau is old, and *malarkey* comes from the kind of brain that's been mummified in a Canopic jar. There's a new indie-punk glam scene that comes in from campus stations late at night on my clock radio, and those new rocker chicks and club queens and androgyny philosophers are taking over from white-boy cock-rockers like The Who and The Stones and Rush and Styx; and I'm trying to figure out why all the cool black rock-and-rollers are selling their souls to disco, and why the hell Grace Jones is singing synthesized Broadway tunes when she could be kicking ass with real skin drums. My dad says there's a generation gap. It's the fucking Grand Canyon. All he sees is this freckled kid who doesn't say what's in her head and he makes her feel dumb and small.

He has piercing blue eyes. He can make you feel ashamed for nothing; like shame is made of live seeds germinating in a forbidden-fruit core. The shame seeds sprout in my stomach like kudzu vines, invasive, embarrassing, with budding leaves that grow out my nose and ears. They creep up the glands in my throat and get in the way when I swallow. I've taken a chicken leg that I can't eat. The shame in my throat gets bigger when I think about the dead chicken. It's my job to feed the chickens. They come when I call them, let me take their eggs, and then my dad chops their heads off and we pluck them and eat them. I just shut up and help Mom clear the plates.

Mom's still dressed up from church, sort of. She's wearing the floral cotton dress that she made with a Vogue pattern: high femme. She even made the matching cloth-covered buttons. But the weather is too cold and the farm house is too drafty for the dress, so she's got a plaid lumber jacket draped over her shoulders and she's taken off her good shoes and put on grey work socks, the kind that are made of itchy wool and have the little white-and-red band at the top. Over the socks, she's got on a pair of men's Kodiak work boots. She says nothing, but she's smiling. She is fifteen years younger than my dad. I went through her nightstand once to try to figure her out. No diary, no pills, no makeup, just a little jar that said *vanishing cream*. You think she's right there, but she's not: receding like the Cheshire cat until all that's left is her smile and her busy hands. My grandpa pounds the table with his fist, vehemently agreeing with my dad: "Kids today; and that music—no religion, no respect." He knows the script so well he doesn't need verbs. In his time music was decent. Men were men.

Dad dropped out of grade eight and started working in a Pittsburgh steel mill, turning gun barrels on a metal lathe at fourteen. That's what it meant to be a man. "When I was your age," says my dad, "we didn't have milk. We just poured coffee on our oatmeal." He had the last of his teeth all pulled when he turned thirty-three, just after getting married. He clicks his dentures together and smiles as Mom takes the percolator off the gas stove and fills his cup with coffee. Her grandmother's inheritance paid for his dentures. It's an open secret. She thinks of her silence as dignity, appropriateness. It's the routine, the predictability that creates our roles, our purpose; a meaningfulness that seals away the sin of doubt.

Sunday dinner is always served at noon. Mom puts the chicken in the oven before church, comes back, and serves it. She gets up and down during dinner, checking the pie, picking up dropped utensils. Then she washes the dishes. Dad gets annoyed if Mom leaves any dirty cooking pots in the sink while we're eating. "Dirty dishes are unsightly and unsanitary," he says. "Discipline," he says, "discipline and faith: that's what makes people strong in the face of terror. It's the narrow gate that guides a soul from the path of destruction." He will not allow us to work on the Sabbath, except for Mom cooking and cleaning, which doesn't count. Everyone else has to sit around all day and be quiet. Mom smiles. "Would anyone like dessert?" *Oh, God, in whom I do not believe, please don't let me become my mother!*

"Yes," I say, less patiently to my customer, but still smiling, "that's eight different desserts, all fresh not frozen. Would you like me to recite the list again?" Mostly, it's families at dinner hour. Lots of sticky little kids who have temper tantrums after their second glass of pop and start to throw their food on the floor. Half the job is cleaning. They call it side work: getting the crumbs and the crispy cockroaches out of the toasters, washing the counters, polishing glasses, refilling the Heinz ketchup bottles with some generic red shit that comes in big drums with plastic pumps at the top.

Steve elbows past Cocoa with disdain, letting the kitchen door swing back in her face. Cocoa readjusts her boa as Steve recites his tight-ass rules: "We have a no loitering policy here; washrooms are only for paying customers. If you would like to be seated, you can leave your name at the hostess stand." He turns to me: "If you don't have anything to do, Windex the pie case."

The pie cases are a bitch to clean. Throughout the evening, the pies molt millions of electromagnetic crumbs that stick to the mirrored shelves and the sliding glass doors. You have to take out the glass doors and then fit them back into the tricky little oovy-groovy slots that keep them on a track. By the time they fit back into place they're all smudged up again and some prick has ordered another piece of crumby pie.

"Nice work," says John, looking at the clean pie cases. Normally, I wouldn't give a rat's ass about this *noblesse oblige* shit, but with John, it's just who he is, not like he's trying to be some gauche fancy man. John treats everyone with respect. "Are you okay with that table of six?" he asks. He comes from old money, and he has a taste for opera and etiquette and for the sorts of men who would always break his heart.

My dad turned eighteen a few weeks after the Allies declared Victory. He enlisted on his birthday. In Kassel and Dresden and Frankfurt, the stench of bodies greeted the occupying troops. Men in uniform were like my dad, kids who left school to work in mills and munitions factories, or farm boys with big clumsy hands, or teenaged store clerks trying to grow hair on their peach fuzz faces. German bulldozers moved mounds of rotting corpses into mass graves. Some boys passed out. They were there to clean up the rubble and rebuild.

"The war only ended on paper," says my dad. "The Allied planes stopped their bombing runs with not much left to knock down. Just the old men and the Hitler Youth were left. 'Guerrilla armies' they would call them now, worse than trying to fight real men. The U.S. troops would be too honourable to shoot a child," he says. "In the time it would take for an American soldier to look into the young boy's eyes, the kid was going to shoot first." Dad's voice gets a little higher, a little less certain. "You don't know what it's like to face a child with a gun and know you have to pull the trigger first." He is unaware that his voice has escalated, that he hasn't blinked and his eyes look both fierce and watery, like he is on that edge of uncertainty, the wider gate yawning open. I want to ask him if he faced that child, if he pulled the trigger, but this is *verboten*.

We hold our breath. The air is combustible. The clock ticks. Then he pauses and breathes and recognizes us all again, as if he has just been away. "That's why," he says, "you're not join-ing the cadets and you're not wearing army pants. Young girls in army pants! That belittles the men who gave you freedom. If it weren't for men in uniform, you would be speaking German now—or worse, Japanese." I think it might be cool to speak Japanese, and freedom? "What freedom?" I ask under my breath. The Greyhound journey is anti-Odyssean, travel-ling anywhere to get away from home.

Wait staff place orders through an intercom that is connected to the kitchen, and our voices boom throughout the restaurant.

It's pretty intimidating to hear your voice carried through the whole big place, and when we get new waiters, they always say "oh shit" the first few times when they're holding the talk button down. Joyce is from Jamaica. This is her first night. She persistently presses the broadcast button and orders a "large cock." The kitchen guys whistle encouragingly, and Billy offers her a taste of his cooking. John, deadpan and well manicured, gently suggests that she might try saying "Cola" instead of "Coke." Steve has little veins that stand out on his neck. "This is unacceptable, Joyce. Wait staff pour their own fountain drinks. We're not on island time here." Joyce puts on a browbeaten face, but she sticks up her chin and mutters some rhythmic curse involving the word *bumbaclot*. She sings it softly, swinging her hips as she walks past Steve.

I've got three dinner plates on my left arm and two on my right. The one higher up on my left arm is sizzling hot, burning the tender crux of skin where the inside of my arm bends. Steve stops me so he can rearrange the garnishes. I clench my teeth and count to ten and give him the evil eye. He has never been a waiter. He just took some community college course on how to boss people around.

My dad trained for an elite force: *Blitz Polizei*—the Lightning Police. Their badge had a *C* for *Constabulary* with a lightning bolt through it, proclaiming *Mobility, Vigilance, Justice!* They chose him because he was an eagle-scout, sharpshooter, and state clay-pigeon champion. Lots of guys could shoot nineteen out of twenty clay pigeons, but he was the only one who never missed. The Constabulary was special-ops. Recruits underwent IQ and psychological tests, watched violent propaganda films. "Some guys," he says, "would have killed a German with their bare hands after seeing those films. Those were the fellows they weeded out, the ones who believed what they saw. Those ones got put on KP; spent their whole tour of duty peeling potatoes. The rest of us got six weeks of German language lessons so we could talk to people there. I don't remember much now, but 'HALT': that's the same in German and English." My dad made sergeant in eighteen months. He turned down the job of Chief Detective of the Pittsburgh Police Department when he came home.

As the kettle whistles for my mom's tea, my dad finishes the war and immigrates to Canada with my grandfather, leaving the world of Eisenhower, dishwashers, paved suburban driveways, and TV sets. Kids started taking drugs and burning their draft cards. He doesn't understand the peace movement. There's really no way of explaining it. He is still in the Lightning Police, spit-polishing his boots, saluting the flag, enlivened at every Sunday dinner by moral outrage. On the rare afternoons when he takes a nap, he tosses and moans, and yells out "HALT" with such anguish that he scares me. Living in the past is not nostalgia, it is shell shock.

My uniform is thick orange polyester. It might stop a bullet, but is designed only for the front lines of the service industry: they're restaurant fatigues. An orange-polyester bodice with little puffy sleeves tops off an orange polyester A-line skirt. Ornamental brown buttons grace the front; a zipper fastens up the back. Ribbons of brown rick-rack encircle the edge of the sleeves. Cocoa's finally got her coffee from the fresh pot. "Girl," she says, "you is so ugly it looks like you got beaten wit' an ugly stick." I try to catch a glimpse of myself in the mirrored pie case. For sure my frizzy hair looks like a lop-sided Afro and my freckles stick out against the whiteness of my face. "Not much I can do about it," I say. "If people have money here it's for sympathy tips anyway; bourgeois assholes hiding dimes under their plates like it's some retarded Easter egg hunt."

A guy with a comb-over and an outdated plaid suit sits in Stacey-Jane's section. He says something to her and she starts chewing on her pencil like she's got to think about it hard. She goes over the menu, a tri-fold laminated behemoth with extra cardboard attachments for seasonal desserts and daily dinner specials paper-clipped to a long tail of pleated cocktail pictures. She's heading over to me with the menu, trailing leaflets and table-tents. "Do we have something called a blow job?" she asks, "I don't see it anyplace. Is it like a dessert?" Her voice is so plaintive and musical, like church bells ringing throughout the restaurant. I take a deep breath. Someone in the front suppresses a giggle. Billy yells out, "Come into the kitchen and we'll help you figure it out, honey." Cocoa is holding her breath so hard she looks like she's going to explode but she waits, breathes deeply, relaxes, and then takes a big swig of coffee to get back her equilibrium. "Do you serve blow jobs where you work, Cocoa?" Stacey-Jane asks. Cocoa twists around and sprays her mouth full of coffee across my freshly Windexed pie case and three banquettes.

She coughs uncontrollably. As she wipes her face with a napkin, she smudges the gold lightning bolt on her cheek and spreads her rouge back toward her ears. I look Stacey-Jane in the eye. "Did that man ask you for a blow job?" I narrow my eyes, trying to make him squirm. He grins back, gesturing toward Stacey-Jane with his hand on his crotch.

Michael is the campiest waiter. "We get that a lot here," he says to Stacey-Jane. Billy yells out from the kitchen, "Sure bet you do, Michael." Michael touches up Cocoa's makeup while trying to explain the facts of life to Stacey-Jane. Oblivious to the giggles and immune to embarrassment, Stacey-Jane seems to have a magical, impermeable protective coating. "Steve's the head waiter," Michael explains. "You can always tell by his dirty knees." Michael demonstrates, dropping to his knees and sticking out his tongue like a begging dog. Stacey-Jane nods like she's taking notes for biology class. It is impossible to shock her.

Then Steve appears out of nowhere like he's got supersonic ears and ESP. "Since no one here seems to be working, I'm docking everyone's pay for an extra break." Cocoa just walks away grinning, which pisses me off. She could have stood up for us and instead she's writing her name down at the hostess stand. She knows better than that. You have to wait for the hostess to take down your name. Besides, she never sits down to eat here. There's a line forming as she edges past the crowd toward the cold grey Toronto night. I hand her a new takeout coffee and she just leaves, lifting the hem of her gold lamé dress over the threshold.

The lineup at the hostess stand is out the door, and the hostess is running around seating people. Steve has taken it upon himself to stand at the podium and read out the names. "Mike," he says. No answer. "Mike. Mike Hunt," he says firmly. "Mr. Hunt," he tries again, "Mr. Mike Hunt." Parents with small children look at each other uncomfortably. The cooks in the kitchen crack up. Steve has no idea why. "MIKE HUNT," he yells. "MIKE HUNT." I'm laughing so hard my cheeks hurt and I have to cross my legs to keep from peeing. It's almost worth the extra side duty. We scrape the crusty bits of dried mustard from the condiment trays and wipe the kid goober off the high chairs and booster seats and polish the utensils before the movie rush. Every once in a while someone giggles for no real reason, just while standing there scraping the relish trays. I'm still giggling when my head hits the pillow.

∞∞∞

The police are chasing me. It's dark, and I'm wearing my orange-and-brown uniform, except it is too short and I'm not wearing underwear and I keep trying to stretch down my skirt but it keeps riding up and feeling shorter. My section stretches out onto the street and up some stairs. I'm holding plates of fried chicken and there's the man whose coffee I forgot and the table of six who are yelling at me to take their order but I know if I get closer they'll grab me. I'm trying to take a plate of green beans to the table, but they're stuck to the counter. Turning into worms under the heat lamps, they start to wriggle. They stand up and start dancing, and they're yelling at me, "I CO UK I CO UK," and I can't figure out what they're trying to say, and the heat lamps turn to strobe lights and the restaurant is like the dance floor of Katrina's with mirror balls and drag queens. Cocoa's looking at me like I've done something wrong. I can feel the shame vines creeping into my throat, sprouting leaves out my nostrils. I run down to the commissary and pull open one of the giant walk-in freezers. I know I've killed someone but I don't remember doing it. I open the freezer door and dead chickens are hanging there upside down with their feathers on, and they start to look at me, giving me the evil eye like I've killed them, and I know that I have even though I don't remember doing it, and a man in a uniform fires a lightning bolt from a gun and I fall like I'm going through a trap door that trips the alarm, and I jerk back awake as I land.

We don't really see that my dad is afraid. He's just a carrier, and we're all infected. He can smell rain, he says. I learn to smell it too. Dark clouds on the horizon begin to roll across the sunset, yet the air is eerily still, hot and humid. The usual noises of birds and animals have stopped, leaving only the high-pitched buzz of the crickets and cicadas. The chickens strut single file into the henhouse without being told what to do. Everyone moves slowly, except Dad. I want to help him turn off the power and lock up, but he says everyone must stay in the house. It is too dangerous. The wind picks up, making little dust devils in the driveway as we watch him from the window, turning off the power in the workshop and then the barn; we wonder if he will be struck by lightning or carried off by a tornado. He puts a padlock on the Wizard of Oz cellar doors, then comes back to the house. The wind follows him in and blows the papers around the living room before he closes and locks the door behind him.

I'm too old to cry, but my little brother and sister are crying and saying they're scared. The big elm tree could fall on the house, Dad says. It is a giant, lopsided leviathan with muscular rough-barked limbs that reach toward our bedrooms and tickle the roof with its branches. The big elm is monstrously sublime—a centenarian that whispers the ancient language of earth and sky. It lisps and chatters in the summer breeze and in a storm its voices howl and scream. The wind wails now, a siren song. We sit in darkness. My mom lights a kerosene lantern that casts shadows around the room. It is story time.

"A kerosene lantern can explode," says Dad. "I knew a family once who came home and set their kerosene lantern down on the woodstove. The whole house went up in a fireball, two kids just about your age," he says to my brother and sister, "and parents and grandparents too. They all lived in the little house with the woodstove and kerosene lanterns. They were good devout people but they were ignorant. They didn't know any better. The bodies were so badly burned they had to get forensics experts to identify them through dental records." The air is heavy when he pauses. "Maybe we should blow out the kerosene light, Mom?" I ask. She pretends not to hear me or my dad. She's rocking my little sister to sleep, humming "Ghost Riders in the Sky." Neither fear nor irony can deter her constant drone. Sheets of rain pummel the ground. We can't see out the windows anymore.

The wind sounds like voices crying in the tree limbs. "We had a neighbour, once," says Dad. "Old Joshua was his name, a loner type. He lived down the road in that big old brick house all by himself. His wife died years ago, before I knew him, the baby too. He used to go out in the storm, thinking he heard them in the wind. One night he put on a big scarf, wrapped it around his neck a few times, and headed out into the storm." I'm holding my little brother. I feel less scared when I comfort him. "He went through the dark windy night knocking on neighbours' doors. 'Did they hear a child screaming?' he asked. Perhaps they had—a baby crying—or maybe a young woman in distress. He was sure now that he had heard a woman's screams in the night and a baby crying." I listen to the wind, and I can hear them, the young woman, terrified of death; the baby who would cry briefly, motherless and alone with no one to save it. Maybe Old Josh could still find them. We know he can't, that he shouldn't look, that he will find only ghostly fiends instead of his real wife and child. "In the morning," says Dad, "after the storm had passed, the neighbours didn't see Joshua in his garden and that night no lights went on in his house. When he didn't show up at church that Sunday, some of the townspeople started talking. Maybe they should put a search party together and look for Old Josh.

"We found him swinging by the neck from a tree limb, down by the canal," says my dad, "hanged by his own scarf. We found him under a circle of turkey vultures. Crows had already picked out his eyes. Funny thing is there was a woman's hanky stuck way up in the tree limb—the old-fashioned kind with handmade lace, not like the ones they make today." My little brother looks up; his eyes are saucer-round. "It must have been hers," he exclaims, "the ghost of the dead lady." Dad shrugs. "Nawh," he says, "it probably just blew out of his pocket. Old Josh probably had it with him the whole time." The thunder crashes; we know it has hit nearby trees and it may start a forest fire. We are startled by the clock chiming nine. "Bedtime," my mom announces brightly. "It's a good night to remember your prayers before bed!" Dad can't resist one more story. "Good thing we turned the power off," he says. "I knew a family not too far from here that got so scared by a lightning storm that they all joined hands and got down on their knees to pray. One little barefoot boy stuck his toe right into a loose 220 outlet. He electrocuted the whole family at once."

I lie awake listening to the wind in the trees, wondering if the big elm will come crashing down through the ceiling. Dad insists that we go to sleep in our own beds like normal. It's about the importance of routine, of discipline; it's about having faith in the Lord and not being a coward in the face of adversity and the importance of learning to be alone in the darkness and never trusting your ghosts. My sister sleeps soundly in her bed on the other side of the room. My mom is sitting up with my little brother, who is too afraid to go to sleep. He has a room of his own. I can hear her singing to him across the hall. I try to imagine walking out in the rain like Old Josh, except that I won't believe in the ghosts. I will have my own magic and draw down the thunder. But every time my eyelids close, I see Old Josh swinging by his neck from the tree, staring with empty eye sockets, drawn in by the under-world voices.

⌾

We're ticking down the minutes until the nightclubs close. There is a feeling of ozone descending like just before a lightning storm. The air smells like rain despite the pervasive sub-odour of french fry grease. Everything is extra quiet, only a few semi-sober customers drifting around before last call; then the hungry drunks come crashing in. The late-night crowd looks like they've never met a mirror they can trust—a mob of unkempt vampires, their skin looking pale and minimally undead under the fluorescent lights. This is a Toronto institution; the city's only all-night restaurant. A cockroach emerges from behind the red vinyl banquettes, having feasted on nearly three decades of crumbs from the much-touted "homemade" apple pies. "Just like Mom makes."

"How was school today?" Mom asks, as she spoons soup into our tin mugs. I shrug in response. The heat instantly transfers to the tin handle and I pull my sleeve down around my hand so as not to get burned. "Don't stretch your sweater out of shape, honey. Sit up straight and ladylike." She smiles at me like I'm three years old. "Just wait for the soup to cool." I am fifteen. Nothing about me will cool soon. Dad is annoyed. He came in at five and the table wasn't set. My math assignment had encroached on the place settings: papers on the chairs, a text-book flapped open where the serving dishes should be. "There's no point in learning algebra if you can't even tell time," he quips. My grandfather shakes his head. "Blue Stocking," he says affectionately and rubs my head. That's his name for me. "You're going to be too smart for your own good," he jokes, "too big for your britches." It's not really a joke. My mom laughs as she chivvies my little brother and sister into their seats after they wash their hands. "Let's say grace," she says. It's a children's rhyme that she made us memorize. My little brother and sister kick each other under the table and giggle: *Thank you for the world so sweet / Thank you for the food we eat.* I'm the only one who doesn't open my mouth or close my eyes.

Suddenly, the gates of hell open wide. It is an absurd horror show. Het couples make out in the booths; some fight and cry.

Drag queens dance on the tables and the crowds of generally wasted zombies come looking for coffee after getting stoned. Two girly het-girls are necking and feeling each other up while their boyfriends are banging out a rhythm on the tables with their fists, cheering them on. There's an itchy junkie at the takeout counter. I watch him scratching the track marks on his arms, then trying to twist his fingers around to the unreachable itch between his shoulder blades before I realize I'm digging my own nails under the back of my bra strap, scratching where the sweat and polyester meet. Every so often he twitches as if to shake off a bug. I twitch too. I realize I've been staring at him and make myself look the other way.

Cocoa Cherry sashays in. This is her kingdom, and she always makes an entrance. She yells out, "We real cool. We left school." A middle-aged man, who has spent his single-malt evening at the Rose and Thistle, yells back in a thick Glaswegian brogue, "Lerrnsum rrree-al English, yabitch!" We shout out our Gwendolyn Brooks tribute with our own twists—a different rhyme each time. I yell back to Cocoa Puff, "We work late. We tempt fate." She stands on a chair and points at me: "You jail bait. You can't wait!" We high five as I stack the coffee cups in my left hand. She turns to Michael, who's running his ass off, and we get Brooks's poem back on track: "We jazz June. We die soon." It's true.

No one's making more coffee—every station has run out. I brew more, running from station to station while my unclaimed food orders start to wilt. Once there's some coffee going, there aren't any cups. The dishwasher can't keep up. I grab some dirty mugs, quickly wipe the lipstick off the rims, and fill them up again. I glance back at the kitchen. "Kumar," I yell, "we need more cups." He doesn't understand English, but I have to say something so that maybe the invocation alone will make the cups appear. I can see the bread on the sandwiches curling up under the heat lamps and feel a panic of urgency as the bacteria breeds: mmm salmonella sandwiches—the perfect ritual end to a night of debauchery. I have a table of eight reasonably sober women who all want more coffee, and they've been waiting forever for their food: four skinny-mini salads, one Mu-Mu Hawaiian burger, and three orders of chicken Wing-Dings. I can't bear to say "Wing-Dings" again over the PA system, it's just too humiliating. But I realize that Stacey-Jane has unwittingly picked up my order from the kitchen and is serving it to a table of jocks who are flirting with her.

I have a table of drunken hockey fans. "Go Leafs Go!" they chant. "Leafs all the way, the Habs are gay." I figure they won't even notice if I give them dirty spoons, they're so loaded. But there are more people coming in, and the hostess is seating them at dirty tables because the bus boys are hopelessly behind. There's a drunken Leafs fan following me into the kitchen looking for a clean spoon and, reaching down, he makes a sloppy grab at my thigh. I accidentally kick him in the lip and he starts bleeding. Steve is coming toward me and I know I'm in trouble for assaulting a customer. I pretend like nothing has happened and dash away with a coffee pot, giving the last thick dregs to the semi-sober women. I pause at the pickup window and yell at Billy, "Where the hell is my Mu-Mu Burger?" "Moo," says the grill man. "Moo Moo," says the next line cook. The kitchen exists in a different time zone that's two hours behind. "Why don't you ask the fucking cow?" asks Billy. "What am I, a psychic?"

I grab more dirty teaspoons out of the bus pan and run them under the tap. There are never enough utensils. The clan from the pub is getting too mouthy. "Hey sexy, give us a smile—smile you fucking bitch—are you waiting for the coffee beans to grow? Hey, girlie, I bet you can't count to six. Them taking all our jobs: all those stupid fucking faggots and filthy foreigners." The accidental alliteration makes them think they've said something clever, and they laugh. "How many fingers am I holding there, lassie?" One: he's shoving his middle finger in my face. I walk away like I'm deaf. He pinches me on the ass. "Don't do that!" I yell and they laugh.

There are two girly-girls flirting with the table of hockey fans and they're still holding their cocktails from the bar, just standing there in my section without a seat. One is chewing on the ends of her teased-up hair; she laughs at me. "Can I get a milkshake?" I have no idea if she's serious. I have no idea how I'm going to get through this. My feet feel swollen; blisters rub against the insides of my shoes. I try to forget I have feet. I slip sideways out of myself for a moment and just try to feel whole again in a perfect split second of calm certainty. If you believe strongly enough in the weirdness of the universe, some goddess of the absurd might just come down and save your queer ass. And it happens.

I open my eyes just in time to see Stacey-Jane in front of a toaster. Smoke is billowing out and little flames follow as she cremates the delicate, white Wonder Bread. She has a glass of water in one hand and a metal fork in the other. John is a moment behind her. Everything moves in slow motion as he lunges to pull out the toaster plug that moment too late. Almost simultaneously, she douses the toaster blaze and attacks the burnt offerings with her fork. Everyone in the room takes a collective gasp before the bang of the short circuit sends us into darkness. There is silence. For a second I think we might all be dead. "Sweet Baby Jesus!" blubbers out Stacey-Jane in the sexiest, trembling, most innocent sobbing voice that carries through the darkness.

She throws her arms around me and we embrace in the dark as she weeps on my shoulder. And there in the darkness, she clutches me close. Her fingers reach around my front and she touches my breast, smoothing it with her palm, like it was the most natural thing to do right there in the righteous dark in the middle of a crowded restaurant after near-electrocution. Steve, flashlight in hand, finds the breaker panel and Stacey-Jane jumps back to earth as the fluorescent lights blind us momentarily. The magic moment is over, and Steve orders the bus boys out of the dish-room to clean up the mess.

ANDREW MacDONALD

THE PERFECT MAN FOR MY HUSBAND

The news arrived with the fanfare of the last tiny float in a very small parade, the one nobody wants to see, the one that fell behind and never caught up. He told me he had cancer, the worst kind, and that it had spread to so many corners of his body that there wasn't any hope. That got me. No hope. Who says that to his wife? We were having dinner, this was before he got really bad, sharing one of those little plates where they poured balsamic vinegar and olive oil, the vinegar slipping around in bubbles. The bread stick had been torn in half. I looked down and saw that it was in my hands.

I put my piece of bread back on the plate and asked my husband, "What do you mean, no hope?"

"Exactly what it sounds like." He drank some carbonated water, sucking it through his teeth. By the face he made, I could tell he had trouble getting it down his throat, as if it hadn't gone all the way to his stomach and had chosen his Adam's apple as its home instead.

This was our Cancer Dinner—what we'd call it over the next few months, when the endlessly multiplying cells really started ransacking his body. I would come to grow fond of this moment, the way Eve must have grown fond of the split second before she bit into the apple and damned us all. It's rare in life you can point definitively to The Moment Everything Changed. We could do that.

Palming a piece of bread into a tiny ball, I threw it across the table and at his chest. I pretended his chest was the universe, that the ball of bread was a missile with such potential for catastrophe that it would end all moments. The bread ball bounced into his glass of water. We both looked at it sadly as the water molecules slowly pulled it apart, the bread falling open like a strange underwater flower you needed grief to discover.

After a few tests, a few rounds of chemotherapy, the oncologists sent my husband home. The reasoning was that if he was going to die, he might as well do it somewhere comfortable. It was a deadly beast, the cancer, and it was beyond reproach. So I went about trying to make him comfortable, starting with the purchase of an ounce of the highest quality marijuana I could find. The dealer, a college student from the apartment complex across the street, said to take it easy, that a gram of the stuff would take me to outer space. Good, I told him. The rings of Saturn sounded very hospitable at that moment.

In the early stages of our courtship, my husband and I would smoke a bit of pot on the porch and watch for patterns in the stars to announce themselves to our scrambled minds. Since then, he had gotten a job teaching at a private high school and couldn't find room in his life for drugs.

"You're smoking it," I said handing him the joint. "We'll go back in time to four years ago when we first met."

He saluted grimly. "Then as now, you're the boss."

I wrapped his shawl tight around his body and lit the joint where it dangled, between his chapped lips. His eyelids fluttered when he sucked in and he coughed out a cloud that hung in the air like a fist. "Goddamn," he said. "That hits you right in the brain."

"If you could have one wish," I said, sucking in my own lungful of smoke, "other than having more wishes, what would it be?"

"More genies."

"That's addressed in the contract, section one B. No extra genies." I replaced the joint on his waiting lips. Its glowing tip lit him up in a pleasant way, like a wet drawing of a sunset, near translucent, patted down over the contours of his face. It was a calm, safe thing. His eyes got milky, the lids at half-mast.

"You really want to know?"

"What kind of a wife would I be if I didn't want to know?"

So my husband said to me, "I wouldn't mind getting laid."

"Your wish," I said, putting my hand on his leg, "is my command."

Which ended up being a natural transition to my husband telling me that he meant he wanted to sleep with a man.

There are pictures you have of people you love, a kind of X-ray that you think reveals their inner lives and shines it bright on the wall like a kabuki shadow puppet play. And then, when the curtain is pulled back and the puppets behind it look nothing like the images you had imagined, you're forced to pick up the Lego blocks of reality and rebuild them in a manner you can live with.

He saw my expression and let the joint fall out of his mouth. It landed on the shawl and sparked until we both frantically patted it out. Our hands met a few times, violent with slapping sounds. Once we'd beaten the joint into a stubbly mess, I took out a spare I'd rolled in case the first one suffered a premature death.

I handed him the replacement joint and asked him, the way you'd talk to someone hard of hearing, "Repeat what you just said."

"What did I just say?"

"That you want to sleep with a man. Is that what you said? Did I hear you right?"

He frowned. "I thought you knew."

Did I know? I might have known. There were signs. Then again, if you told me my husband had been a closet uni-bomber, I could have found signs supporting that claim as well. He was anti-social sometimes. He was the only person I knew who liked licking the glue on envelopes. If I'm not mistaken, the uni-bomber liked doing that, too.

"Sorry," he said. "I'm stoned. Very, irredeemably stoned."

I considered the joint. It still lit up his face like the wet sunset thing. "Did you ever find me attractive?"

He stopped to think and he did so in a way that I found terribly honest, as if I'd just put him in charge of ending all the genocides going on around the world and he had to confront the way that we as Westerners fit into that sort of thing. "I do find you attractive," he said finally. "Kind of the way you can tell a piece of art is beautiful without actually, you know, necessarily wanting to sleep with it."

"So that's it, then," I said to him. "You want me to seek out a male partner who can be with you in ways I can't."

Had you given me a card and asked me to briefly describe what intercourse looked and felt like, I would've said, "Earnest and Fairly Fulfilling." Past lovers had been more passionate, more acutely attuned to the power of friction on the clusters of nerve in the sexual parts of my body. But my husband did his best, and his best manifested itself nearly every time we slept together, which amounted to twice a week. Children hadn't been possible on account of my uterus. According to the doctor, it had the warped shape of one of Dali's clocks. A part of me felt ashamed that I couldn't give him children and assumed my infertility accounted for our subpar sex life. I explained that to him.

"Fuck my disfigured uterus," I said.

My husband sighed. "When have I ever talked about having kids?"

"When have you ever talked about putting a penis inside your mouth?"

Digging himself deeper into his shawl, my husband conceded that it was a good point.

The man I was considering had dark hair, very short with a swoop of bangs. In the picture my co-worker Hattie showed me, he almost looked like a woman. He modelled for a hair product company, she told me. You wouldn't call him handsome or beautiful. More like striking. Hattie described him this way: "Looking at him in person makes you feel like you've been hit by something very sharp."

"And this is a good thing?"

"This is a good thing."

Hattie was the only one so far who had agreed to help me find a man for my husband. Most people said very bad things to me about the status of our marriage. These were the kinds of people who exchanged crystal swans and called it love, while simultaneously thinking up elaborate ways to inflict harm on one another. My mother believed in traditional marriage norms, even when one-half of the marriage was dying of cancer, as my husband was.

"What you're doing will crush you," she said.

"I'm already being crushed," I said, referring to the cancer and the crushing weight of its metastasization.

"But this one will crush you more," my mother said.

When I told him about the conversation, my husband said, "Maybe she's right," and that was the only time since he got cancer that I couldn't stand him.

I'd tried some other things before deciding to find him a man to sleep with. For a week I bound my breasts with tensor bandages left over from the time I sprained my ankle. Little hairs sprouted on my legs and under my arms, and I stopped waxing the fine thin line of down that stretched thin as dental floss just above my upper lip. I even bought a wig. Wearing it transformed me into one of the Beatles. When I tried it on and approached my husband and said in my deepest voice, "You need your plumbing fixed?" he blinked twice. Only one blink would have done.

You wonder: What kind of man should my husband sleep with? I thought of me, but as a man, and realized maybe that was the point, that he wanted a "not me." Which in some lights, might seem horrible. In the light I chose, it meant that his attraction to men could only be an inversion of his attraction, or lack thereof, to me, such that in loving men, according to some curious physics, he was also loving me, too.

—

The plan was for Alex and Hattie to show up to our apartment in tandem. From there, Hattie and I would gradually fade away as my husband and Alex interacted. My husband was having one of his good nights, and even though I don't believe in God, I thanked Him or Her or It for small graces. I'd pre-emptively gotten the bed ready, washing the sheets so when the time came things would be in place. Pillows were fluffed. Scented candles and condoms placed at convenient locations throughout the room. Anticipating a night on the couch, I made sure to have an old sleeping bag curled up behind our television set in the living room, ready for retrieval.

Things started poorly when Alex showed up minus Hattie. "Food poisoning," he said apologetically. He handed over a bottle of shiraz. "I wasn't going to come, but she made me promise I would anyway."

"And a good thing you did," I said, modulating my voice to sound cheery and absolutely comfortable with Alex's presence. I took his coat and called my husband over. "Would be a shame for all the food I made to go to waste."

My husband introduced himself. I searched his face for evidence of enchantment. They shook hands and I tried to determine the nature of that handshake. Was it gentle and sensual? Firm and flirty? Thirty pounds lighter than he usually was, my husband practically swam in his collared shirt. His pants didn't fit him well, but he smelled nice and I'd shaved him, so his face had the glow of a nice stone zapped by a laser beam.

"I was just thinking," I said, engaging in damage control by leading them to the kitchen, "that you two could talk. It's my understanding that you've been out of the closet for a long time. My husband here could probably use a few pointers."

"Jesus Christ," my husband sighed. He touched his temple. To Alex he said, "You'll have to excuse her," which I took to be a good sign, since it implied collusion on their part, a gendered taking of sides.

I'd prepared a dinner of salmon and coleslaw and mashed potatoes, knowing my husband could get portions of each down. Their talk amounted to a lot of polite, empty banter. Hattie had simply told Alex that my husband recently came out, on account of an unspecified illness that was not, Hattie made sure to make clear, HIV. Since he didn't know he was on a date, being test-driven by both of us (or just me—I later learned that my husband thought I was joking about setting him up with men), Alex didn't pick up a lot of the cues a person on a date would normally pick up on. Twice I encouraged my husband to compliment him. Twice my compliments evaporated into the ether.

Occasionally I tried to raise the stakes by introducing sexuality into the conversation. "What's your favourite sexual position?" I said. "How do you feel about pornography?"

"I don't watch it much," Alex said, eyes lowered to the food on his plate.

"Us neither," I said, though I added that my husband might, since prior to this point, it was probably the only way he'd been able to experience gay sex.

I waited for Alex's good looks to stab my husband's heart sharply the way Hattie said. My husband asked me to help him to the washroom. I wasn't sure I wanted to leave Alex alone in the kitchen, where he might steal the nice forks and knives my grandmother left me when she died. It turned out my husband didn't need my help. He squeezed my upper arm until it ached. "You can't do what you're doing, Abby."

"What am I doing?"

"You can't force someone to want to have sex with me."

"Pardon me for thinking that the rest of the world would find you as pretty as I find you."

"It's not that." He let go of me and looked into his hands. "I shouldn't have said what I said to you. It wasn't fair."

I took a deep breath. "How many times have I done something very bad and you forgave me?" I said, touching his face up near the sideburns, where his skin was slightly more pale. "You've got cancer. If that's not grounds for getting something you want, I don't know what is."

My mother had actually been the one to put it in my head that a man could smell when a woman couldn't give birth. Despite having only one child, she thought of herself as kind of like that stone Venus from Willendorf, hips rounded with fertility. In her mind, all roads to motherhood and relationships led to her.

Even though it was ten at night, long past her bed time, we rang my mother up. My husband and my mother never got along, but only because he hated her because she acted like she hated me. Who knows, maybe she did hate me. We lit another one of the joints. My husband dialled since, after a few hits, I couldn't translate the symbols on the phone's dial pad. He handed me the phone. We were in the outer space of marijuana intoxication.

As the phone rang, I could picture my mother taking off the stupid little mask she wore to bed. I could picture her hair coiled around pink plastic cylinders that made bunches of follicles curl.

"He's a homosexual," I said when she answered.

"Who is this?"

"Gay. Flaming. So the thing you said about me being a defective woman? Stuff it."

She recognized my voice and said, "I know he's a homosexual. Are you all right? Do you need me to come over?"

Slamming the phone down, I reached for the remains of the joint and lit it.

"That must have felt nice," my husband said, coming up behind me and rubbing my shoulders with weak, skeletal hands. I turned in my chair and buried my face into his stomach.

"Screw you for dying," I said. His fingers made electricity behind my ears.

"I'm not dead yet," he said. It occurred to me that what he'd said was true.

Hattie called me up and said that I'd probably be fired from work, since I hadn't called in to explain my absence. It wasn't a particularly meaningful job—I worked at a non-profit organizing fundraising events, only I knew the non-profit was covertly for-profit, so its success or failure didn't faze me.

"I say we fight the bullshit," Hattie said. "If they fire you, I know a friend of a friend who's a workplace rights lawyer. We'd gut them real quick."

I said I didn't care. We went for lunch and she asked how my terminally ill husband was doing.

"Mostly like shit. He can barely walk, but he puts up a good front." That morning, he puked on the floor of the bathroom and passed out in it. How he had anything to throw up was beyond me. Without him knowing, I'd been keeping a diary of his food and fluid intake and found that in the last three days he'd consumed the equivalent of a two-inch cube of cheese, three thumbs of orange juice, and a soggy bowl of cereal.

"I was always jealous," Hattie said. She picked out a leaf of spinach. "You two always had this thing. I can't explain it."

For the last three years, she'd been on a series of hopeless first and second dates that ended short of her expectations. As far as I could tell, she had a lot of sex but felt an emptiness in her gut when she wasn't in love with someone.

"It's too bad he wasn't looking for another woman." She swallowed the spinach leaf and pursed her eyebrows. "Sorry. I'm a shit."

"No arguments here."

I watched as she took the water carafe at the centre of the table and filled up both our glasses. "Have you found a guy for him?"

Stabbing at my own salad, I answered, "Negatory."

Since the awkward dinner with Alex, I tried to set up one more date, this time with a nice, clearly homosexual man I met at the grocery store. But the man had a boyfriend, and besides, my husband said he wasn't thinking about screwing men. Jokingly, he said that he wanted to keep his soul pure so that he could gain access to the kingdom of heaven.

"Don't be an asshole," I said, picking up one of the pillows we'd designated as a surrogate for him and punching it.

"Oof." He doubled over, as if I'd just thumped a voodoo doll of him. "Uppercut to the kidneys."

One day, when he didn't seem to be dying as much, he took me by the wrist while I was skinning potatoes and brought me to the living room. He was sleeping in there now. Going upstairs took too much out of him. There were scented candles that he lit with as much grace as he could muster and erotic movies with titles like *Love in 49 Positions* and *Having Sex in the City*. I don't know how he set it all up without me noticing. The couch was pulled out and neatly made, with condoms on a nearby table. My husband took my face and kissed it, transferring an explosion of mint toothpaste into my mouth. The taste went straight inside my body, into my veins. I stepped back slowly, the way they say you should when dealing with angry bears, and said, "What's going on?"

"I want to have sex with you." He started unbuttoning my blouse. I was still holding the potato peeler.

"You can't just tell me you're gay and then ask to have sex with me."

"But I'm dying." This had been our mantra, our reason for doing things like decorating our bedroom with old *Mad Magazine* covers and buying a fish just because neither of us had ever owned one before. "Aren't I allowed to ask for what I want?"

"You don't want this."

"How do you know?"

What should a wife do when she has to argue against her husband and herself? He put his hands under my shirt and said he liked how small my breasts were. I told him I liked how small his penis was and he got that it was a joke right away. I asked him if he wanted me to wear a baseball cap to make me more masculine, if he wanted me to use a tensor bandage to keep my breasts clamped down. "Do you want me to try to be Ringo again?"

"No, I want to have sex with you." His pants came off. I joined him under the covers. "Give me a minute," he said, his hands disappearing below his waist. He started trying to get hard. A glaze of sweat formed on his face. "Almost there," he said.

"Let's just sit here a minute and breathe," I said. At first my husband positioned the parts of his face—nose, eyes, eyebrows—in a scene of frustration. Then he relaxed and after a while, our breathing synchronized without either of us noticing. Kissing him on the forehead, I took the potato peeler back to the kitchen and ran the blade against the vegetable's ruddy skin.

A lot of animals go off on their own when they're about to die. When I was eight, our spaniel dug a hole for herself under the house and burrowed there. We found her later that week, serene in her little grave. Apparently elephants do that too. Apparently so do husbands.

I brought his breakfast into the living room on a tray. Usually he drank the milkshake I made and picked a bit at other things. This time he looked at me and said, "I want you to go back to work."

"And I want a golden toilet. Sometimes we don't get what we want."

"I mean it. At least to talk to them about you coming back when things escalate to the point where they can't escalate anymore."

The way he said *escalate* made me think of moving stairs, of my beautiful gay husband standing on an escalator and slowly going to heaven. It was an unnecessary, melancholy thought. "It doesn't matter if I don't go back. I'll find another job." In fact, head hunters sometimes called the house, so we both knew that was the case. In the end, I told him I'd go. "But only because I need to pick up some more pot on the way."

As usual, the signs were there. Before digging her own grave, our spaniel seemed unusually calm. Everything she did felt premeditated. On my way out, my husband slapped my ass and told me he loved me. Is it perverse to associate the words *I love you* with entombing? The playful gesture of ass-slapping with sinking submarines filled with men forced to accept their watery fate?

At work, my superior, Vargo, told me a joke. "What's worse than a paper cut?"

"A lot of things."

"Don't ruin it," Vargo said, and he repeated, "What's worse than a paper cut?"

"I don't know, Vargo. What?"

"The Holocaust." His head tilted back, mouth opening like a Pez dispenser. "Isn't that bad? I think it's so bad. Bad, bad, bad." Because I felt sorry for Vargo, I laughed too. He told me that I could come back to work whenever. He asked about my husband and touched my arm and I remembered that Vargo tried to sleep with me when I first started working at the non-profit.

On the way out, Hattie made her hand into a phone and mouthed the words, "Call me."

While I was listening to Vargo's joke, my husband collapsed on the front porch. I sorted out the timing and the exact second Vargo assaulted me with his tasteless punchline, our neighbour was calling an ambulance. And somewhere on the coast of Brazil, a butterfly flapping its wings had caused all of this.

My husband was still in his bathrobe when I got to the hospital. The nurse at the triage said he'd been acting delirious. He saw me and apologized six or eight times. "I told them not to take me. I even tried to fight back. It's going to be expensive." A ludicrous sight that must have been, that bathrobed husband of mine, warding away the rescue attempts with darting punches, a beetle on its carapace.

I asked if it was bad. He shrugged. "It's been bad since day one."

The hospital room smelled like vomit. On the other side of the curtains, a woman with a Yankees baseball cap stretched over her head waved at me. I waved back, feeling as though one of us was in a car going someplace, and the other was standing very inert, very still. "I think she tried to eat herself a couple hours ago," he said. I looked at the woman again and saw the imprints of what could have been teeth on her hand.

We sat in silence as the tubes put things into him and sucked things out. I let him fall asleep, but not before I made him promise not to die on me before I could take him out of this place. All I could think to do was walk around the hospital, looking for someone, anyone, who fulfilled my idea of what a gay person looked like. What did I plan to do when I found him, the perfect man for my husband? In times of crises, your nervous system dilates your pupils, raises your blood pressure, increases your heart rate, parts of your brain shut off, and you can only comprehend survival. It was a simple equation: if I could do this thing, find this man, I could negate so many other things. The word *cancer* didn't even occur to me as I tried to find the perfect man for my husband.

My husband wasn't dead when I came back empty-handed, no potential candidate on my arm. The fact hit me, right then. He probably wouldn't be getting out of the bed he was curled up in.

"Doctors are like weathermen," I whispered into the thinning hair of his crown. "They're wrong about everything. They used to recommend spraying people with DDT." He grunted a little bit, which made me think what I'd said had entered him through a sort of osmosis.

Crawling into the bed with him, I transformed my body into something like a plaster mould. The space I would make between our bodies would be an imprint, the way you'd make a mask of someone's face. I told myself if I didn't move I could keep the shape of him forever, that when this version of him was gone, I could fill the shape up over and over, making a new him when the old one had to go and leave me. My eyes were closed when my husband put his mouth on my ear. Not just on it, around it, as if he were trying to swallow me starting at the place I could hear. After coughing a little, he pulled back a bit and touched my hair and whispered, "There are no monsters here."

SARAH MEEHAN SIRK

MOONMAN

When the sky turned black, I thought of my father. But that makes no difference to you now. "Where were you when it happened?" you ask, and I say I was at work, in my cubicle, in the centre of the city. Which is not untrue. Hunched over my keyboard, the computers blinked off with a defeated drone, the lights flickered out, and the silence of a city cut from its power rose up from the ground. A quiet more unnerving than darkness, just like Moonman had whispered.

"How did you get out?" you ask, meaning methods, vehicles, escape routes. You want to hear about the path you assume I took west to the wide roads and stiff stalks of corn, whether I knew about the tunnels in advance, and so on, so you can amend your own plans of now-constant preparedness, mental networks fizzing as they rewire.

I don't tell you that when the black clouds thundered across the sky I didn't go anywhere, and my first thought was of the man least capable of protecting me from the end of the world.

—

I saw him the way he was, with a mug of red wine and a pack of Player's Light, on the other side of the screen door that led out to our small backyard. He could sit out there for hours on summer evenings, smoke lingering around his head in varying densities like a dirty halo. He sat and smoked, looking out, facing elsewhere, while Mom dried the plates and glasses with a blue dishtowel and went upstairs to put Alice to bed.

I'd sometimes pretend he was out there on the step listening to a Jays game on the radio, unwinding after work like most dads did. I imagined that if I opened the squeaky screen door he'd shift over to make a spot for me and tell me that there were two out in the top of the fourth, with runners on first and third. We'd sit just listening for a while and, when the game began to drag, he'd talk about stats and trades and the players he watched when he was my age. Near the bottom of the seventh, when the score was 11–2, he'd tell me to grab our gloves from the garage so we could throw the ball around until it was time for bed.

Instead though, like most nights after dinner, I was inside lying on the rug in front of the TV, and he was out there alone sitting quietly on the back step, wishing he were somewhere else.

I was ten when he came home on a Saturday afternoon with a used guitar. He ruffled my hair as he walked across the front porch where I was colouring with Alice, and let the door bang shut behind him. His fingertips left trails on my scalp like swaths cut through a wheat field. I followed him inside and watched from the living room doorway as he leaned the banged-up guitar case against the couch. He grabbed a glass from the cabinet in the dining room and whistled on his way into the kitchen, where he rummaged through a high cupboard, clinking bottles together until he found the one he was looking for. I'd never heard him whistle. He returned, the glass half-filled with a nectar like dark honey, and stopped when he saw me, his lips still pursed in melody.

"Hey, Simon," he said. "Wanna hear something, little man?"

I nodded and moved closer as he set his glass down on the coffee table with a clink. He pulled the case onto the couch, clacked open its locks, and lifted the lid to reveal a plush red interior cradling a scratched black guitar. He ran his fingers along its strings before pulling it out and nestling it into his torso. For a couple of minutes he tuned the instrument, his eyes closed, head cocked as though listening for some secret. And when he started to strum, a whole different man took the place of my father.

Something dropped to the floor in the upstairs bathroom, and a second later my mother was there on the stairs, her hair pulled back with a kerchief, yellow latex gloves on her hands glistening with water.

It was just before Christmas when he left his job at his uncle's car dealership. My mother wore a hood of silence as she peeled carrots and potatoes over the sink, her dark hair hanging forward like a curtain so none of us could see her face.

"Maggie, you're not even trying to understand," my father said.

He leaned beside her against the counter, with his arms crossed tight over his broad chest, shaking his head and staring down at the tile he kept poking with his big toe. Mom peeled harder and faster until the carrot in her hand looked more like a weapon than a vegetable.

"Babe," he said, "come on. You think it was easy for me to make this decision?"

As though he wasn't there at all, she chopped up the potatoes and carrots, dumped them in a pot of water, and set it on the stove. She grabbed plates and cutlery from the shelves and drawers, set the table for three, and opened the oven door to check on the meat.

"It's pork," she said, slamming it shut. "Dinner will be ready in an hour."

She wiped her hands on a dishtowel, tossed it onto the counter, and didn't say anything to Alice or me on her way through the living room and up the stairs.

"I'm really getting tired of this martyr shit!" my dad yelled to the ceiling on his way out back, the screen door clapping hard against its frame.

Alice and I sat like statues on the living room floor in front of *Wheel of Fortune*. I thought that if we didn't move, if we didn't say anything, we might blend into the carpeting. I was relieved when Dad came back in a few minutes later and went upstairs.

"Big money! Big money!" Alice called out as she clapped her hands.

I elbowed her in the ribs: "Shh!"

The bedroom door opened and shut above us, and I heard the bass of their voices getting louder and louder until something slammed against the wall, rattling the trinkets in the china cabinet beside me.

Footsteps in the hallway above. Fast but not running, my mother came down the stairs, my father close behind.

"Maggie, wait," he called to her. But she was already out the front door. Because I didn't hear the creak of the porch steps, I knew she hadn't gone far and imagined her leaning over the railing, which, in a way, was just as bad.

That spring I turned eleven and got a bike for my birthday. By then my father was writing music during the day and playing Bowie cover songs in bars a couple nights a week. My mother was working the overnight shift at the radio station, where she was a part-time producer. I'd heard her on the phone with someone not long before she started working nights, saying Alice and I wouldn't even know she was gone, that she'd be around for bedtime and home in time to take us to school in the morning.

"My aunt is going to stay over the nights that both Chris and I are working," she said into the receiver. "I don't know, Fran. It's going to be tough for a while, but I think it's only temporary. I mean, my hours and his . . . *situation.*"

And then she laughed in that conspiratorial way mothers share while talking with one another about their husbands and children. A laugh, it seemed to me, that rarely involved joy.

I couldn't tell her that she'd been wrong. It didn't matter that she was home when we went to bed and when we got up for school in the morning—her nighttime absence echoed through the halls. We always knew when she was gone. I lost the feeling that children are supposed to have when they drift off to sleep: that knowledge that their parents, their mother, is in the house somewhere, her protective warmth flowing from room to room in the dark. Without it, I lay awake for hours listening to every creak, every rustle, and every snore that rose up from Great Aunt Audrey, who slipped into an impenetrable slumber on a chair in front of the television minutes after the front door was pulled shut and the key turned in the lock.

In search of a direct line to my mother, I brought the old brown clock radio up from the basement one night, plugged it in by my bed, and tuned it to her station. I knew I wouldn't hear her voice, but it didn't matter. I could see her in the windowless studio I'd visited on a PD day, sitting at the control board pressing buttons, adjusting volumes, directing the show in silence. The studio felt as serious as an operating room and everything in it seemed very important, including my mother, without whom I believed the whole thing would fall apart.

I burrowed deep under the covers with the radio and slowly increased the volume.

"They know more than they'll ever let on, while they ply us with television and hamburgers and the Super Bowl, pounding our brains into a doughy pulp. You can't hear them, but they're laughing. Right now. Laughing at us."

The voice stopped. A man's voice, almost whispering. I felt like I'd caught him in the middle of telling a secret. I waited a few seconds before reaching for the tuner, thinking maybe I had the wrong sta—

"Laughing!" he boomed, the radio tumbling from my hands and clunking to the floor. Aunt Audrey's snore broke into fits before returning to its sinusoidal cadence. I picked up the radio and settled back under the blanket.

The voice was whispering again.

"Laughing. At us. And you can bet your last ounce of gold that they'll be laughing harder as they watch us try to peeeeeel our flabby bodies off the couch when it comes time to fight back."

Pause.

"To fight the new world order."

Pause.

"If, that is, we ever open our eyes to what is happening. To what—really—is happening."

Longer pause.

"I'm Moonman and this is *The Age*, on the Striker Radio Network."

I crawled deeper under the covers where it was hardest to breathe and decided that when Moonman came back from commercial I'd focus on the silence between his words. It wasn't hard to do. And I could swear, if I listened hard enough, that I heard my mother in that silence, that I could hear her breathing. She was always there in the soundlessness. Quiet on the board signalling to Moonman to break, quiet in the kitchen packing our lunches for school, quiet with Alice asleep in her arms through the crack of the bedroom door.

I tuned in to Moonman under my blankets every night she was gone. I listened to him talk about the Illuminati, about life in other galaxies, about Area 51 and what really happened in Roswell, New Mexico. I learned about the symbols of the new world order, the secret histories of world leaders, and the imminent "end of the world as we know it." Moonman knew more than anyone I'd ever met, and every night I felt like he was sharing secrets of the universe with me alone.

If I wanted to, I could blame him for what happened. I could say he planted seeds of curiosity about the world at night, that he inspired me to explore the dark, that listening to him made me feel brave and independent and old enough to creep down the stairs past sleeping Aunt Audrey, into the garage and out onto the street with my bicycle.

But, really, I think it was rage that sparked it. Rage or insomnia, or just the plain white terror of being left alone in the dark. Or some of all three.

I rode off into the starless city night, pedalling hard and fast, weaving through neighbourhood streets, toward the main road. Darkness rustled the leaves high overhead and I was breathless with adrenaline and the metallic taste of the night air that in no way resembled that of the day. I knew where my dad was. He'd pointed it out to me one afternoon when he picked me up from school—the pub where he played his music.

I had to blink against the bright street lights when I turned onto the main road, standing up as I pedalled along the wide sidewalk, zipping past people out for a nighttime stroll or huddled in dark doorways smoking cigarettes.

"Hey—kid!" someone yelled. "Little late for a bike ride!"

I slowed down and rode close to the storefronts as I approached the pub, slipping into the shadows of the awnings that lined the way. I heard music. A man's voice singing something familiar. "CHRIS COATES, TONIGHT 9 P.M.," written in pink chalk on a sandwich board outside. I hopped off my bike and leaned it against the window of the shop next door. When I was sure no one had seen me, I crouched down beside the planter box in front of the pub and slowly raised my head to peek into the window.

He was right there, sitting on a stool with his back to the street. His feet were perched on the lowest rung, his heels bouncing up and down, keeping time. A column of sweat soaked through his shirt along his spine. On the small stage floor beside him was a bottle of red wine and a half-empty glass, and everything was hued pink and green by the lights cast from the ceiling above him. My father strummed his guitar while he sang hard and loud into the microphone. Even through the glass I could hear that his guitar sounded brighter and more desperate than it ever had in our living room.

I looked past him into the pub where candles flickered like grimy stars on each table. A group of college kids was making its way to the pool table at the back, the girls stirring candy-coloured drinks with tiny straws. Two older men in plaid shirts drank beer and ate nuts at the bar while they watched hockey on televisions that were hung from the ceiling, and three young women sipped white wine and looked around the room instead of talking to each other. One couple sat facing my dad, a blond woman leaning back into the man she was with, a number of shot glasses and beer bottles scattered on the table beside them. The man seemed to be having a hard time keeping his head from bobbing around. The woman was staring at my father. When the man said something in her ear she swatted at his face with long fingers and didn't take her eyes off the stage. I looked around for others listening the same way but, outside of a few people nodding their heads to the music now and then, no one else seemed to be paying much attention.

When he stopped playing, the blond woman was the first to clap. She sat up straight and pressed her elbows against either side of her chest. A few others turned to applaud as well, but none as vigorously as she did. I heard my dad say something about taking a break and I dropped down again as he slid off his stool.

I peeked one last time and saw him standing in front of the stage, pouring more wine into his glass. He was talking to the woman. She smiled with big white teeth and tossed her blond hair over her shoulder when she laughed. The man she'd been sitting with had fallen asleep with his chin on his chest and was being nudged, hard, by a chubby waitress as she cleared the empty bottles left on their table into a black dish tub. Dad walked in the direction of the bar, the woman chatting close beside him. He smiled at her in a way that was moist and young, a smile that bared too many teeth and a hunger I couldn't recognize.

I rode home. Fast. The wind felt colder, like it was scratching my throat with long frigid fingernails. I was suddenly very tired and I wanted my bed. My radio. My blankets. My mother's inaudible breaths in Moonman's pauses. I stood on my pedals and pumped hard, turning from one street to the next in wide arcs. A block from my house, I took a corner too quickly.

I remember headlights. And that is all.

Nauseous in the aluminum lighting.

Thick throbbing in my ears.

Mom and Dad shadows cut out against a white ceiling.

Alice's singsong voice at the end of a long, warbling tunnel.

Can't talk. Can't move.

Nurses checking tubes and dials, stroking my forehead when they looked down from far up, into my eyes. In the light, a dull, faraway inescapable pain.

Dad somewhere in the room with his guitar once. Or always.

Mom hovering in the quiet spaces between.

I left the hospital near the end of autumn. The surgeon came down to see me on my last day and ruffled my hair and told me to buy a lottery ticket on the way home. When my mother wheeled me through the front door, I knew right away the house was not the same—a new emptiness in the hallway, the coat rack gone, the spider plant no longer trickling its spindly leaves from a stand by the stairs.

I was lifted ("Careful! Careful, everyone, the scar on his back still hasn't healed . . .") to a hospital bed wrapped in *Star Wars* sheets in the middle of the living room. The television that had been on a stand against the opposite wall was now perched on a stool by my bed between stacks of comic books and bouquets of helium balloons. The couches and chairs were now clustered in the dining room, the big table itself nowhere to be seen. New drapes had been hung on the window over- looking the porch and the street, silky sheaths that let the sunlight in while hiding me from curious neighbours, my experience of the outside world, in turn, reduced to dreamy, shimmery snatches of ordinary life.

There were pictures missing from the hallway. For days, I stared at an edge of wallpaper that was lifting near the railing, trying to remember which one had been there.

A steady stream of assistants paraded through the door for a long time, nurses and therapists checking scars, lifting arms, bending legs, taking measurements. ("He's progressing well, Mrs. Coates. Kids have a tendency to bounce back.") I asked for a radio. Mom was always home now, but on wide-awake nights, when everyone was sleeping, I still listened to Moonman in the dark.

Since he was usually somewhere in the stream of nurses and therapists and caregivers, it took a while before I realized that my father didn't live with us anymore.

Huddled under a blanket on the porch one afternoon, still feeling achy and watery from an infection, I watched my parents standing by my dad's car parked across the road. Mom stood with her arms crossed, looking past him far down the street. Dad fiddled with his keys. Mom said something and nodded a few times before walking back up to the house.

He opened the car door and was about to get in when he looked up at me. I pretended I couldn't see him. Drugged, groggy, it wasn't hard to stare out at nothing in the distance. My mother came up the steps and with the back of her soft hand touched my forehead, then my cheek, and kissed me before going inside, the door banging shut behind her.

"See ya in a bit, soldier," my father called out.

"Oh," I said, acting like I just realized he was there. I lifted my arm, held up my hand. "Okay."

He slid into the driver's seat, started the car, and unrolled his window. The radio was blaring. He flicked it off and lit a cigarette. For a moment he sat there in the puffs of grey, before driving off with his hand holding the door.

My mother married Stephen when I was fourteen. Their ceremony quiet, silvery, cozy with night. He was a gentle but faraway man, a serious look in his pale eyes behind the small round glasses he was always adjusting. His long, thin black hair was tied in a ponytail that curled down his back, grey wisps framing his bony equine face. When he moved in, he brought heavy boxes filled with books, two lamps, a pair of jeans, and three black T-shirts. He bought a globe at a garage sale to show me how countries were drawn in the decades before the First World War. He touched my mother whenever he could.

One evening on the porch when he was writing notes, I asked him if what he talked about on the radio was true. Without looking up, he said he didn't know what truth meant anymore. Sometimes I liked when he responded that way.

"I mean, are those things really happening?" I asked.

"Some of them already have," he said, consulting one of the open books on the table beside him.

"But I mean, the really bad things, like the end-of-the-world kind of stuff."

"It's cyclical, Simon," he said, removing his glasses and rubbing his eyes. His voice bent in the direction of his on-air delivery. "And it's relative. There's a rhythm and a plan. Most is beyond our control."

"But I mean—"

"Simon," he said, lowering his pencil and looking straight at me. "Are you asking if I believe there will be change, even significant change, in our lifetime?"

He held his breath and my gaze as though expecting some deeper understanding to reveal itself in my eyes, some realization I would come to that would prevent him from having to say what he really thought. But I was long accustomed to his pauses by now and thrilled to be his private audience for what felt like a particularly omniscient insight. I leaned forward, blinking.

After a moment, he released a lung full of sour air.

"Yes," he said, returning to his books and jotting down a note. "I do."

You call and tell me how you remember the salespeople and middle managers and secretaries and vice-vice-presidents chatting about weekend plans as they descended the windowless concrete silos of office building stairwells, cellphones in leather holsters, name tags swinging from lanyards around their necks. "All the sheep," you say, but not without pity. You gave them a quick smile of reassurance because that's all you could do as you and everyone else poured out to the sidewalk. The grid of city streets locked with idling cars, drivers leaning out of their windows, squinting at the horizon, nearly decapitated by cackling bicyclists whizzing past. Everyone with phones to their ears, looking east, then south, then west, then north, then at the useless phones in their hands as one network went down, then the next, then the next, and then all we had left were the people in front of us, people slowly being covered in ash and soot that fell from the sky like black snow.

It was so much like how Moonman said it would be. He'd warned us. He'd hoped we'd fight back in time enough to prevent it from happening, that we'd "wake up and see through the lies," the attempts to tranquilize us. But his was only a voice in the night. And half the time, when you were tuned in, listening under the covers, it was impossible to tell if you were just dreaming.

On spring and summer weekends, Stephen rose early and drew a map of the garage sales in the neighbourhood that had been advertised by handmade signs taped to lampposts, charting the most efficient course from one to the next and home again. He rarely came home with anything. He said to me once that buried treasure was hard to find.

On winter weekends he sat in the worn wingback chair he had pushed to the living room window, flicking the newspaper from page to page, raging under his breath at our collective blindness in the hazy, dusty light.

Now he's on an island with my mother. I think. I like to think. Somewhere where an evening sun glistens orange and gold off the sea as they sit watching it on a mat she wove from palms, her head on his shoulder. Alice in a tree house nearby yelling "Big money! Big money!" at an old TV set that washed up on shore.

My father went back to the car dealership to pay for the portions of my treatment the government wouldn't cover, and moved into an apartment above a drugstore. He set up a bench press by the living room couch, his guitar in its case in the bedroom corner where it remained partially hidden by an Ikea wardrobe. When I went to visit him he'd chain my wheelchair to the bike post out front and carry me up the two long flights to his door, holding my chest close to his. He took each step slowly. We didn't speak as he ascended, so the journey felt long. I once broke the silence by telling him he didn't have to be so careful, that I wasn't made of glass, but still he went slowly. Another time, during my grade twelve exams, I was exhausted and let my head drop on his shoulder, nearly drifting off as we went up and up and up. I heard his heart beating faster, and sounds of broken breathing. When he sat me down on the plaid chair he said he was going to order a deluxe pizza and went over to the phone on the wall with tears in his eyes.

I'd like to think he's on an island somewhere too, playing Bowie songs to a ragtag commune of tanned and shaggy octogenarians who listen and bob their heads as they sip hooch out of coconuts. But I can't picture it, as much as I want to. He was the first person I thought about when the ash clouds rolled over and I realized what was happening, but I'm still not sure if it was because I wanted him to save me or if it was the other way around.

My producer Cal says the lines are already lit up. He says we're on in two. I glance up at the old digital clock counting down on the wall of the studio then return to highlighting my notes and stacking them in three piles. Hour 1, Hour 2, Hour 3. All twelve lines on the phone are blinking in front of me.

Cal stands at the control board with his left hand on the fader, the fingers of his right hand counting down in silence.

Five. Four. Three.

Two.

One.

The theme song comes up. It's a song my father wrote a long time ago. It's not even that good, but it's been shared millions of times since I started playing it off the top of the show. I let it play for a while then click on my mic.

"It's Wednesday," I say, pausing as the music comes up again. "We're all still here. For now."

You tune in from all over to find out how to survive. You think I've got the answer. You say I'm the only voice you can really trust now, and you whisper it over the line as if I'm the only one who can hear you, as if the quiet dark around you isn't rustling with perked-up ears. You think I'm genetically predisposed to outlive everything, so you buy my duplicate genes by the ounce and inject them into your veins, not even waiting for the zone nurse to come around and help. You press your radio to your ear to hear what I will say next and panic when the signal is lost. You know but do not care that as we rebuild our cities, our countries, our continent, I've built an empire on you.

You do not know that when the sky went black I went nowhere. That the elevators stopped working and I watched everyone cluster to the windows and then file toward the red exit sign leading to the stairwell, looking at me sympathetically as they passed. Someone will be up soon, they said, squeezing my shoulder. You do not know that I was alone in the dark when my phone rang, and it was my mother telling me in a low, quivering voice to go into the washroom and lock the door. She said she had Alice. She said don't worry, just go. Then the network went down and that was that.

I don't tell you that I didn't make it out that day. I don't say that I rolled my chair into the washroom and breathed in recycled air and drank toilet water in the dark for what felt like weeks. I don't tell you that I was rescued by a man in a make-shift haz-mat suit who was pulling the office building apart for wires and copper and wood. I don't tell you I was nearly dead. You don't even know that I can't walk. That is no way for a hero to be.

I've told you elaborately concocted tales that even I believe half the time. I run through them again in my mind before I say, "Let's go to the phones. "

Cal says, "Chris is on Line 1."

"Chris," I say, "Welcome to *The Seed*."

"Simon," he says.

I don't say anything. No one knows my real name.

"Simon," he says. "It's me."

My finger hovers over the drop button on the phone. I push it.

EMILY BOSSÉ

LAST ANIMAL STANDING
ON GENTLEMAN'S FARM

I came out in the morning to find three wattles frozen in the mud outside the pigs' pen. They had turned greyish overnight, the melting ice on the ground waterlogging them into plump, fleshy petals. Maybe this is just something chickens did. Shedding wattles. Dropping chins to attract roosters. Chickens, am I right? There were clumps of feathers and down drifting across the half-frozen mud, but no signs of blood, as though the chickens had decided to reconfigure themselves into clean chunks, as if that just worked better for them. The rooster nodded sleepily on top of the fence post, undisturbed by their disappearance. The pigs blinked.

I went into the kitchen and dug around in the junk drawer until I found the zodiac calendar I'd picked up with my Triple Seven order. Pig and Rooster were not listed under the "no match" column. In fact, they were a "match," though not an "ideal match." This made good enough sense, as the chickens were slowly becoming part of the pigs but, judging by the pools of yellow bile floating on top of the mud, the chickens were fighting the merger. I called Paul to see if he thought this meant anything.

"I really don't know what the hell kind of meaning you're looking for here, Davey."

I unrolled the calendar again. "I don't know, something about my perfectionism being consumed by, uh, loyalty or, shit, I don't know."

"Your pigs just ate sixteen chickens and the first thing you do is look at a zodiac on the back of a takeout menu?"

"Why would they eat them? All? In one night?"

"This has nothing to do with the zodiac, dopey, and everything to do with the fact that pigs eat fucking everything."

"Even chickens?"

"Sure, if they can get 'em. And once they taste flesh, well, that's the end my friend."

"What now?"

"Give them some Pepto-Bismol. And stop looking at that fucking pussy zodiac."

I began to really feel that the pigs were going to die.

<hr />

The night the envelope from LANDE & WOLFE arrived was the night someone held up the juice bar. I was trying out college on the West Coast and ended up at Shooting Sprouts instead.

One night just before closing, two jerks in bell-bottoms and down vests come in and start massacring my face. The guy on top of me has his knuckles up my nose while the other one jimmies open the register with a crowbar. The guy whaling on me has all of these rainbow patches on his vest, like he's winning a badge for robbery tonight, and he actually has feathered hair. Feathered hair. Once they have the money they leave me in a puddle of spit and blood, the door chiming after them. "Woah, real tough guys!" I scream at them from the floor. "Fucking Farrah Fawcett assholes!" But my mouth is pretty mangled, filling up with metallic, salty liquid, and suddenly something thicker, sweeter—

After vomiting in the sink where we clean the blenders, I decide I need to get the hell out of this city. If I ever get my face tenderized again, it's going to be over something I really believe in. Not a day's worth of wheatgrass profits. When I get home, there it is: a big brown envelope with a note from my mom written on kitchen stationery and something from LANDE & WOLFE on legal letterhead. I open the legal letter first, and it says my uncle Phillip died and left a lot of his estate to me, something about property, something about chattel, a meeting, turnover, so on, so forth. The note from my mom is shorter, saying something along the same lines, but also God knows why Phil would leave this to me as he hasn't seen me since I moved away, and I just don't know the first thing about husbandry, but it's just a hobby farm, really: a little more than a dozen chickens, eight pigs, one goat, a rooster, and a dog. Maybe it would be good for me, and if I can stand the thought of going back to Devon it's mine. Then, at the bottom: *P.S.—tell Paul I say "hi." Yours, Mom.* I've never heard of another mom who signs her letters "yours." Good old Eva.

I'm on the next bus out with as much as I can stuff into the duffel bag I stole from my deadbeat roommate. For a second I think I see Joanna sitting about six rows in front of me, slack jawed and stringy haired, her roots about six inches of grey fading into an orangey urine colour. She's looking straight ahead just like she rides the bus over and over back home, but I can't imagine Paul letting her out like that, and he's been in charge of her since Mrs. Estey died. We stop at some trucker place called Chatter's, and I call Paul collect. It's around 3 a.m. back home, but he picks up the phone on the second ring. I tell him my uncle's dead and I guess I've come into some land or something, and I'm coming home toot sweet. Paul inhales and exhales noisily into the phone.

"Paul. Seriously. This is some Jane Eyre shit."

"Oh man," there's a sound of something falling over, glass hitting glass and shattering. "College boy."

"Wait, listen, are you okay? Did you fall over?"

"You cheap bastard, why the fuck are you calling me collect? You own a goddamn farm."

There's a woman in line behind me who's wearing a lot of velour and tapping her foot.

"Listen Paul, I have to go, someone else needs the phone. But, um, are things, uh, are they pretty much the same back there? At home?"

There is another deep inhale and exhale on the other end of the line. "Different. Very different. We just got a Dixie Lee."

There's no time to say I think his half-retarded sister is on the bus.

No one knew exactly what was wrong with Joanna Estey growing up, and I don't think anyone ever really tried to find out. When I moved to town Paul staked me out as a friend right away. We were nine, and he wore his Green Lantern pyjama top to school like it was a shirt. He kept trying to get the other kids to call him "The Rooster" because it sounded cool. That's how he introduced himself.

"Hey, I'm Paul, but everyone calls me The Rooster."

Paul was clearly the biggest loser in the class, but he demanded respect from the other kids by insulting them, and he had a BB gun.

He brings me to his house after the first day of school and starts naming off a list of endless brothers that reads like a nursery rhyme.

Dave does laundry, for the ER.

Ian joined the army, married a stacked nurse.

No one talks to Randy; he's living with Dennis (and not in the macho kind of way).

Norm's a lawyer; don't talk to him much.

Ben moved to Toronto, goddamned bastard.

And Percy is twelve but just lies in his crib.

Paul stops in front of his house, which is smaller than mine, even though there's only Mom and me to fill it. The middle drags the rest of the house toward it, like it needs more boards at the centre for warmth. The porch is supported by huge sheets of corrugated tin propped up between pillars, ending three inches from the roof. Someone tried to cheer up the entryway by painting the inside green. The effect isn't cheerful; it just makes everyone at the door look like they are about to throw up.

Just as he puts his hand on the door Paul turns to me. "Before we go in, I have to tell you about my sister. She's fifteen." His eyes dart toward the door handle.

"What, is she like, mean or something?"

Paul shakes his head. "No you dope, it's not that, it's just that, well, she's kind of gross."

Sisters were annoying, pigs maybe if they were fat, but no one had ever told me they had a gross sister before. "She's *gross*?"

Paul grabs the rusting door handle and pulls it so it shrieks under his hand. "You'll see. Just go in the living room. She's watching TV. She won't even notice."

Paul's foyer has a strange phlegmy smell, like moulding boots and mushrooms. I step over piled hills of shoes, none of which seem to belong to a woman. The whole place looks dingy, and there isn't any of the usual cheap junk on the walls—no "Bless This Mess," or souvenir crucifixes, not even a badly framed family picture. Around the corner is Joanna. She is sitting in the middle of an aggressively ugly couch that blooms mustard coloured out of the orange shag carpet. She stares straight ahead, mouth slightly open, blue reptilian eyes dead in their sockets. Her face looks like old skin under a Band-Aid. I take one look at her, this teenage girl with saggy boobs and some grey hair, and have to concede in a whisper, "Yeah Paul, I guess she is kind of gross."

"Told ya, dopey." He slaps me on the shoulder, pleased I'm seeing things his way, and pulls me through the hallway, toward the back door. The house is only this hallway with rooms on either side, not even a second floor. We reach the last room and Paul signals for me to stay back and stay quiet, he knocks softly on the door frame, his voice changed. "Ma?

Ma? I'm home." The lights are off, but I can make out the shape of a woman, squat, dressed in shapeless eggplant-coloured cotton. She is leaning over a crib, and touching the face of a child. It's a boy, folded onto his side, his eyes shut and limbs twitching slightly. He is fully dressed in overalls, checked shirt, even a bow tie, shoes with unworn treads. She doesn't look up, but mutters something at Paul.

"Say hello to your brother, Paul. Don't be rude."

"Hello, Percy. I'm going to my friend Dave's house for dinner. That all right?"

Mrs. Estey turns toward the door to make sure I exist, then turns back to the child in the crib. "Sure, sure, that's fine." Paul pulls me out through the back door and into the sunlight, tilts back his head, and crows in triumph. He looks at me and grins.

"That's all right, eh, Davey?"

I shrug. "I guess so. It's just my mom and me."

"No old man, huh? Me too. C'mon!"

Their backyard opens up onto fields and the back lot of a strip mall, full of corroded train tracks and discarded junk. There is a claw foot bathtub, piles of old *Penthouses* mixed in with Nancy Drews baking under the sun. Small paths cut through the grass leading to the more populated areas of the suburb, and Paul darts in front of me instinctively heading for the paved and shaded neighbourhood ahead of us, assuming I live there or somewhere like it. Panting, I slow down and notice a house raised above the rest on a hill, old-fashioned with columns and lacy trim, even a part that goes higher than the rest, capped in black tar shingles with an iron railing around its square top. There are rusty whirligigs on the lawn and porch, moving slowly, measuring something heavier than air.

"What's *that* house?"

Paul barely slows down, pulling me ahead. "Mr. Murray's. He sells houses. Me and Joanna go over on Thursdays."

"What, so he like, babysits you?"

"I guess. C'mon, I'm hungry, I want to go."

"What's wrong with your sister anyway?"

"I dunno. Just slow I guess. She just watches TV and rides the bus. C'mon, Davey."

"Why do you go over there?"

"We just do. He helps out with Percy. Now stop screwing around, dopey, I'm goddamned hungry."

My mom, Eva, does not get mad when I bring Paul home, even though I didn't ask first. Maybe it's his pyjama top, the way he eats his casserole so fast, even the burnt parts where the corn is fused to the tuna, or because he says with her curled black hair she looks like Lynda Carter, the way he strokes the binding of the books in our living room, how he's never had tapioca pudding, how he doesn't make pretend gagging noises when she plays James Taylor, how he slips up once and says "shit," blushing deeply. And when he leaves, he says, "Thanks Ms. Anderson. You can call me The Rooster if you want. Everyone does."

She says, "You can call me Eva," and is all of a sudden someone who is not my mother, or at least not only my mother.

That night when she comes to turn off the lights, she leans over to kiss me and pauses, touching my cheek. "Paul is welcome over any time. You be a good friend to that boy." I wonder what she means.

The pigs all died together in the corner of the pen, their skins glistening with the early morning frost, bound to the surface of the mud like ballooning flesh-toned fungus. I waded out into their deaths, boots breaking through the half-resistant slop until I was standing over them. They were strangely hairy, covered in white humanoid fuzz tapering across their snouts and ears. The one closest to me fluttered albino lashes weakly but couldn't move his head, mud getting sucked into his throat with each inhale, slopping up his bare gums and down into his great swollen esophagus. The rest of them lay there, in a bloated naked orgy, six obese corpses.

I vomited as quietly as I could in the slop bucket. Then I went inside and called Paul.

"They're all dead, Paul. All of them."

"Get in the car, Joanna! Okay what, Davey? Who's all dead?" "The pigs, Paul. The pigs are all dead outside."

Paul sighed. "Shit, son. The pigs. I thought you were going to say your neighbours or something. They're just pigs, dopey. Relax, I'll be right there. 'They're all dead.' Jesus."

When Paul got there I was standing in the pen and the pig was still blinking at me in desperation with his straw lashes. Paul looked scraggly, maybe stoned. He had a three-day beard growth and he was not someone who should grow a beard. It was a reddish blond while the rest of his hair was dark and curly. "This one's still alive," I said, nudging it with my boot. It wheezed softly. I gagged into the slop bucket.

"Jesus Davey. Where the fuck do you think bacon comes

from?" Paul stuck his hands in his pockets and sucked his teeth thoughtfully. "Did ol' Phil have a gun? He did. Over the stove or something, am I right?"

"Yeah. Yeah. A rifle. Over the mantel."

The pig gave a soft little gasp. I swallowed hard. "Oh all right," Paul conceded. "Go in and get the gun, dopey, then call the vet."

I looked into the doghouse on the way past, just to confirm the night hadn't resulted in a total catastrophe, that no one had decreed all life on the farm must be wiped out. I bent down and saw two brown eyes blinking at me like a pilot light. Somewhere, the goat was bleating. "Good dog," I whispered.

Joanna held the door to the house open. Had been holding the door open. She stared straight ahead as I brought the gun out, straight ahead as I went back inside and dialled the vet, straight ahead as the shot sounded. She held it open as Paul came inside, then gently let it go so it latched shut.

"Let's get some food in you," Paul said to me, as if he didn't just shoot a two-hundred-pound animal. "Joanna, how do you feel about riding the bus for a while?" She didn't respond, just walked toward the truck, signalling that yes, a bus ride would be fine.

I grabbed my coat. "Triple Seven?

Paul shrugged. "Where else?"

When we get back from dinner, the bodies have been moved from the pen to the pasture and the vet has left a note on the door: *Intestinal torsion. Change in diet? Call me.*

It is a Thursday in the summertime, so there is no school, which means there is no way to tell what day it is—time by the hour is non-existent. In the field behind Paul's house we are running madly, cartwheeling over rusted nails and mattress springs, dancing around tetanus. Paul has brought an enormous bag of peanuts in shells that taste like sawdust on the tongue, animal feed, pulpy masses spit onto the ground. Paul begins to throw them in the air, and I run through them, and they are suddenly a swarm of locusts rising and descending onto the field. We throw handfuls in the air and run through them screaming "REPENT" and "WRATH OF GOD" when Paul says, "Shit it's Thursday, isn't it?" And he's running up to the house on the hill saying, "Go home, go home, go home, Davey, you dope."

But I don't know if Mom's home and I have no key, so I follow, begging, up to Mr. Murray's, to the weather-beaten board porch, which is assembled fancily, but unpainted. And Paul says, "Fine, stay, you goddamned leech, but don't come in. Just stay."

The heat is awful, there is a bug screaming at the same frequency as a smoke detector. I move into the shade of the door frame and begin to toss peanut shells into the wind, seeing if I can throw them into the gears of the whirligigs on the lawn, prying pebbles from my shoe treads and weighting the shells down, cutting slits in them with my nails, fitting them together to form lopsided flightless rotocopters.

It's been a long time since Paul went in. It's very hot.

If I go inside then Mr. Murray will offer me something to drink, water at least, maybe something sweet with ice, or I can just ask him where the nearest tap is, if there is a hose around back. That's it, just ask if he has a hose around back.

The door is well oiled; it opens without a sound. It is cool inside, and even though the house seems huge and old there is no dust. There is an electric chemical smell. There are pictures on the walls all the way up the staircase. There are sounds, little susurruses, hushing, murmuring, rustling, the shushing of the trees blowing outside. But there is no wind. More susurrusses, fabrics moving, murmurs. Voices? There is a door at the top of the stairs. Open slightly already, a man's voice and whispers, he is soothing someone, there is a toneless animal groan. Eye to the crack, and there is a strange tangle of bodies. What is this configuration? A toneless animal groan. Blue reptile eyes dead in their sockets, she is bent over and makes eye contact with me, staring straight ahead. He doesn't see me, green lantern visible over the curve of his sister's back. The man is secondary.

What? What? What?

Backing away as quickly as I can, over the landing trying to get down the stairs, but I run into a sidetable and it's upended. The bedroom door is thrown open, a man's voice is yelling but I've bolted, vaulted, over the railing across the field, tripping over tires, flying across deposits of broken glass, into the shady neighbourhoods, down the street through my own front door. It is open, unlocked. My foot is bleeding. I've stepped on a nail. "Mom?" I say. Then again, "Mom?" She comes to me and says, as I did, "What?"

⌘

The dog's death was more manageable somehow. It was a death I could get my head around: there was one of him. He was covered in brownish golden fur, with burnt-black patches, some kind of shepherd-lab mix. And people's dogs died. This was something that happened. He had never greeted me, never licked my hand or come to say hello, never barked protectively over the house, the pigs, the chickens. It's not that it wasn't tragic—he lay on the floor of the potting shed, great blue tongue lolling out of his mouth, blue foam coating his nose and teeth, eyes closed in release from what must have been a painful end. I bent down and stroked the fur on the bridge of his nose. When I say to myself, "My dog is dead," it sounds natural, but the blue foam is toxic and synthetic.

Just there, an inch from his head is a pile of what I think is chicken feed. Large sunflower seeds, smaller grains, black granules. A meal that would only be appealing to a dog that hadn't been fed on time, and yes: in the sand-like particles there is the faint ghostly tint of a tracing agent. Eradi-Rat.

When I call Paul he's not surprised. "Didn't you even think to put it on a higher shelf?"

"No, I guess I didn't." I can see the dog's tawny body from the kitchen window, and I don't even bother to ask if there's any meaning in this. The rooster begins to lurch his way purposefully toward the potting shed, death drive in full swing. "Shit, I have to go. Rooster's going for it."

"I'll bring a shovel over, and you owe me some takeout."

Paul arrives with Joanna in tow, both of them looking worn at the edges. Paul smells strange and peppery—the result of smoking dozens of joints and not washing his hair, his curls like sponges. "Joanna, sit on the step," he says, and she does. We carry the dog between us, Paul holding his front legs, me his back, eighty pounds of dead weight to be slung into a hole we've yet to dig. We don't say anything while the shovels break ground in the pasture, digging through layers of mud, throwing rocks aside and finally, lowering the body down, reversing the process, smoothing the top of our handmade grave.

We're pretty hungry after that.

The Triple Seven is a mediocre Chinese place where the lo mein is all right, but they serve you onions chopped into quarters if you ask for extra veggies. Before it was the Triple Seven, it used to be a restaurant called Jives, which served pub food but made the wait staff wear bowler hats. Before that, an Italian place. Before that, a novelty fifties diner. Before that, Mr. Murray's house. But Paul insists that egg rolls beat fried chicken, which is all you can get at the Dixie Lee. It is the place to be if you don't cook and hate poultry.

Joanna sits silently in the back of the truck. When we get out, so does she, but she stays glued to the truck, doesn't budge even though we're all the way to the restaurant door.

"C'mon Joanna," Paul says, about to go in. I see her turn herself around. There are some box stores around the lot now—a Zellers, a hair salon, but you still have a clean view of the tree-lined neighbourhoods. "C'mon, Jo." He's sweet, convincing. "You can get the buffet." She turns herself around again, facing downhill toward the field, and spots her own house, she must. The sagging middle, corrugated tin, green porch. A family passes us on their way into the restaurant. Mother, father, a boy of about ten, a girl of thirteen or so. Joanna turns to Paul. She opens her mouth and pulls back her lips, baring remarkably white and beautiful teeth. She screams, and screams, and screams. She bellows as the owners walk out, as Paul pleads with her, touches her arm. She enters a state of catatonic noise, a deep desperate cry that draws everyone out-side to observe, that renders us unable to load her back into the car. She wails as the owner calls an ambulance, howls along with the sirens, refuses to stop as they carry her in. Paul remains frozen beside me as she disappears through the double doors. They close, muffling the sound, but it's too late: the parking lot remains haunted.

⟳

Mom—Eva—brings me over to the Esteys' the day after it happened. Friday. She is there in Paul's foyer, the heel of her nude pump spearing a deflated orthopedic shoe. Mrs. Estey is taking up most of the door frame, making it so that Mom can't get through. Mom is calling over the top of Mrs. Estey's hair, which she's dyed a strange purplish orange, like she mixed together two kinds of Kool-Aid and went at it. "Joanna, sweetie," Mom is calling, "Joanna, honey, come here a sec."

Mrs. Estey stands there, arms folded, her lips withered over her teeth, like her mouth isn't hers and they're shrinking away from the alien parts. "She won't come. *The Waltons* is on."

"Paul? Paul, honey?" "He's off somewhere."

I watch them through the screen, sometimes hearing them, sometimes not. The holes make it look like they're moving on dotted comic book paper, adding lines around their arms and mouths, making them look shady and cool. I wonder if I'll be able to see Paul again. Mom is getting louder, trying her hard-est to explain something to Mrs. Estey, whose face has stayed the same this whole while. There's a strange edge to her voice. She is all Eva, raging and begging at the same time.

"Do you know what he does in that house?"

"He's a Shriner. He's in real estate."

"Do you know what he does?"

"He gives me money for my Percy."

"Mrs. Estey, you have more than one child. Paul and Joanna—"

"He's sleeping."

Joanna has come to the door frame and stands slightly behind her mother, her teenaged body looking as if it's gone through seven babies, her mom's exact shape. She smiles vacantly straight ahead, focused on Eva, who is beautiful in her skirt suit. Joanna's blue eyes glint as they catch mine through the screen. Her smile shows a lot of gum, and it's more like she's rolling her lips back slowly over her teeth, not really smiling at all. I start to feel sick, because all doors toward her lead to the same thing, and I'm not sure what that is.

Eva is worn down now, each word hard but important work. "Do you know, Mrs. Estey. Do you *know* what that man does with your children in his house?"

Mrs. Estey shrugs. "Of course I know. He loves 'em, that's all. He loves 'em."

My mom, because she is my mom now, throws her hands up like she's been burnt, her mouth open, and takes me, and we're in the car, speeding toward home, and she is shaking but not mad at me, and then we're home and she says go to your room, but not angry, very quietly. I stay there for a while and think about Paul and try not to think about Paul. When I go into the kitchen she's sitting there at the table, her head frozen in her hands, her fingers spread across the sides of her skull as though she is trying to stop her thoughts from spilling into the kitchen.

I grab a pop from the fridge, even though I'm not supposed to have sugar after seven. "Mom?" It's seven-thirty. "Mommy?"

She stays there, a maternal statue, her sadness collecting in droplets on the table.

Paul doesn't come to school for a week, but I think I see him running by sometimes, out around the big boulders on the playground, up to the soccer field and away.

⸺

The goat was the only one I bothered to name, the rest of them I called by their Christian names—dog, pig, chicken, rooster—and that seemed to do. But when Paul and I drank with the goat, we had to name her. It was a week after the dog died and the goat had moved into the doghouse. It seemed cute and homey, a little *Green Acres* or something. Paul and I went out with some stubbies and popped the caps off, watching the goat settle into its house and trying to think of a name.

"How about Zsa Zsa?"

Paul pulls out some rolling papers. "That's a fucking pussy name. Zsa Zsa the goat. What are you, trying to attract women with your goat or something?" He tosses me the paper, and goes back inside, coming out a second later with a carving knife and the good cutting board. He sits down, balances the board on his lap, and begins to chop some weed.

"All right then. Daisy. Daisy the goat." "That's more like it. Daisy. Fuckin'-A."

The sound of the knife echoes out over the pigpen, into the clearing where the livestock is buried. Paul's beard is longer, it's even more weirdly mottled: splotches of orange vivid against his dark, black hair, like his face is trying to camouflage itself. He lights himself a cigarette, then lights one for me too.

"Thanks man."

Paul starts laughing quietly as he rolls. "You remember that time we were sleeping over here and a bat got into the bedroom? And you went out to get Philip and he comes in sauced with the gun, tells us to plug our ears, and fires four times straight into the ceiling. Shot bat everywhere. What did you used to call him?"

"Drunkle Phil."

"What did we call my junkie uncle?"

"Crackle Basil."

"Or, when Phil woke us up and made us pluck ten chickens?"

"A gentleman farmer's dozen." I toss my cigarette butt over by the goat house and keep an eye on Paul. He places the cutting board carefully next to the step and stands up slowly, flicking his lighter at the end of the joint but never quite lighting it. "So, where's Joanna tonight?"

"She's on the bus."

"They run this late?"

"She's on the bus to the Restigouche Hospital Centre." Paul touches the flame to the tip, watches the moment of ignition and lets it burn without inhaling. "I just couldn't fucking do it, Davey."

"Did something happen?"

He draws the smoke in as hard as he can. "Did something happen. Did something fucking happen. I don't know, you tell me, Davey. Did something happen?"

"I just meant—"

"For fuck sakes, something is wrong with her. Very fucking wrong. You saw her the other day, screaming like that. You know what the crazy thing is? That's the most sensible reaction I've ever seen her fucking have, to anything, to anyone. She started screaming and I'm like terrified, yeah, but also like, 'Fucking right!' My life in that goddamned backwoods shithole house, just crazy people and mutes and me." Paul in profile. Paul serious. Paul on the verge of something, almost in motion. "I need to not be here."

"Move in with me. The place is big enough. You can raise the animals—well, the goat, I guess, and the rooster. You can keep them alive."

He turns away from me, facing the pigpen, his anger palpable and overwhelming. "I don't want to raise anything." He picks up the knife by the handle, tosses it, catches it by the blade between thumb and index finger. "I don't want to raise fucking anything. Why the fuck didn't Mom bring her in somewhere? Wouldn't you do that, if your daughter was like her? Or would you spend your time watching your other kid die in a crib, like it's all that exists?" Toss, catch, fingers wrapped around the handle. "What the fuck was wrong with her?" He barely moves, just contracts and lets loose, his arm in close, now extended, fingers fanning, releasing the handle. The blade end over end until it's buried in or beneath a mass of speckled feathers on the fencepost. There is an explosion of wings and sounds, a frantic baying roar that goes on and on, but the blade is buried in the fence post, not the bird. Paul and I sprint so that we are standing over the rooster whose throat is extended, making a strange, strangled screaming noise, garbled and electronic, lasting half a minute. Paul crouches down in wonder. "What the fuck was that?"

"I think it was crowing."

"Jesus, Davey. Well, at least your rooster works."

We stare at the pasture and smoke our brains out.

⸎

When Paul comes back to school we don't say much to each other for a while. I sit next to him in math and hear him breathe in and out as he methodically pours glue onto his hand, lets it dry, then peels it away like a second skin. We start riding our bikes around a lot, just to listen to the gravel and dirt pop under the tires. If we're feeling really conversational we'll stick some cards in the spokes and pedal as fast as we can, the short crackles and hisses speeding up until the wheels sound like they're purring. When we go through tunnels and under bridges the noise swells into the growl of an engine beneath us, and I can't believe we have so much power at our feet—that we can propel ourselves places with a roar just by adding a piece of paper.

Our games change. We try to make noise and take up space without any particular goal. We bring bags of ice behind the school and go up to the top of the hill. We stick our hands in until they ache and we can feel it in our teeth. Then we pitch the ice as hard as we can against the brick wall, watch it shatter, then grab another handful and break that too. We play something called scream run, which is where we go up to the soccer field and run its length yelling the whole way, zigzagging so our feet touch every inch.

What Paul likes to do most is ride our bikes to the town limits, just where the light pollution stops and you can see the stars hanging over the highway. If we turn back to look at the town there is an orange fog suspended over everything. The horizon is clouded by people and the things they use to get from point A to point B. We stare at the town for a good ten minutes, then turn and stare at the highway, the way out his brothers chose for the great Estey exodus. We are silent and stand on the side of the road, watching the pavement cut through the hills, slicing the land into great swaths of earth that fall away from the asphalt without protest. We stay there for a long time, like landmarks hovering on the edge of town until there is a shift in energy all of a sudden, and things feel calm, and maybe even all right.

Paul breathes in and out, and if I close my eyes I feel like he's working my lungs too.

<hr>

I haven't heard from him in three days, not since he almost knifed the rooster. The nights have been cool and clear, and when I step out to feed Daisy there are deposits of hoar frost on the ground, the wheelbarrow, the chicken wire around the goat house, trees like rock candy. I go over to the house and light a cigarette. I've trained her to come up to me and put her hooves on my shoulder, and she'll take the butts right out of my mouth. Ah, Daisy, all the company I have: yellow eyed, clever footed, teeth strangely human and square. I almost trip over the axe, and have to grab for the Triple Seven napkin, caught in an updraft, moving in bits of harsh ice in the sunlight. This is what the napkin says:

Davey, had to go at least for a while. Going out west, here that's what everyone is doing now, worked well for you. Will write. Know where you live. Came to say goodbye but you were sleeping and were always a bitch to wake up. Daisy has goat bloat. Can't get her out, will have to break the house. Must have eaten dog food. Goats are sensitive.

Take care dopey.

Paul

P.S. — Don't be too sad. The rooster lives. Cock-a-doodle-doo.

I bend down and see the top of Daisy's head in the door, mouth slightly open in surprise, a mound of frost on the visible yellow eye. I blow gently on the crystals and they dissolve into a line of liquid, coursing past her tear duct. I can see her distended sides, pushing the body up so that the legs barely touch the ground. If I try to pull her out I'll have to break all four of her legs. I bring the axe down as hard as I can on top of the dog house, wood splintering outwards, everything caving inwards, frost and dirt and wood chips drifting onto the body like dust motes. Every last thing from my childhood has crossed the town limits and moved on. The awful, the wonderful, the people who loved me and are dead, the people who never loved me and are living, the people who I love who are alive but unreachable: sealed in carbonite, on the moon, in a different dimension. How to reconcile the smell of phlegm and fungus in a foyer with a small boy crowing hopefully in a superhero shirt. What is behind doors leading to Joanna. What are the best and worst moments. The removal of a goat corpse from the rubble with the departure of your only friend.

Somewhere, something or someone is crowing wildly.

There, in the wreckage of the paint and the boards is a single gleaming bone, too big for a chicken leg, too small for a dog. Unchewed, unmarked, stripped clean and hopeful, even though it will never turn into anything else or rejoin with a larger body. I put it in my pocket and take a shovel in my hand, Daisy in my arms, and move out to the pasture where the rest of the bodies are buried.

As I break ground, it strikes me that nothing looks so bad if we take the skin off cleanly. Even me out here surrounded by twenty-four corpses of varying sizes. If we take the meat off the skeleton I look happy enough as I bend up and down, digging a hole for Daisy, also smiling contentedly on her side.

My mother at the kitchen table, smiling into her hands as a small pool of salt water collects without explanation below her on the tabletop.

Mrs. Estey, smiling into Percy's crib, Percy grinning back, immobile.

Joanna on the bus, smiling at the road.

Paul on the bus, smiling westward.

Joanna and Paul in the house on the hill that day, nothing strange or deadening, nothing traumatic or bad, because they are not people at all, but two skeletons of relatively the same size balancing against one another. And I can smile as I see them touch because they are both bent and smiling as their jaws and joints work. They smile steadily, one into the back of the other's head, and they really mean it.

RON SCHAFRICK

LOVELY COMPANY

was at work, finishing up for the day, when I got a call from my father. It scared me a little, seeing his name on the screen like that in the middle of the afternoon. Usually I was the one who made the calls, nearly every evening since my mother passed away three years ago. He only ever phoned when he was upset about something, often late at night when his eighty-year-old mind started playing tricks on him, getting him wound up into thinking that so-and-so was trying to take away the house, or that someone else was siphoning money out of his bank account. And so it naturally fell to me to reassure him, often unconvincingly, that everything was all right, that no one was stealing from him, and that certainly no one was trying to take away the old farmhouse he had built more than forty years ago, the house I'd grown up in and where he continued to live.

"What's wrong?" I said.

"Nothing's wrong," he said. "Something's got to be wrong for me to call?"

I leaned back in my chair.

"You know what?" he said. "I think I got a girlfriend now."

Since my mother died he sometimes carried on like this too, crackpot talk of girlfriends and romance, thorny words that jabbed me with something like embarrassment, even though no one could overhear our conversation. He said that one of the personal support workers from Community Care wanted to introduce him to another one of her clients, a woman of similar age and who had also lost her spouse a few years ago.

"I just talked to her on the phone," he said, "and she sounds like a *real nice lady*."

My father's emphasis on these last three words made it seem like an incontrovertible fact. He also sounded so cheerful—a departure from his usual prickly self—that I didn't want to point out he could hardly consider this woman his girlfriend if he'd not met her yet.

"She wants to meet me this Sunday afternoon," my father said. "She's going to come over for coffee. Around three o'clock, she says. And you know what? I'd like you to be here." He said this last part in such an oddly proud way it was as if he were asking me to be the best man at his wedding. "You think you can do that? You think you can come down for the afternoon? I want you to meet her too."

I had planned on going to see a play that afternoon (a modern adaptation of an old Oscar Wilde comedy) with Michael, my ex. It was the final performance; I even had tickets. But there was no way I could *not* go home with this potential crisis looming, and so I told my father I'd be there.

"What do you think?" he said. "What would you say if I got hitched up again?"

I hated the way my father talked at times, how he'd say things like "hitched up"—an expression he'd likely picked up from the TV that was on from morning to night ever since he'd quit farming and retired. When my mother was alive, he was the most taciturn man I'd ever known, stiff and emotionless, a product of Hitler's war and the effect it forever had on him growing up in bombed-out postwar Germany. But since my mother died, he'd become in many ways what I can only describe as a pathetic man: he was often emotional and cried easily, and he nattered on embarrassingly to complete strangers when I drove him to doctor's appointments or to the mall to get his hair cut. A few times I'd even witnessed him being inappropriately affectionate with the PSWs who came to the house to cook and clean, trying to corner them into hugs just as they were on their way out the door, and I'd have to look away and remind my father afterwards not to do that, that he risked losing the services provided him if he kept it up. "What?" he'd say testily. "I'm not trying to *sleep* with her."

He'd never been like this when my mother was alive: not once did I ever see a scrap of affection between them, not even a kiss. Theirs was a marriage of quiet indifference and tolerance—very German in its way—and for the last twenty or so years they slept in separate beds, my mother annexing my old bedroom shortly after I moved out to go to school. (Her snoring, she once confided, kept him up at night.) When I think about it now, it's a wonder I was even born; it must have been a fluke, a one-time deal that led to their only child.

"You wouldn't like it, would you?" he said. "I can tell. You're not saying anything."

He was right. I suppose I had the child's natural aversion to the idea of a stepmother, even if she was at this point still immaterial. And when I tried picturing her, what I saw was of fairy-tale proportions: a willowy, birdlike woman with thinning grey hair and a hearing aid, the better to hear my father with; bony, talonlike hands, the better to tear him up with; and shiny white false teeth, the better to chew him up and spit him out with. And maybe not so unlike my father's delusional worries, my own thoughts also wandered down an irrational path. I feared this predatory old woman would take advantage of my father's slow but progressive descent into dementia to win over his affections and influence him to sign over the property and what little my father had in the bank to her and her wicked offspring.

"Well," I said, "we'll have to meet her first before we can talk about that."

"Y'know, your mother and me, we were together for fifty-three years," my father reminded me, as he often did. "It's not easy now. I get lonely."

"Yes," I said. "Yes, I know you do."

As soon as we hung up I realized I didn't even know what this woman's name was. But I also knew that if I called back to ask, my father wouldn't remember it either. She was still just an idea in his head. Not a real woman.

I drove home on Sunday morning, a two-hour journey down the 401 from Toronto. It was a bright, sunny June morning, warm, and in a way it seemed a shame to be spending such a marvellous day behind the wheel. Michael and I had been separated for about half a year by this time (we were legally common law for seven), yet I clung to the idea that, no matter what, we could still be friends, that his encounters and brief relationships with other men didn't bother me, and that maybe one day we could get back together again. And so, in a completely thoughtless moment, the day after my father called, I handed the tickets over to him. "Here," I said, "take whoever you want," as if trying to make some kind of magnanimous gesture of open-mindedness, as if to say I was above petty jealousy and bitterness.

"You sure?" he said.

Michael was a tall, good-looking man with dark hair, dark eyes, and a dark band of stubble that no razor could ever come close to cleanly shaving off. But as soon as we broke up, he made a prodigal return to the gym and within a couple months lost the paunch I'd always known him to have, along with the scrawny arms and sagging glutes, and, at thirty-eight, he managed to reverse the flow of aging and become once again the handsome man with the winsome smile he was at thirty.

"Great!" he said, flashing teeth he'd also had professionally whitened, and I regretted it instantly.

When I got to town, I stopped at Zehrs and picked up an apple cinnamon coffee cake, plus a precooked barbeque chicken and a tub of coleslaw for lunch. Then it was back onto the highway and into the country, past newly planted fields of corn and hay and orchards of apple and pear trees in their long and perfect rows. When I at last pulled into the driveway, I saw that the front and back lawns were freshly cut (my father must have eagerly fired up the tractor mower, keen to spruce up the place) and that the barn doors stood open, revealing the back end of the '92 Dodge Caravan inside, which had not been driven since my father gave up his licence a year earlier. And I wondered what this woman—whatever her name was— would make of this scene: the tiny brick bungalow that was our house, the barn that had once held more than two thousand laying hens, the dilapidated greenhouse, and the surrounding acres where potatoes and green beans and onions and cucumbers had once been planted but which were now fallow fields of tall, monstrous-looking weeds. I wondered if she'd find all this somehow quaint, or if she'd want to run away, the way I did when I turned eighteen and set off for university. My father came to the door. He was wearing his usual blue jeans and a short-sleeved plaid shirt—his Sunday shirt—and I could see that he had shaved. "Oh good," he said as he opened the screen door, "you got cake," forgetting that he was the one who asked me to pick it up in the first place.

In the fridge I found a casserole dish of rigatoni in tomato sauce—"noodles," my father called it—that one of the PSWs had likely made the day before. I heated it up in the microwave and we ate that along with the chicken and coleslaw I'd brought. "Y'know," my father said when we sat at the kitchen table, "she says she's looking forward to meeting me." Like the other day, he sounded proud, the way he reported this bit of information, as though no one had ever said that to him before, and when I think about it and the solitary life my father had always led, I wouldn't be surprised if that were true. And then he said this odd thing: "The way she talks, she sounds like she's always crying." I could tell he found this trait both attractive and reminiscent of my mother. A lachrymose woman, my mother wept not only at sad movies but also, somewhat disturbingly, whenever she saw scenes on the news of natural disasters, war, or violent crime.

"You see," my father said, waving a forkful of rigatoni, "*you* got a partner, so why shouldn't *I* have a partner?"

I didn't entirely follow my father's logic (what if I had a disease?); I also didn't tell him about the breakup. Although he'd met Michael many times over the years, my father and I weren't close and I hardly ever told him anything related to my personal life. I also offer this as an example of the recent changes in my father's diction. I'd never heard him use the word *partner* before; usually, he only ever said *friend* (as in, "Your *friend* there, does he *have* to come to the funeral?"), as if the word were something unpalatable he was forced to chew.

Shortly after three I heard the crunch of tires on gravel. We were both watching TV, my father and I, and when I went to the window I caught a brief glimpse of a young woman behind the wheel of a silver SUV and the shadowy figure of an old woman beside her.

"Company's here," my father said, clicking off the TV, and together we stepped out onto the porch. "Hello, hello," he called out, waving happily, as he went round to the passenger side of the vehicle.

"Hi, I'm Lisa," said the young woman when she slid out of the driver's seat. "I'm in on Tuesdays and Thursdays for your dad."

Since my mother died, I'd met several of these personal support workers. I'd met Courtney and Brittany (ridiculous pop-star names) and Stephanie, but it was the first time I was meeting Lisa.

"Isn't it exciting?" she said, leaning in conspiratorially. "I told Barbara all about your dad. Y'know, I just thought they're both around the same age, they've both lost a spouse, they're both lonely. So I figure, why not?"

"Yes," I said, smiling politely, observing up close that this woman was probably half my age, a kid of maybe twenty-two or twenty-three, a recent grad in social work no doubt. "Yes, why not."

"So I said to Barbara, 'There's someone you just *got* to meet,' and she told me she was *so* excited after they talked on the phone. 'He sounds like a *real* sweetheart,' she kept saying on the car ride over. Look at her, here she comes, all dolled up."

And there she was, being led by the elbow by my smiling father, not at all the thin, wiry widow I'd expected, but a plump, regal-looking woman, like a dowager of some distinction. She was dressed in a white skirt and a matching white jacket over top of a white blouse flecked with tiny blue polka dots. A string of pearls hung from her neck and a pillar of tightly curled white hair crowned her head. "Hello, luv," she said, extending her hand. "I'm Barbara." And I heard what it was that made my father think she sounded like she was crying: it was the warble in her voice. She was English.

"Well, I'm off. Barbara—" Lisa called. "I'll be back at five, okay?" She turned to me and whispered, "Let's hope it works out," and made a fingers-crossed gesture as she climbed back into her tank-like Ford Explorer.

"What a lovely home you have," Barbara said when we entered the living room.

"My wife and I built it," my father said, aiming her in the direction of the couch as he took his usual place in the armchair. "Have a seat."

"So . . ." I said, clapping my hands together. "Coffee?"

"Tea, dear," she said. "I'd love a cup of tea—with milk and sugar."

"The usual for me," my father said, referring to the thick, syrupy black coffee he consumed throughout the day.

As I poured water into the kettle and got the coffee maker going, I felt compelled to make as much noise as is possible when preparing coffee and boiling water so that I didn't have to listen to their small talk. Perhaps it was because it embarrassed me that my father was on a date, and because I found the whole thing sad and symptomatic of the many changes he was undergoing. For the first time I wondered what my mother would make of all this, but just as quickly I saw her dismissively wave away the whole thing and tell my father, "Ach! Do what you want." Although whether she meant that, I couldn't be sure. I also realized I was in the uncomfortable and unnatural position of being my father's chaperone, and I did not look forward to the conversation that would follow once Barbara left, the talk my father and I would have about her suitability as his bride and what she could bring to the marriage table, and the fierce quarrel that would inevitably ensue.

They were both laughing at something when I came back into the living room, and for a moment I caught the glimmer of something in their eyes, like a look of recognition—or relief: something that said, *So glad to meet you. At last.* "Did you put in sugar, luv?" Barbara said as I set a tray bearing two cups of coffee and one of tea onto the coffee table. She smiled at my father. "I have a weakness for sugar, you should know. And cream. And wine. Yet I'm as healthy as a horse, I'm told."

"Me, I love my coffee," my father said, raising his own cup as if making a toast.

In a way she did look like a bird, I thought, as I settled into the armchair opposite my father. A large, flightless bird, like a turkey, the way her neck was stooped and the thready skin beneath her chin flapped. She also had a long, beaky nose and small dark eyes, and I wondered if she'd been pretty when she was younger.

"So you're from England," I said, after a moment's silence. She was sipping her tea and without turning her head she swivelled those avian eyes in my direction and smirked, as if what I'd said was the kind of banal observation she'd heard countless times and might have hoped I was above making. "How long you been in Canada?" I said, flustered, not knowing what else to say.

"Very good tea, dear, thank you." She set her cup on its saucer. "More than forty years, to answer your question."

"Really," I said reflexively, and glanced up at the little clock on the wood-panelled hi-fi. The play would be well under way by now, I thought, and I wondered whom Michael had gone with, not that I knew any of the contingent of men in his life now; they were all just a slew of names to me, interchangeable.

"And before that we were in South Africa, Robert and I." Barbara turned to my father. "You remember Robert?" she said. "I told you about him. On the phone?"

"Your husband you're talking about," my father said, midway between a statement and a question.

"We were there for several years," Barbara said, fixing her gaze back onto me. "He was a banker, you see. But you can imagine it. The political situation . . . the strife . . ." She shook her head disdainfully. "So when a similar position opened up in Toronto, naturally he seized it." She picked up her tea again, but instead of drinking from it, she cupped it in her palm and gazed at the picture window as if she were staring at a photo from long ago. "Nineteen sixty-eight it was when we came here."

"That was the year me and my wife built this house," my father said. "Nineteen sixty-eight."

"And it certainly is a lovely home," she said again, gazing disapprovingly about the room as though mentally disposing of the old curtains and wallpaper and putting up everything new. "But I had no idea how far out in the country you are. I said to Lisa, 'Where *are* you taking me?' That's certainly going to make it difficult for this to work out since neither of us drives anymore."

For this to work out. The words echoed in my head and, like a stalled truck, sat there.

"But why did you give up your licence, Bert?"

"I get disorientated," my father said. "One time I was coming home from"—he gestured vaguely to the corner of the room—"what's it called now? The mall over here? And I ended up way the heck over by Highway 20. I said to myself, 'What the hell am I doing here?' And that's not the first time it happened either. I was supposed to go in to write the test, but I just figured, ach, forget it."

"So you're at home all the time now," Barbara said.

I saw then what Lisa must have meant by "dolled up": the subtle application of a faint but sparkly blue eyeshadow, nails that were painted a dazzling red; even her toenails were painted. The complete opposite of my mother, I thought. She was never one for cosmetics of any sort, my mother; occasionally she'd apply a clear polish to her nails, but that was the extent of it. Farm work was ill-suited for such extravagances. Barbara's well-pedicured toes reminded me of my mother as she lay dying in the hospital, comatose from all the morphine they kept pumping into her: when the nurse pulled away the blanket to point out the mottling that had started in my mother's bloated feet and legs—the sign that death wouldn't be long in coming—I saw her long and filthy toenails, chipped and uncared for, and a strange and inexplicable combination of shame and sadness welled up within me.

"I'm stuck here," my father said, throwing his hands up in the air.

Barbara shook her head. "You must get so lonely," she said, as though she'd stumbled upon the thing that linked them together and that, hand in hand, they could conquer.

"Oh, I got the girls coming by every day," my father said, downplaying any suggestion of loneliness. "They bring me my groceries and do the cooking and the cleaning. And I keep busy. There's always grass to cut, and I do a little gardening in the greenhouse."

"Oh, I know all about loneliness," Barbara insisted. "I suppose this young man doesn't know anything about *that*"—she smiled wistfully in my direction—"but thank goodness for my Lisa is all I've got to say. I just wouldn't be able to manage without her. She's a wonderful darling. Bathes me in the morning, makes me something to eat. Makes me my tea." She sighed a little, as if the occasion called for it. "I'd die if it weren't for her."

—

Somehow we got onto the subject of church. Barbara said she belonged to an Anglican one in town, that it was walking distance from her house, and she wondered if we belonged to a church as well (we did, a Lutheran one, but we never went). She talked about her daughter, a woman who lived in Calgary with her second husband but seldom called home. "You're lucky to have this young man living nearby," Barbara said, once again smiling in my direction. "Angie wouldn't care if I were dead or alive." And then she sipped her tea, no longer delicately like before, but greedily, hungrily.

"The cake!" I said suddenly. "I forgot the coffee cake. Would you like some? Cinnamon apple, I think it is."

"Just a small slice for me, luv," Barbara said.

I was glad to get out of the room for a few minutes. My smile and false cheeriness had become an enormous strain and, like a diver at last reaching the water's surface, I felt I could finally let go and breathe.

"Tell me, Bert," I heard her say as I clattered about in the kitchen, looking for clean plates and forks, "have you ever been on a cruise?" I suspected my absence from the room offered an illusion of privacy necessary to pose this question. "I'm looking for someone to go on a cruise with," she said.

"A cruise!" my father said. "I haven't been on a boat since I came to Canada in '57."

"Here we are," I said, smiling again as I returned to the living room. "Three coffee cakes."

"Thank you, dear, looks lovely," Barbara said. She turned to my father. "Oh, I *love* cruising. Robert and I used to go all the time. He took me to Barbados and Panama, the Italian coast and—where else did we go?—oh yes, and Alaska."

"For how long?" my father asked.

"A week," she said, lifting a forkful of cake to her mouth. She smiled wolfishly. "But two is better."

"Hey, this cake is good," my father said. "How much you pay for this?"

"Yes, very moist," Barbara said. "Excellent choice."

"It was on sale," I said. "Zehrs."

When a quiet moment had passed, Barbara said, "So, what do you think of my proposition?" She added enticingly, "The sun . . . the sea . . . lovely company . . ."

I could see my father turning it over in his head, trying to picture it the way one might catch the first glimpse of sun as it rises above the ocean.

"Y'know," my father said, reaching for his coffee cup on the end table. He looked at me and smiled. "I always said one day I'd like to travel the world."

I'd never heard my father say such a thing before, and I wondered if he meant it. Could he see himself in a bathing suit and sunglasses, lying on a deck chair next to this woman in similar attire? Could he see himself having cocktails in the evening, dressed in a dinner jacket and tie, mingling with other passengers? Could he see himself and Barbara dancing hand in hand on the dance floor? What would they have to talk about? What would he have in common with these people, the kind of people who take cruises?

"What more could you want, Bert?" Barbara said. "Nothing to worry about . . . Everything all-inclusive . . ."

I couldn't picture it. The images wouldn't come to me—or rather, they did, but they seemed comic somehow, like it wasn't really my father but a stand-in, an actor. What came to me more easily was the image of my father in his usual flannel shirt and grubby blue jeans, the old well-worn slippers he plodded around in both inside and out, and the slow dawning of disappointment both he and Barbara would feel in each other as the two of them sat on the bed in their cabin, turning away from each other, realizing too late the mistake they had made in going on this trip together. My father had rarely, if ever, spent a night away from the farm, and I knew—even if he didn't—that the world beyond the property lines frightened and intimidated him; it contained people who were cruel and judgmental, and this world could best be viewed from the safety of his armchair as it played itself out on television. Ordinarily, my father would have laughed off such an outrageous suggestion—*A cruise! You think I'm some kind of big shot?*—but my father had changed, I no longer knew him, and I needed to protect him.

"How much is a cruise?" I said, hoping the answer would quickly deflate any notion of embarking on such a doomed voyage.

"Three thousand," Barbara said, then sheepishly added, "Maybe closer to four."

"Four thousand!" My father clanked his dessert plate onto the end table. "Oh, no," he said. "And who's going to look after the house?"

Barbara seemed stunned by the question. "Well . . ." she said. "You have neighbours, don't you? They could look in on the house once in a while. No?"

"Yeah, well . . ." my father replied, and the rest of the sentence fell away.

An awkward silence settled over the room as the three of us focused on the cake in our laps. When I at last set my empty plate back on the coffee table, I turned to gaze out the picture window at the leaves on the trees, shimmering in the sunny outdoors, and again thought of Michael and whomever he was with, the two of them laughing no doubt at the goings-on onstage, perhaps a hand suddenly reaching out for the other in the dark.

"That was lovely, dear," Barbara said, laying her empty plate on the coffee table. She brought her hand to her mouth, covering a deep but barely audible rumble of a belch. "Very kind of you. Thank you so much."

"Is there tennis on TV?" Barbara said, when the silence had stretched into minutes.

"You like tennis?" My father reached for the remote and began flicking through the channels.

"Oh, I adore it, dear. We used to play it all the time in the summers, Patrick and I."

Patrick? Was that her husband's name? I was certain she had called him Robert. Maybe Patrick was her son. But something about the sound of my voice and its present false-ness prevented me from breaking up the silence that had once again enveloped the room. Anyway, what did I care? This woman meant nothing to me and I couldn't wait for her to go home.

"And you, Bert?" she said. "You like tennis?"

"Ach!" My father waved away the idea. "I don't care much for sports. I like gardening. And TV. I like the old shows. *The Waltons. Little House on the Prairie.* Those were the best."

"Doesn't look like there's any tennis on, does it, darling?" she said to me.

"Oh, I like this," my father said, pausing the clicker on an old western from the eighties.

"And what do you like to do on a Sunday afternoon?" Barbara asked, turning to me suddenly.

"Oh, he's always got his nose in a book," my father said, upping the volume on the TV.

Barbara, still gazing at me, smiled. "Patrick was the president of the literary society in town," she said, seeming to recall a distant memory. "He was a big reader too."

By this point my father had taken on the trancelike blankness of one absorbed in a movie. I looked up at the clock and tried to think of something to say, and when nothing came to mind I also turned to the TV, as if this were a final and irrevocable act, one I wouldn't be able to undo once committed. On the screen were two men—one in a bowler, another in a cowboy hat—and a woman in a frilly pink dress typical of the period, the three of them riding in a stagecoach that was under attack by Indians on horseback. With a shower of poison-tipped arrows, the Indians killed the stagecoach driver, leaving the horses to run wild and the stagecoach to go out of control.

"That's not Roger Moore, is it, darling?" Barbara said. Without turning around I said it wasn't, though I couldn't remember the actor's real name. "I adore Roger Moore," she said. "Such a handsome man."

That was the last thing anyone said for a long time and I felt the increasingly onerous weight of the silence. But after a while I began wondering if maybe my father and Barbara *weren't* uncomfortable at all, if maybe they didn't mind all this dead air and were simply happy to have each other's company. Maybe *I* was the only one who felt that constant chatter was necessary to abate the loneliness. Then suddenly Barbara said, "Well, I don't know how we're going to do this, how we're going to maintain our friendship."

Was that what it was? A friendship? Already? If someone I'd gone on a date with spoke of going on cruises and maintaining friendships within the first hour, I would have picked up the pungent scent of a clinging desperation and run the other way. But maybe it was different here. Maybe their age was the necessary excuse to forgo the usual plodding steps of getting to know each other.

Or maybe not. Maybe she was simply desperate.

"Any suggestions, luv?" she said, giving me what seemed to be a meaningful look. "You think you could drive me here sometimes? When you come down to visit your father?"

I didn't like this burden she was imposing on me, the way she was already worming her way into our lives without even giving my father and me the chance to talk about it, without allowing things to evolve *organically*.

I looked across at my father for some kind of sign, but he no longer seemed to be listening; he was engrossed in the drama unfolding onscreen, a smile lighting his face. "I could," I said weakly, shocked that her incursion was a matter of asking a simple little question. I cleared my throat. "Sure," I said. "The next time I come down." On the TV screen the man with the cowboy hat was arguing with the woman in the pink dress, the latter now holding a matching parasol over their heads.

"Oh, I have an idea," Barbara said. "Why don't I get you to drive me home today on your way back to Toronto, and that way you'll know where I live for next time. Would you mind, darling? Would you do that for me?"

I knew the idea hadn't come to her as suddenly as she made it sound, that she had probably been mulling it over for a while.

"Would you mind?" she asked, smiling plaintively. How could I say no? "Good," she said. "It's settled. Then I'll call up Lisa and tell her she doesn't need to pick me up. Where's your phone, Bert?"

"The phone?" my father said, snapping his attention back to the present. He stood up and indicated the kitchen. "It's by the stairs where you came in."

"Hello, Lisa?" we heard her say a minute later. As if waiting for this signal, my father leaned in and, grimacing, once again rattled me with an uncharacteristic choice of words.

"Not my style," he whispered.

We watched the movie till the end, and when the woman with the parasol at last kissed the man in the cowboy hat—quickly and hesitantly at first, then long and passionately, the two of them grasping each other tightly—Barbara said, "Oh!" Followed by: "Oh, yes!" And, more longingly: "Oh . . . that's nice."

"Well," my father said, giving the armrests a good slap. "That's love!"

"That's *sex*, I'd say," Barbara replied, and the two of them laughed.

I felt myself redden. "Well," I said when the credits started to roll. "Shall we get going?" The little clock on the hi-fi chimed five; it would be just after seven by the time I got home.

"May I give you a hug, Bert?" I heard Barbara say when I was in the kitchen getting my few things together, and through the half-open living room door I could see her put her arms tightly around my father, while he appeared some-what cool in his response: not at all like the scene we'd just witnessed. Had she attempted a kiss? I don't know; I quickly turned away.

"Thank you for the lovely tea," I heard her say when I loudly jangled my keys. "It was wonderful to meet you."

The play would likely be over by now, I thought as we buck-led ourselves into my Civic. There would be the suggestion of dinner—a bit too early, they'd both agree—or maybe they would return to one or the other's condo, ostensibly for coffee, a quickie before going out to eat being the mutual understanding.

"You all right, luv?" Barbara said as we pulled away from the house. She waved to my father, who was standing on the porch, waving back. Then, just before turning back inside, he locked eyes with mine and gesticulated "Call me" with extended thumb and pinkie, something I'd never seen him do before.

"Sorry," I said, "I was just thinking something."

"I don't know that your father entirely enjoyed my visit," Barbara said when we hit the on-ramp for the highway.

"Oh?" I said. "What makes you say that? I'm sure he did."

All afternoon I hated the sound of my voice, its straining timbre and undeniable ring of falseness, my inability to lie convincingly. It was true: I knew that my father hadn't enjoyed her company and, frankly, I was relieved.

"Well, he seems like a very sweet man, your father."

I did not attempt to respond to this. He was many things, my father, but that was not a word I would have chosen. "He's recently been diagnosed with dementia," was what I said instead, something I'd wanted to tell her all afternoon, the underlying message being: *lay off.*

She looked at me quickly. "Well, you certainly have your hands full, then, don't you? Patrick had dementia when he died."

"Who is this *Patrick*?" I said, surprising myself with the sudden gruffness of my own voice. "Is he your husband or is Robert? I thought he was your son."

"My son?" she said, and gave a short, sharp laugh, like a bark. "Whatever gave you that idea? No, no, my dear. Robert was my wonderful, sweet husband. And Patrick . . . Well, let's just say he was a very"—she hesitated—"let's just say he was a very *special* friend of mine." She paused a moment, allowing that to soak in, then sighed dramatically. "Yes, dear, I know what you're thinking, and it's true. There were three of us in that marriage."

I turned to look at her and I could tell she liked the sound of that, that it set her apart from (if not above) most people.

"Robert was the love of my life," Barbara continued. "That will never change, and Patrick was someone I met twenty-seven years ago when I was in the park one day reading a book. Now I don't want to go into details, darling, but let's just say we became very, very good friends. All three of us."

I did a shoulder check and glided over to the passing lane. I didn't know what to say to that. I honestly had no idea.

"You're not shocked, dear, are you? You don't think I'm some kind of wicked woman, do you, luv?"

Now it was my turn to laugh, a real, true laugh, not one of those polite, forced exhalations through the nose. "No," I said, looking at her. "No, I don't." And I didn't. In fact, in another context I probably would have liked Barbara very much. But she was aching for passion, for love and kisses, the kind of thing she had shared with Robert and Patrick but would not find with my father, nor would I want her to. And for a moment, I saw my mother rouse from her eternal slumber, briefly survey the situation and, pleased with today's outcome, roll over and promptly fall back asleep again.

"You're lucky," I said, thinking of Michael and whatever his name was, and cast a glance in her direction. "That sort of situation doesn't always work out for people."

She looked as though she was about to ask me something, but then quickly faced the highway again. "Yes, darling," she said. "I think I was lucky that way. I was loved by two very dear men in my life. And it's a good thing to be loved. A very, very good thing indeed."

I expected her to ask me if I was married or had someone special in my life, but when she didn't, I knew that my father, in one of their long pre-meeting phone calls, had told her I'm gay. And I was glad she didn't; I didn't want to get into it. What she said instead was this: "You ever go to the theatre, darling?"

I glanced over at her. "I was supposed to see a play today, actually."

"It's been ages since I've seen a play," she said. "Patrick always used to take me after Robert died, the two of us spending the night in Toronto. Wonderful productions we saw. I so miss that now.

"Here we are," she said after we exited the highway and turned onto her street. "The house on the left, dear. Isn't it lovely? Yes, Robert knew how to take care of me."

I pulled into the driveway of a suburban white brick split-level, a house that had once been the gleaming happy home of a young family but that had slowly taken on the slightly shabby look of neglect: the lawn was crowded with dandelions, rust trailed the bottom of the eavestroughs, and the driveway was sun-cracked and warped. A widow lives here, the house seemed to be saying.

I helped Barbara out of the car and, slowly and carefully, up the three steps to the front door. "Would you like to come in, dear?" she said when she'd dug her key out of her purse. "Have a cup of tea?"

"I really should get going," I said, anxious to be on my way.

She held her purse in both hands and looked at me fixedly. "I'm not going to call your father," she said. "I'm going to leave the ball in his court, as they say. But it would be nice to get to know him. Y'know, go out to see movies with him, maybe go to Toronto and see something onstage, spend the night."

You still don't get it, I thought, do you? My father could not give her what she was looking for: she was too educated for him, too worldly, and what she was looking for, like my father's own futile search, was some unattainable ideal, illusory and out of reach and still deeply rooted in the past. He was looking for a *hausfrau*; she was looking for Roger Moore.

"I'm sure he'll call," I said, knowing that he wouldn't, and I smiled, an honest smile that came without any effort or strain because I knew it was over, that neither my father nor I would ever see her again. And I'm guessing she knew it too.

"I think I'll sit outside for a bit," she said, suddenly reaching for the plastic patio chair behind her. "Lovely evening. Nice weather."

I got in the car and backed out onto the street, but when I waved, she was no longer looking in my direction but at the ill-tended rosebushes. She was already elsewhere, perhaps along the Italian coastline, decades away, alone with her memories.

As I expected, my father never ended up calling her. Or if he did, he never told me about it. But I doubt it. What I didn't expect was the departure of the good spirits he'd been in during the week leading up to that one and only date. He became his old cantankerous self again, snapping often at the PSWs, accusing them of trying to poison him or filching money out of his wallet. Once, he even got it in his head that Lisa had called him a "stupid old man" behind his back. There were tears, apparently—Lisa's, not my father's—and the next time I went home the doctor decided it was time to add risperidone to the cocktail of meds he was already on.

Since the afternoon he'd stood on the porch and waved goodbye to Barbara, I assumed my father had forgotten all about her, that he was glad to be rid of her, and that as soon as she walked out the door she would have slipped into that chasm of non-memory known as dementia. But that October, while we were having Thanksgiving dinner and my father was on his second glass of wine ("C'mon, just another glass. If I can't live it up now, when can I live it up?"), a commercial for an online travel company came on TV. Cupping his wine glass, my father turned to me and in a slightly drunken, downcast voice said, "The sun . . . the sea . . . lovely company . . ." And that's when I knew she returned to his thoughts from time to time and that he regretted the outcome of that afternoon. "What more could I want?" he said.

It was just the two of us in the house at the time. A year earlier Michael had sat at this table too, the presence of a guest adding, however illusory, to the festive spirit of the day. But something momentous must have happened to Michael the afternoon he saw the play because I've not heard from him since, except for the card I received in the mail inviting me to his wedding, a tastefully chosen card I quickly tore up and threw out. Of course, neither my father nor I mentioned his absence. In fact, his not being there reflected an even greater emptiness in my father's life, magnifying it to grotesque proportions: no loving wife, no daughter-in-law, no multitude of grandchildren, not at all how my father imagined his last few years would turn out. We were just two aging men alone together, eating turkey and watching TV.

And yet I think about it occasionally, the mistaken sense of satisfaction I felt that warm June evening when I got back to Toronto and called up my father, thinking this intruder in our lives had left for good and we could happily carry on as before.

"What's she going to do for me?" my father grumbled into the phone. "You think she's going to cook and clean? Oh no, she's not going to do that. And what's she thinking? That I'm made of money? Going on cruises and whatnot ... Silly woman. No," he said. "No, she's not for me. *She's* the one who needs help. *She's* the one who needs someone. Not me."

He carried on in this way, and I believed every word of it.

CHARLIE FISET

MAGGIE'S FARM

The girl and the boy speed farther and farther away from Piacenza, where they should have detrained. The girl's perched on the edge of her seat, rocking back and forth slightly as she looks out the window at the blurred landscape painted with the burnt umber sunrise. The boy is completely silent, clutching his stomach as if his chronic, anxiety-induced cramps are gnawing away at him. He's never worked on a farm before. On top of that, they both dread being late to meet Margaret. She hired them on faith, without even meeting them. They've also put a lot of faith in her by buying the ticket to Alessandro with the last of their money. But Margaret doesn't know it counts for anything because she doesn't know how desperate they are.

"Do you think there'll be another train?" the girl asks.

"Yes, of course," says the boy.

"What if it doesn't leave until tonight? Or tomorrow?"

"I don't know," the boy says. He's looking at the floor, as

if the view through the window is making him nauseous. "Maybe there's a bus."

"How are we going to contact Margaret? She won't know where we are—she'll think we decided not to show up at all."

"We'll find a phone at the next station," the boy says. "We'll call her."

"But she'll already be waiting for us."

"Don't worry."

"I am worried," says the girl. "How are you not worried?"

The boy licks his lips, but makes no reply.

"We need this job," the girl says. "You know how much we need it."

As it turns out, Margaret isn't waiting for them at the Piacenza station. When the boy telephones her at the next stop, he discovers that she hasn't yet left her farm.

"Well, what did she say?" the girl asks, as the boy hangs up. They're standing across the street from an old church, their backpacks slumped against the clear plastic wall of the telephone booth. Pigeons strut along the cobbles, pecking at empty shells that lie at the feet of an old man selling hazelnuts roasted on a portable barbeque.

"She said we should take the bus back to Piacenza," the boy says. "There's one every half hour."

"Did she seem upset?" the girl asks. "Irritated?"

"No. She said she's running late, too."

They wait at the station for Margaret. The girl, sitting on her pack, her elbows on her thighs, is just beginning to reach an unbearable level of anxiety when a tiny Ape pickup truck pulls up in front of the station. The horn honks.

A tall, thin woman in her early forties climbs out of the driver's seat. "I'm looking for a couple of Canadians who need a lift," she calls, with an English accent.

"You're Margaret?" the boy asks, as they shake hands. She has a strong grip; firm and dry as firewood. But her eyes are watery.

"No, no. My name's Diane. Don't mind me, I didn't have enough time to change."

She's wearing blue overalls and tall rubber boots patterned with skulls and crossbones. Mud stains on her knees and hay in her greying blonde hair. When she picks up the girl's bag and hauls it into the back of the Ape, it's as if she's slinging a bale. She hops behind the wheel.

"Are we all going to fit in there?" the boy asks.

The Ape is comically small. Usually they're portable produce or flower shops—the girl wonders if maybe that's why they're called "bees." There's only one long, narrow seat in the cab.

"We'll have to squeeze in, unless one of you wants to ride with the luggage," says Diane.

All three of them pile into the tiny truck, the girl sitting in the middle with her knees pulled up and her arms crossed in front of her and resting on her lap.

"Are you Margaret's barn manager?" the girl asks.

"Me? Oh no. I just arrived in Italy a few weeks ago. I got a flight from Heathrow to Malpensa Airport for one pound. You have to book far ahead to get a deal like that. Those flights are going to be the collapse of the airline industry."

On the ride out into the countryside Diane tells them that she's just finished working at a trail-riding business in the forests of Romania. The Romanian language came very easily to her, and now she's hoping to pick up Italian.

"That's one of the reasons Margaret hired me," Diane says. "She needed someone to talk to the Romanian boys she keeps hiring. They don't speak any English at all, and very little Italian."

"How did Margaret hire them?" asks the girl.

"Oh, the same way she found you. She casts her nets very wide." Diane gives them a sideways glance. "Is this your first job in Europe? You look so young."

"We're nineteen," says the boy. "We were backpacking, but we thought we would stop for a while and try something different."

The girl is relieved that the boy doesn't tell Diane they've been eating only apples and cheap baguettes from grocery stores for the past week, and sleeping in stations because they can't afford hostels.

"The farm is a little slice of heaven on earth," Diane says, "except, she's had awful luck maintaining the place. It's so hard to find good help, and Margaret's not a farmer. The place is just a hobby farm, really, but she's let it get a bit out of control. She buys up animals whenever she gets the chance—not just horses. Goats and chickens. She says she likes to have fresh eggs for her guests. But I haven't seen any guests and I'm sick of crawling through their coop on my hands and knees."

"Guests?" the girl asks.

"Margaret teaches horse whispering."

"Horse whispering?" the boy asks.

"Back in the Old West there used to be cowboys who'd shut themselves up in a barn with an unbroken horse. When they came out a few hours later, the horse would be tame. The whisperers never revealed their secrets. But when the towns-people pressed their ears against the barn doors to try and listen to what the horse whisperer was doing, all they would hear were mutterings, whisperings." Diane drums her fingers on the steering wheel. "Margaret uses her techniques on rescue horses or horses that have never had any contact with human beings. She insists on following the tenets of her own brand of horsemanship very closely. It's a way of life, really. As long as you listen to her—I mean, do exactly as she says, to the *letter*—you'll be all right."

They drive deeper and deeper into the countryside. Finally, Diane pulls the Ape up to a tall gate that is surrounded on either side by orange trees. She jumps out of the car and presses a button on the gate's intercom.

"Hello?" says a voice on the other end. "Diane? Are the new girl and boy here?"

"They're here, Margaret."

"Tell them to come up to the intercom, please."

They stand in front of the intercom. Margaret says, "Hello! Welcome to my farm."

She has a beautiful Italian accent. But her words are rushed, as if she's pulled herself away from something very important.

"What a beautiful property you have," the girl says, though they've yet to see beyond the gates.

"Thank you. I am so very lucky to have such a beautiful place to keep my animals. I have arranged things so that you may stay in the guest cabin. Please unpack your bags and have lunch, and then we can get started on the afternoon chores. I have some work to do in the office, but I should be down presently."

The gates slowly open. Diane drives the Ape through. They buzz over a dirt road that slopes downwards through the hills into a small valley where a grey stone farmhouse sits nestled in a grove of trees. The girl can see the roof of an English-style stable just beside the house.

Diana parks the Ape in front of a log cabin at the top of the valley. She gives the girl and the boy a brief tour, showing them how to work the stove, which burns bags of woodchips. There are already towels in the bathroom, and Margaret has filled the fridge and the cupboards with groceries.

"Why don't we meet back at the barn at one-thirty or so?" Diane says. "That should give you enough time to eat something and get settled. Just come down to the gate when you've finished, and I'll let you in."

When Diane leaves, the girl and the boy search their new home.

"Look here!" the boy calls. "What the hell is this thing?"

The girl finds him in the bedroom, touching a bundle of dead leaves that are wrapped in string and hanging from the ceiling.

"It looks like voodoo," the boy says.

"Voodoo? They're just dried herbs. That's how my mom hangs them."

The girl reaches up to touch a sprig of mint but withdraws her hand when she sees that the silvered, pale green leaves are wrapped in cobwebs and blanketed in dust.

"Come look at the kitchen," she says, taking the boy's hand. "Look at all the food Margaret bought us . . ."

They sweep through the cupboards, pulling down boxes of things they want to eat, not bothering with the kettle or the range or even utensils, but eating out of packages with their bare hands. They talk excitedly about what they'll do with the money they earn.

When they have combed through the lower cupboards, the girl stands on the counter so she can see what's in the upper cabinets. She finds that they are filled with pots and pans that have rusted through with filth. They'd have to be thrown away. But when the boy asks her what she sees, she says: "Nothing, just some cookware."

He helps her down from the counter, and the girl wraps her arms around his neck. She presses her body against his and kisses him on the lips.

"I'm so glad we found this place," she says.

"We're very lucky. We won't stay long," he says. "Just until we have enough money to go someplace better."

As they walk down the hill toward the farm, they have a better chance to view the property. The land falls down into the valley at a steep drop-off just behind the barn and house. The bottom of the valley looks like it might have once been a river-bed. The ground is sodden; mud coats the legs and tails and bellies of the horses standing in the paddocks that divide the valley floor into tile-like squares.

The house and barn are surrounded by a courtyard that's closed off from the rest of the property by another fence with a tall gate. They can see the top of a large chicken coop at one end of the courtyard, and three large cages—maybe for ducks or rabbits—at the other end.

When they reach the gate they find it open.

The first thing the girl notices is the sulphurous, rotting-vegetable smell of fetid water. Wine-dark liquid has settled in stagnant pools on the cobblestones, amidst piles of blackened hay and bits of broken wood. A large haystack stands in one corner, next to a shed that's been stripped of its siding. The girl thinks the haystack must have been there for a very long time; its decomposing strata are distinguishable from each other because of a slight variation in the tint of its layers, which change from crisp green at the top to rusty black at the bottom. A tiny creature skitters out from the bottom of the pile and disappears into the shed. *Moles*, she thinks. *Or rats*.

She glances up at the boy, but he seems to notice nothing out of the ordinary.

"What a beautiful horse," he says, pointing to the corner of the yard, where a blood-bay mule is pulling hay down from a rotten stack.

"That's not a horse," the girl says. "Why's it loose in the yard?"

"I'm just about to catch It!"

The girl turns around to see Diane emerging from one of the stalls, towing a little brown pony behind her. The pony looks as though she's pregnant, or has foaled recently; her bulbous body sways beneath the saddle on her back with every step she takes.

"This is Its mother. It only comes to Its mother."

"Whose mother?" the girl asks.

"That mule," Diane replies. "I've never dealt with mules before. I don't know what to do with It. It's why I was late picking you up today. It gets out of Its paddock and then It goes all around the property, wreaking havoc. Margaret owns fifty acres. Sometimes, It disappears for days."

"Its mother is that horse?" the boy asks. "I thought you said It's a mule."

"Its father was a donkey. Its mother is this pony. So It's a mule."

"Is It a boy or a girl?" the girl asks.

"Never checked. Doesn't matter either way. All mules are sterile. It's God's way of saying they're a mistake. Margaret says It's having separation anxiety."

"Separation anxiety?" the girl asks.

Sensing movement just above her head, the girl looks up. She thinks she sees a shudder run through the curtains in the uppermost windows of the house.

"It doesn't want to leave Its mother, but it's high time It was weaned," Diane explains. "It's almost two years old. We put It in a pen right across the property. But It jumped the fence. We tried putting It in with the other horses, but It kicked the latch on the gate. And then It gets Its mother out too. She never goes further than the round bale. But that mule is a different story. It gets into everything. The feed room. The house kitchen. Once, It tried to climb up the stairs—"

There's a sudden, loud grinding noise from the bottom of the valley where the paddocks are. The ducks and the chickens beat their wings against the bars of their cages as the steadily building hum of distant machinery grows louder and louder.

Diane curses. "Don't tell me that fool is coming up the hill!" She drops the pony's reins on the ground and runs toward the path that leads down into the valley. "Stop!" she yells, waving her arms. "What are you doing? *Stop!*"

The tractor's raised bucket precedes its appearance in the courtyard, as if it's straining bodily to make it up over the final lip. Upon seeing it, the mule bolts from the bale and tears across the cobblestones. But instead of running away from the tractor, It runs directly toward it.

The man driving the tractor swerves violently to avoid the mule, and the tractor's front wheels skid on the mulch of rotten hay that covers the wet cobbles. The tractor teeters dangerously at the hill's highest point before beginning to roll back down the path.

A few seconds later, there's a loud crunching noise followed by the sound of glass breaking. Everyone in the courtyard rushes to the top of the path to see that the tractor has crashed through a paddock fence and into a large rock that is embedded in the valley floor. Its bucket lies on the ground beside it. The mule is cantering along the fenceline, in the near distance. It throws a buck in midstride.

"Oh God," Diane breathes, holding a hand to her chest. "Margaret's going to throw a fit. You," she says to the boy, "go get that mule, please." She turns to the girl. "You, catch the pony and un-tack her. Margaret's going to want me to ask the driver what the hell happened."

The boy gives the girl a wide-eyed, terrified look before taking the halter Diane is proffering toward him. He has never caught a horse in his life. But Margaret hired them with the belief that they both had experience working with horses.

"Hurry!" Diane barks. "I can hear her coming down the stairs!"

The girl watches the boy walk toward the path that leads down into the valley. At the head of the path, he meets the man who'd been driving the tractor. The man walks slowly and dazedly. His overalls are muddy up to his chest, and he's missing one work boot.

A loud voice cuts across the courtyard, issuing from the direction of the house. "What happened? What happened to my tractor and my paddock?"

A stout woman strides toward them. Her cheekbones are patched with ruddy splotches, and her chest heaves in and out with exertion. "Who has done this?" the woman asks. "*Who?*"

"It was the mule, Margaret," Diane says. "The new boy's gone to get him. This is the new girl."

Diane introduces them, and Margaret clasps the girl's hand between her small, clammy palms. "Oh," she says. "I am so terribly sorry that you have to see this on your first day, your first hour, on my property! What must you think of me? Did you have a pleasant trip up?" she asks. She's looking across the courtyard, down toward the valley. "You know, you really should have planned it so you wouldn't be late for the train."

"I'm so sorry," the girl says. "There were no signs marking the stations—"

"What is the pony doing with her saddle on, walking loose in the courtyard?" Margaret asks Diane.

"I was going to use her to get the mule," Diane says. "But then the tractor rolled down the hill. The girl's going to catch her right now."

The girl rushes to grab a lead line from a hook on one of the stall doors. Then she stalks the fat pony, who's grazing on the rotten hay that's strewn atop the cobbles. The girl does her best to listen to what Diane and Margaret are saying.

"Ask him what happened, please," Margaret says, speaking to Diane and referring to the man in overalls. He's standing nearby, a clueless expression on his face.

Diane says something to the man in Romanian, and the man quickly replies.

"He says he doesn't know how to drive the tractor," Diane says.

"Of course he can drive it," says Margaret. "That's why I hired him." The man says something to Diane.

"That's not what he says. He says he never knew how to drive it."

"Ridiculous! He's been driving it all week. Ask him why he was driving so fast."

"He says he was afraid of rolling back down the hill if he didn't drive fast enough. He wants to know why the mule wasn't in Its stall."

A strange look comes over Margaret's face; her eyes narrow, as if she cannot comprehend the question.

"Diane, can you please ask Vasil to come into my office?" she says.

Diane laughs nervously. "Oh, sure. But do you mind if I have a quick cig first?"

When Margaret leaves, the girl brings the pony over to where Diane's puffing on her cigarette.

"What's going on?" she asks, taking off the pony's saddle.

"She wants me to fire him," Diane says. "I'm the only one who can speak Romanian, and she needs me to tell him to get off the property."

Vasil seems to have just noticed he's missing a boot.

"How do you know that?" the girl asks.

"Because she's done it two times before, in just the time I've been working here. Just put the pony in a stall when you're done with her. It doesn't matter which one."

Diane flicks her cigarette onto the cobbles, stamps it out, and then disappears through the door of the house, calling Vasil's name and motioning for him to follow her.

The girl suddenly remembers the boy. She's just about to go looking for him when he appears at the top of the path, with the mule in tow.

"I can't believe you did it!" the girl says.

He's holding the line as one would hold a dog's leash, but the mule's trailing behind him, Its large, dark eyes mild and attentive.

"How did you get a halter on It?"

"I just walked up to It and—"

"*No!*"

The boy and the girl turn around to see Margaret standing in the doorway of the house. "No!" she shouts again. "No, no, *no!* There must be nothing, no halter upon that horse's head!"

"What's wrong?" the girl asks.

"I have not yet introduced It to the halter. Take it off. Right now, please!"

The boy begins to unclip Its halter, but before he can lift it over the mule's ears It jerks Its head away and wheels around. It throws a buck and then bolts across the courtyard, sliding to a stop in front of the rotting round bale.

"There must be no processed . . . no manufactured threads upon the horse's skin," Margaret says. "It is unnatural. It demeans and dominates the horses."

"None of your horses wear halters?" the girl asks.

"Most of my horses come from other farms, and have suffered irrevocable damage at the hands of those who have mistreated them. Those wear halters. But I bred this horse myself. It has been submersed in my training techniques since birth. At the moment we are struggling because I am attempting to separate It from Its mother, and I have been so busy that I have neglected to take the proper measures to ensure that the separation goes smoothly." She reaches into her pocket and pulls out a small glass vial that contains a colourless liquid. She presses the vial into the girl's palm.

"Here," Margaret says. "This should take care of It."

The girl looks at the vial; she opens her mouth to ask a question.

"I trust you are comfortable, up in the cabin?" Margaret says, cutting her off.

"Oh yes. It's very nice. Thank you for getting us groceries—"

"Good. I am glad you are happy. I have more woodchips for the stove, should you run out. I apologize for the business with the tractor." Margaret lowers her voice. "But I believe that man was trying to vandalize my property. I caught him stealing just yesterday evening. He took eggs from my hens and he picked through my root cellar, and he even took a pint of milk from my goat. What did he do with this milk? Did he drink this? It's filthy, disgusting behaviour."

The girl stares at Margaret.

"Now, I have prepared a schedule for the both of you," Margaret continues. "The girl will wash the floor in the kitchen and clean the bathroom at the top of the stairs. The girl will also please keep the fires highest in the kitchen stove and in my study. Come in, follow me, come in here . . ."

Margaret leads the girl in through the front door of the house and turns immediately to the right, into a large farmhouse kitchen. A white enamel woodstove sits in the corner by the windows, which are heavily shuttered by shrouds of lace curtains. Diane is standing by the sink, her arms folded across her chest. The Romanian man is nowhere in sight.

"Do you see how cold it is?" Margaret asks. "It is terrible. Terrible. Keep the fires very high. This fireplace is very big and hot, so the wood must be restocked continuously. You can find wood in the barn opposite, and you can use the wheelbarrow to move it in here. Diane will show you. But before the house chores—though not before you've stoked up the fires—you must help to clean all of the horse's stalls. And you must help with the morning turnout, and the preparation of the evening feed. If you have any spare time, you will help to muck out the paddocks."

Margaret's eyes fall upon the boy. "Do you have experience with the chickens?" she asks.

"No."

"Diane will show you what to do. And you will feed the ducks, as well. And muck the paddocks. Can you drive the tractor?"

The boy shakes his head.

"We will perhaps get Vasil to teach you how before he leaves—he has just informed me that he must return to his family in Romania. Diane, you will ask him, please. I have more work to do in the office. Please, do not disturb me unless it is very important."

Diane lights up another cigarette. She smiles, and nods her head.

"All right," says Margaret, clapping her hands together. "Goodbye for now. Nice to meet you, and welcome to the farm!"

When Margaret closes the office door, the girl holds up the little glass vial Margaret gave her. "What is this?" she asks Diane.

"Let me see." Diane takes the vial and unscrews the cap. She smells the contents. "It's just lavender water," she says, as she hands the vial back to the girl.

"Lavender water?"

"It's part of Margaret's natural horsemanship. It's supposed to soothe maternal separation. Just dump it next to the water tub of whatever paddock you find the mule in. But try to make it look like you're mixing it with the water," Diane whispers. "I think Margaret might watch everything from the windows. I don't want what happened last time to happen again."

"Last time?"

"During the last heat wave It went off Its water completely—horses will do that sometimes, if they smell something funny. They think it's poison, you see. The mule was just about dried to a crisp when I went down to check It. Trust me, it's just easier to let Margaret think you're doing exactly what she tells you to do."

The girl and the boy spend the rest of the day in the yard. The sun's just setting over the distant hills when they finish work for the day and begin the climb back up to the log cabin.

"What do you think of it?" the girl asks. Her shoes are soaked through with mud, and she's so tired she feels like she could sleep on her feet.

"About the mule?" the boy asks.

"No. About the farm. About the work. About Margaret."

The boy doesn't say anything for a long moment. "Well, it beats sleeping in the streets, doesn't it?"

The girl nods her head. "Of course it does," she says.

The next morning they walk down to the barn at half-past seven. The bottom of the valley is completely shrouded in a thick white blanket of mist, making it appear as though the stable and its courtyard are a solitary, floating island. As they reach the courtyard gate it begins to drizzle.

They begin their day by helping Diane with the morning feed. Diane tells them that there's no new hay on the property, so they pick through the rotten hay beside the stables.

When the rain picks up, Diane pulls out a cigarette and moves underneath the eaves of the barn while she smokes. She exhales bluish clouds that coalesce with the puffs of mouldy dust that the girl and boy churn up from the hay with their pitchforks.

"I was up all night in the kitchen, drinking a bottle of wine with Margaret," Diane says, as she looks out over the valley. "She was afraid to go to sleep with Vasil still on the property. She thought he might try to rob her."

Vasil sleeps in a small camper on the other side of the manure pile. The camper is completely inert, the blinds drawn. But a pair of tall rubber boots sit on the top step of the little ladder that leads up to the door.

"When is he leaving?" the boy asks.

"We don't know," Diane says. "I translated for Margaret, but he only went into his trailer and drew all the blinds. Hopefully he'll be gone by tomorrow. He was talking to me yesterday, after I told him Margaret had fired him. He told me that he has a daughter back in Romania, and a young wife. He came to Italy to try and find work so he could send money back to them. It's almost the same thing that happened to that nice Hungarian couple who used to live up at the log cabin. They were managing this place before I got here. They left in the middle of the night."

"What?" the girl asks.

"They packed up everything, and were gone before morning. Margaret was devastated."

"Why did they leave?" the girl asks. Suddenly, she remembers the rusted pots in the upper cabinets, the linens still hanging in the bathroom, and all of the groceries left in the cupboards and the fridge.

"I suspect it had something to do with the pay," Diane says.

"Have you been paid yet?" the girl asks, tentatively.

"No," says Diane. "You know, the trail-riding business in Romania owes me thirty-five hundred dollars in back-pay. I don't suppose I'll ever see that money. That's just the way it goes with horse jobs. I always say you'd be silly to do this sort of work for the money." Diane flicks the butt of her cigarette away and turns to the boy. "Let's get the yard taken care of first, then I'll show you how to collect the eggs. Have you built up the fires yet?" she asks the girl.

"No."

"You'd better go do that, fast. Margaret gets very irritable if the fire in her office isn't built up. Don't worry, she's probably still in bed. She's never up before noon. Since she had it out with that farmer, she's been moping around the house. He came to deliver the hay last week, but she wouldn't pay him. That's why we've been using the stuff left over from last spring."

When the girl checks the wood caches in the office and the kitchen and in the sitting room upstairs, she finds them all empty. So she spends the next two hours carting in load after load of wood to pile beside each of the stoves. Soon, all of the fires are burning. But the girl has trouble keeping them hot, and often they subside to coals within minutes.

While she's stoking the flames in the kitchen stove, the girl notices that the room is packed with hoarded objects: the windowsills are lined with half-empty wine bottles and stacks of collapsed cardboard boxes. The clutter's general equilibrium is punctuated throughout by empty pickle jars filled with quantities of strange objects: the rinds from fancy cheeses, tabs from cat-food tins, and a collection of small, black pebbles that shine dully in the light.

The girl does her best to clean around the jars and bundles. She scrubs the pots and pans and other dishes that have been left in the sink, rearranging the cupboards so that all of the bowls and plates strewn atop the counter can fit inside. She dusts the lace curtains and sprays down the windows. All the while, she keeps running up and down the stairs to throw wood on the fires. But the fireplaces are so big that it seems like she could stand beside them all day throwing in wood and it would make no difference.

At one o'clock, she stops for a break. As she pulls on the rain slicker she found in one of the cabin closets, she wonders if it belonged to the Hungarian couple who left in the night—she's almost sure that she and the boy have been eating the groceries they left behind. She debates telling the boy, and wonders if he's drawn the same conclusions.

Out in the courtyard, Diane is standing in front of the boy, holding her pitchfork teeth up while the boy shovels straw into a wheelbarrow.

"Look," Diane says. "Do you see all of that, at the bottom? It's not clean at all. It looks like you just kicked a bit of straw over all the shit and piss."

"I'm sorry," the boy says. "I must have missed that stall." He doesn't meet their eyes as he shovels forkful after forkful of the spoiled straw.

"Just make sure it doesn't happen again," Diane says.

When Diane leaves to cart the wheelbarrow to the manure pile, the boy says, "I knew I wasn't doing a great job. I didn't think I was doing a *terrible* job."

"I know you're not used to this sort of work," the girl says. "I asked Diane if I could feed the chickens and do the mucking and the work with the horses, and you could do the housework, but she said Margaret won't have it. She's too old-fashioned."

The boy looks very worried. He's covered in mud, and his hair is full of straw. His face is pale and his lips are white.

"If I don't do a good job, Margaret will fire us, just like she did that Romanian guy," he says.

"Never mind," the girl says. "How were the chickens?"

"Not bad. I only had to crawl around on my hands and knees in the straw and look for the eggs. The chickens didn't mind me taking them. But they looked sad once I did. How was the kitchen?"

"I don't know how I'm expected to keep everything running in the house," the girl says. "I didn't think Margaret wanted a maid when I answered the ad. I thought she wanted us both to look after the stable."

But the girl knows that neither of them had cared what the job was when they accepted Margaret's offer. Margaret was the only employer who responded.

They eat lunch together in the house kitchen and, afterwards, they drink tea that the girl boils in a kettle on the stove. Just as they are finishing, Margaret's footsteps sound on the stairs. She appears in the kitchen doorway.

"Good morning," Margaret says. "And how is the work going today?"

"It's going well," the girl says.

"I had to build up the fires in the office and in the sitting room," Margaret tells her. "It is very important that everything is kept nice and warm. It is not acceptable to have a cold house when one has guests. I am expecting a student at the farm by the end of the week. I will be preparing in my study, and I do not wish to be interrupted."

Margaret leaves the kitchen and disappears behind her office door, which is directly across the hall.

"Don't worry," the girl says. "I'll keep those fires high if I burn my hands to smouldering stumps in the process." She lifts up her hands and shows her fingers to the boy. They have already been burned in several places.

After lunch, when all three of them are mucking the paddocks, Diane tells them that she knocked on the camper door on Margaret's orders, to try and find out when Vasil was going to leave. When she received no answer, Diane tried the latch, only to find the door unlocked. There was nobody inside, boots gone from the steps.

"He must have left," Diane says, "when he realized he wasn't going to get any money out of her."

At seven o'clock, the boy and the girl walk back to their cottage to eat supper. Without saying anything to the boy, the girl begins to strip the bedroom and bathroom of their linens.

"What are you doing?" the boy asks.

"I'm just going to give everything a wash," she says. "We'll sleep in our sleeping bags tonight."

At eight o'clock, the boy pulls his boots and coat back on, even though they're still soaked with mud. The girl watches him through the cabin window as he sets off toward the chicken coop so that he can feed the chickens once more before dark. While he's gone, the girl picks through the cupboards and collects all of the unopened packages. She throws away most of what's in the fridge, hoping the boy won't notice.

"Margaret was there," the boy says, upon his return. His pants are soaked to the hips; even his jacket is drenched with mud. He strips off his clothes and the girl hangs them in front of the woodchip stove, on a clothesline that dangles from the ceiling. He stands shivering and rubbing his hands against the heat that pours out of the top of the stove.

"I think she must have been looking down at me from the windows."

"She was watching you?" the girl asks.

"She heard me cursing and swearing at the chickens," he says. "The chickens saw me coming, and I think they remembered me. They knew I was the one who took their eggs away. They were pretending not to notice me, like they usually do. But when I spread the corn they started flapping everywhere and pecking at my hands instead of at the corn. It wouldn't have been so bad, except the mule was there."

"The mule?" the girl asks.

"I think It wanted to get at the corn too. It must be hungry—all It does is pick at that rotten bale in the courtyard. When It saw the chickens flapping around the corn It charged the chicken wire, and Its mane got stuck. Then It threw a fit, bucking and jerking Its head around—I thought It was going to tear the whole coop down!"

"Oh no," the girl says.

"The chickens were terrified, and so was I. I panicked and tried to stand up, but I got my hair caught in the chicken wire at the top of the coop. I cursed and swore and chased all of the chickens away from me, because they were pecking and clawing at my legs. Finally, I managed to get myself unstuck and out of the chicken coop—the mule ran off too. But when I looked up Margaret was looking down at me from her window, just watching the whole thing."

"What did she say?" the girl asks.

"She told me that if I can't control my temper I won't be allowed to go near the chickens. Or the horses. I'll only be allowed to shovel mud in the bottom paddocks."

"Your temper?" the girl asks. "What temper? You don't have a temper!" She stands up and runs her hands through her hair. "She's just looking for an excuse to get rid of us because you can't drive that tractor!"

"I've never been so tired in my life," says the boy. "Margaret would never find anybody to work as hard as we've been working for the pay she's offering."

A few days later, a new man arrives at the courtyard gate, carrying only a worn, leather suitcase. He can speak neither English nor Italian. The girl watches from the house as Diane shows him the trailer and then sends him to work at the bottom of the valley with a pitchfork and a wheelbarrow. After that, the girl rarely sees him. He's up and working before anyone else. He only comes into the courtyard when he's carting a full wheelbarrow up the hill to the manure pile.

"Diane says the new guy isn't working out, either," the girl tells the boy one afternoon a few days later, when the boy comes up to the house kitchen for tea. "She said that Margaret asked her to give him notice last night."

"But he's hasn't even been here a week! All he does is work! Why is she firing him?"

"Diane said he refused to ask the ducks' permission before feeding them or giving them water," the girl says. "He was supposed to ask '*permisso?*' And the ducks were supposed to return with '*avanti.*'"

"That's ridiculous," the boy says. "How could Margaret expect him to say that to the ducks? He doesn't even speak Italian."

"Diane says he threw a fit when she told him he was fired. He started smashing things in the trailer—the windows, the fixtures. Diane was afraid he was going to come after her. But all of a sudden he broke down and started sobbing." The girl pauses. "You never would have thought he was violent, by the look of him."

"Anybody can turn violent if you back them into a corner," the boy says.

"I asked Diane if Margaret said anything about us. It's the third time this week Margaret's told me that I'm not keeping the fires hot enough. But Diane said she hadn't heard anything. I think she was lying. There was another empty bottle of wine in the kitchen this morning, and yesterday, while you were in the fields there was a big fight between Margaret and a man who came to deliver a load of hay. Diane says that Margaret refused to pay him again."

"I guess our chances of getting any money out of her are pretty slim," says the boy.

"At least we have a place to sleep," the girl says. "And we have food."

But that night they eat the rest of the pesto and noodles. The girl knows that their stock will be gone before the week is out.

The girl and the boy spend the rest of the week trying to prepare the farm for Margaret's guest. They pick up all the rotten hay from the courtyard, and sweep the stones underneath. The girl scours the hearths and the boy puts fresh straw in the chicken coop and scrubs the ducks' pens with water.

Margaret's student is due to arrive on the morning of the boy and the girl's first day off. The night before, the boy and the girl do not get off work until nearly ten o'clock. Margaret asked them to scrub all of the troughs and water-buckets before leaving.

"She was supposed to pay us today," says the boy, as they trudge up the hill toward the cabin. His teeth are chattering because the sleeves of his jacket are soaked with water. "Did she give you any money?"

"No. Diane said she still hasn't paid her, either. We're almost out of food. We need to go to the grocery store."

"We can go tomorrow," the boy says.

"I forgot to tell you, Diane said that Margaret asked that we come down to the barn at eight o'clock tomorrow morning, just so I can build up all the fires and you can help with the feed and turnout before the guest arrives."

The boy doesn't say anything; the girl knows he's been looking forward to sleeping in tomorrow morning. He leans forward and wraps his arms around his stomach; his shoulders slump forward, as if he's in pain.

"Are you all right?"

"It's nothing. Just stomach cramps."

"I'm getting so sick of this!" the girl says. "Margaret has no idea what she's doing! I never see her working with her horses, and her stupid horsemanship rules just make the animals worse off! She only runs this place so she can collect things."

"Collect things?" the boy asks.

"She collects everything. She takes away the hens' eggs even though she doesn't sell them, and nobody's allowed to eat them. I just end up throwing them out. She collects broken animals and broken machinery. And you should see the weird stuff she collects in the kitchen. What do you think she does upstairs, besides spy on everyone? It smells awful up there. You know, she might actually need help. Like, mental help. If it was just the farm and the animals, it would be bad enough. But she collects *people*."

"Actually," says the boy, his voice hollow, "people are about the only things she doesn't mind getting rid of."

The girl is beginning to worry about the boy. He should have been getting more and more confident in his work with each passing day, but he is only becoming more and more anxious. And his stomach pains seem to be getting worse.

⚬⚬⚬⚬

The next morning, the girl gets to the house half an hour early so that she can ensure all of the fires are built up. After tidying the kitchen and helping Diane and the boy with the morning feed, she cleans the upstairs bathroom, something she's been meaning to do since she arrived.

She scrubs the sink and bathtub, and she washes the floor. She prunes the plants that are hanging in baskets in front of the window. She throws out a number of cracked, dirty soaps from the soap dish and some rotting rolls of toilet paper she found beneath the sink.

When she's finished, she and the boy go back up to the cabin and eat the last of their food for lunch. Then they put on their packs. Diane told the girl that there's a small hamlet with a general store five or six kilometres down the road from the farm.

Just as they are leaving, they see Margaret's guest pull through the front gates. He's a balding man in his mid-forties; he drives a very expensive car.

"Who would ever take a course with Margaret?" the girl asks, as she watches the guest drive down toward the courtyard.

"I don't know, but Diane says Margaret is very well respected in the Italian horse community. Apparently, her family used to be royalty or something."

"What does that count for? The horses don't give a shit."

The road beyond the gate is smooth walking, and the weather is warm. The light pours down through the lines of orange trees and onto the grassy fields on either side of the road. The girl holds the boy's hand as they walk.

When they finally arrive at the general store they buy frozen bruschetta and cheese, cereals and madeleines and four pounds of ground beef, milk and carrots and a favourite brand of packaged chocolate cake that they can only find in Italy. Then they pack all of their groceries into their backpacks and start off down the road back to the farm.

"Well," the boy says. "That was the last of the money."

"It's all right," says the girl. "Margaret *has* to pay us. We'll stay with her until we have enough money to move on. Then we'll leave. Maybe we'll leave in the night, like the Hungarians."

The boy smiles slightly, but neither of them laughs.

When they arrive back at the cabin they eat for nearly an hour straight, cramming the cakes and the raw noodles into their mouths without cooking them, eating slices of bread and drinking milk straight from the carton.

At eight o'clock, the boy says that he's going down to feed the chickens. The night is clear and pleasant, and the girl decides to go down with him.

As they are walking down the path, the boy doubles over suddenly, clutching at his stomach.

"What?" the girl asks. "What is it?"

"Nothing," the boy says. "It's just the cramps. I think I ate too much. We should have cooked those noodles."

After a moment, he straightens up and begins walking normally again. But the girl continues to watch him, nervously.

When they enter the courtyard, they meet Diane.

"Well," Diane says, "I finally got the mule down to the bottom paddock. Margaret asked me to move It this morning when she saw It chewing one of the fences—she didn't want her guest to see It misbehaving. It's certainly not happy about it."

"What does she teach her students, anyway?" the boy asks.

"I don't know," Diane says. She pulls a cigarette from her pocket and lights it. "They haven't been outside with the horses, that's for sure. They didn't leave her office all day. I heard Margaret lecturing him, so I went to have a peek for myself. But when I got there all I saw was Margaret standing in front of a big dry-erase board, and her student sitting in front of her, looking up at her like she had him under a spell. When she saw me, she closed the door in my face." Diane exhales a puff of smoke. "Oh," she says, "Margaret wants to talk to you, by the way. I was just on my way up to the cabin to get you."

"Me?" the girl asks.

"That's what she said."

"Did she say why?" the boy asks.

"No. Didn't say why." Diane exhales another puff.

The girl finds Margaret sitting at the kitchen table, her hands folded neatly in front of her. "Why are you here?" Margaret asks.

"Diane said you asked me to come," the girl says.

"No, I meant *him*."

"I thought you wanted to talk to both of us," the boy says.

Margaret sighs. She runs her hands through her hair and tugs at the ends. "This is what I mean. You do not listen. No one *listens*." She stretches her cheeks into a quick, taut smile. "I wait all day for you to come back, and you stay away. I fed the fires all day by myself while I am trying to teach my student. I cannot teach when it is so cold, so terribly cold! Feel my hands—" She walks up to the girl and places her small, grubby hands on the girl's face. The girl sees dark lines of dirt beneath Margaret's fingernails.

"Margaret," the girl says, "today was our day off. We went to get groceries—"

"Who used all of this paper towel?" Margaret asks, holding up a diminished roll. "I can't understand, where did all of this paper towel go?"

"I used it," says the girl, "to clean the windows."

"And where are the wine bottles?"

"I washed them and put them in a box underneath the sink."

"What about the kettle? And the pots?"

"They're hanging above the stove, on the rack. Look, there."

"Oh," Margaret says. "Oh, oh, oh, *oh*."

She turns and marches back up the stairs toward her bedroom. At first the girl thinks she's storming out, but then Margaret's voice echoes down the stairwell. "Come with me," she calls. "Come with me, please, now."

When the girl reaches the top of the stairs, she sees Margaret standing in the bathroom, a hand covering her mouth. Her eyes are wet with tears.

"How could you do this?" she asks. "How?"

"Do what?" the girl asks.

"How could you . . . move everything? This is not cleaning. This is destroying. It is a disaster!"

Margaret begins to rearrange all of the items that the girl had cleaned. "This was *here*," she says, moving a toothbrush to a different slot on the wooden toothbrush rack. "And this was here." She snatches up a rose-shaped soap from the porcelain soap holder and places it next to the large bar of soap that sits in a dish near the taps. "And these were here," she says, moving the shampoos and conditioners back to their original positions, in the yellow rust-rings the girl had tried to scrub away from around the top of the tub.

"You must never do this again," Margaret says. "Do you understand? You must never come into my house and touch my things again. We use only one sheet of paper towel to clean the toilet seat, and another to clean out the sink. We do not ever move anything or throw anything away."

The girl watches Margaret without saying anything.

"Do you understand?" Margaret asks, her voice frantic. "These possessions I need to stay in the relationships that they are, or I am unsure of how anything is. Do you understand? Are you listening?" She takes a deep, shuddering breath. "Come," she says, when the girl does not answer. "Come down to the kitchen."

Margaret goes back down the stairs. After a moment, the girl follows. She stands next to the boy, in the kitchen doorway. They are both facing Margaret, who's next to the woodstove, warming her hands.

"I am afraid I was hoping that one of you could drive the tractor—"

"The tractor?" the boy asks. "What does the tractor have to do with anything?"

"The tractor's still broken," the girl says.

"It is still broken because I am very poor," Margaret says. "And I cannot afford to fix it. I'm afraid that I cannot afford to pay you, either. I need to hire someone who can fix and then drive the tractor. That is the type of work I really need done around here."

"If you can't afford to pay us," the girl says, "then why did you hire us in the first place?"

"I thought I could pay you, of course. But, no pay. I can't pay. I am very sorry. What I can do is keep you here for a while. For a few more days, anyway, while my student is here. You work while you are here, and you can keep living in the cabin. But I can't pay you. Right now I need for you to build up the fires—"

"No," the girl says. "We're not going to keep working here." She can hear her voice shaking with the pounding of her heart. "We're leaving. Today. And we want our money."

"What?"

"We want our fucking money," says the boy.

The girl resists the urge to turn toward him, open-mouthed, shocked.

"But I just said that I can't afford to pay you."

"We worked," the girl says. "We deserve to be paid. You're going to give us our money, and then we're going to leave."

"But I don't have—"

"Give us our *fucking* money," says the boy. His voice teeters on the border of utter rage. He takes a step toward Margaret. His fists are clenched, as if he's only just stopping himself from throttling her. "We're sick of putting up with all of your bullshit. We want our money, now!"

Margaret looks as shocked as the girl feels. "How dare you speak to me this way?" she asks, stepping backwards, away from the boy and closer to the stove. "How dare you? I won't have this disgusting, disrespectful language in *my* house. You do not come to *my* house and speak to me this way—"

"I don't give a fuck about you or your house," the boy says. "Give us our money! Aren't you *listening?* We're not leaving without our fucking money, the money we worked hard for—"

The girl grabs the boy's arm to stop him from moving closer to Margaret, but he shakes her off and takes another step.

Margaret yelps. She's bumped into the hot stove. She stays perfectly still, caught between the boy and the stove. Her eyes are wide and fearful.

"We want our money—"

"Shh!" Margaret hisses, cutting the boy off. Her voice is shrill. "My guest is still sleeping! You will wake my guest!"

"We want—"

"Fine!" she breathes. "Fine! I'll give you the money. Move, move! Get out of my way!"

Margaret skitters across the hall into her office, backing into it so she doesn't have to take her eyes off the boy. "You will wait here," she says. "I will return in one moment." She closes the door behind her; the handle trembles as she locks it from inside.

The girl kneels down and looks through the keyhole. She watches as Margaret pauses behind her antique desk, in front of a large portrait of a woman with dark, puffy hair and a husky build. The girl had often looked at the portrait while feeding the fire in Margaret's office. Now she realizes that it must be one of Margaret's ancestors.

Margaret takes the portrait off of the wall to reveal a small, steel safe in a niche cut into the stones above the fireplace. She reaches into the safe and withdraws a thick, brown manila envelope. After pulling a handful of euros out of the envelope, she closes the safe and replaces the picture.

"What's she doing?" the boy asks. He's stepping from foot to foot, as if he's about to charge at the door.

"She's getting the money," says the girl. "It looks like she has lots."

There's a crinkling sound; the bills emerge from under the crack in the door, as if Margaret is the ghost inside a haunted ATM.

"Thank you," the girl says, as she picks them up. "Thank you very much."

"Now go away!" Margaret calls. Even though her voice is muffled, the girl can still hear the fear in it. "You will pack your belongings and leave the premises immediately."

The girl feels very strange as she and the boy start up the hill toward the cabin. She wants to say something to the boy— some words of comfort, or at least support. But she finds she can't think of anything. Margaret gave them even less money than she expected; it won't last long—maybe just long enough to get them to their next job. So instead she says:

"All that food. We bought all that food and now we're going to have to leave most of it behind. We'll never be able to carry it in our bags. And the refrigerated stuff will spoil."

The boy doesn't say anything. In the moonlight he looks deathly pale. His brow is dotted with sweat, as if he's desperately fighting the desire to be sick. He's looking at the courtyard gate. The girl sees Diane standing there, smoking another cigarette.

"She knew," the girl whispers. "She could have said something, at least."

"You really gave it to poor Margaret," Diane says, when they get close enough. "I was listening, through the kitchen window."

"I—I just snapped," says the boy. "It was almost like I couldn't help myself."

"Well, some people just have that sort of temper," Diane says. She blows out a lungful of smoke, making the girl cough.

"That's the thing," the boy says. "Usually, I'm not like that at all. I've never yelled at anyone like that in my life."

"He's not," the girl says. "He's the gentlest person I know."

The girl can tell that Diane isn't really interested in anything she or the boy has to say. Diane doesn't know that the girl and the boy had been starving before coming to Margaret's farm. When Diane shows the cabin to the next set of new hires, and she sees the unwashed dishes piled high in the sink, and the muddy footprints leading to and from the furnace, she won't take into account how tired, how overworked and overwrought they were. She'll just think they lived like pigs.

Diane follows them into the cabin and stands near the door while they pack their bags. The girl wonders if Margaret asked her to watch them, to make sure they didn't break or steal anything before leaving.

"Where are you going to go?" Diane asks.

"To the town with the grocery store," the boy says.

"There isn't a bus station there."

"There's a hotel. We saw one."

"Nobody in that whole town speaks a word of English," says Diane. "There's no bus, and there's no train. How are you going to find more work?"

"Worst comes to worst, we can always just go home," the boy says.

"But first we're going to Venice," says the girl. She doesn't know why she says "Venice." It's the first city that comes to her mind.

Diane looks smug; or, somehow validated. "Venice?" she asks. "I hear it's a beautiful city. But very expensive. Wish I had enough saved up for Venice. Well, I guess this is goodbye, then. You take care of yourselves. Take care, now. Take care."

Diane follows them to the door and watches them close it before turning around and heading back toward the house. But she's only gone a few steps when a shrill whinny sounds from somewhere near the bottom of the valley. The mule's mother, who's eating from the rotten round bale just outside the barn, throws her head up and returns the call, her belly heaving. A split second later, a dark blur shoots into the court-yard, clatters across the cobbles, and then leaps over the courtyard fence.

"It's the mule!" the boy says.

"*Basta!*" Diane cries. "Basta! Basta!"

But the mule charges past her, gaining speed as It mounts the slope that leads toward the main gate.

"Catch It!" Margaret screams. She's hanging out of her bedroom window. "Someone catch It, now!"

But neither the girl nor the boy make an effort to stop the mule as It gallops past them. They watch It come to within two strides of the main gate, collect Itself, and then leap high into the air.

When It lands on the other side, It kicks up Its heels and then bolts down the road. The silvery rays of the moon highlight the glossy auburn sheen of Its coat as It picks up speed, travels around a bend, and then disappears into the night.

"Do you think she'll open the gate for us?" the boy asks.

The girl shakes her head.

They take off their packs and then the boy helps the girl over the fence. The boy passes the packs to the girl and then he too scrambles over, tearing his sweater on the way down. They start toward town, following the mule down the moonlit road.

MADELEINE MAILLET

ACHILLES' DEATH

chilles. Not like the god, in French you say it like "a shill"—the *s* is silent. He was my grandfather and he was strong, he could crack a walnut in one hand, he could do that until he got sick and died. I don't remember what it was—I want to say it was his heart. I remember that they put a hospital bed in his room and that it looked funny with all the normal furniture. I remember that he looked like a child; is it a cliché, to say that dying people look like children? Because it's more than just the way we tuck them in.

The day he died we didn't go to his deathbed because I had lice real bad. My mom shampooed my hair with insecticide and sat me at the dining room table and combed out all the dead lice, wiping the comb on a mottled old towel. She has a very expressive mouth and I think that's why she didn't do it in the bathroom. We had a vanity with a chair and everything and it would've been the best place for it, but she didn't want me to watch her.

"Are there a lot?" I asked.

"Oh yeah, honey, there's lots of these babies," she said in her trying-not-to-sound-excited voice. It was the voice she used when she told my dad she was gonna pop his zit. "Wanna see one?"

There was a dead louse on her thumbnail, its exoskeleton was beige, like a worm. I could see the brown food inside, my blood. But I couldn't see the part that mattered, the piercing and sucking mouthpart.

My sister stared at us. She was doing her homework at the table, because she wanted to gloat or she wanted to be near us. That morning, after my father had stood up from the table with his dirty plate and peered down at my head and told me I had lice, they had checked her too. She was hysterical, the eczema and the asthma made her meticulous about her person. Now, she stared like she wanted to see the lice and didn't want to see them.

"Do you want to talk about Pépé?" Mom asked.

I felt itchy and sorry, but mostly for myself.

"No," we said. We hated feelings talks.

I could feel the comb's metal tines scrape my scalp. Well, the lice were almost gone, it would take two weeks of daily combing. It wasn't fair. I was eleven years old—too old for lice. I was a lost boy in *Peter Pan* and one of the other lost boys must've had them. There was another girl lost boy, but most of us were boys. I had thick, mouse brown hair that I never brushed. It stuck out from my head like a triangle. I had to cut it. And I knew that instead of a girl with wild eyes and wild hair, I would look like a weak-chinned, weak little boy. I had a crush on Eric E. He was my birdhouse project partner. I wanted to be pretty. I wanted him to think I was pretty, but nobody thought I was pretty. I wished I were a boy and had a penis. I would write my name in pee. No, I would pee in a drinking fountain.

"Are you thinking about Pépé?" Mom asked.

"No," I said.

The phone rang and my mom grabbed the cordless, still holding the tiny comb. She stood in the doorway and nodded and asked my father eager unthinking questions, "How's your mother? How's your brother? How are you?"

I watched my sister flip multiplication table flashcards that my mom let her laminate at the school board office. I liked to laminate pictures of whales from *National Geographic*. If you laminate something it says that thing is important and that you know how to take care of things that are important. We all loved the laminator. It was huge and it looked like a loom and it looked like a computer. Trimming the plastic edges with the paper cutter frightened me. I thought of a paper cutter as a finger guillotine and felt afraid of myself.

"What are you thinking about, honey?" Mom asked.

"*Jane Eyre*," I said.

"Which part are you at?" she asked.

"There's a big black dog, but I don't know if it's a real dog or if it's in her head," I said. I wanted to read but it would've been rude. I asked my mom how much she'd gone through and she tugged the section of my hair from my nape to my ear-lobes and said, "Baby, I've gotta go slow." So I stared at my sister, staring at her flashcards, and wished my eyes were blue like hers. Mom quizzed her on her multiplication tables, from six to ten, and she looked pleased with herself, and I hated her, the way you hate your sister.

I twisted up a tress of wet hair and imagined I could wring the lice out. I let it go and it clung to my neck, like a disgusting thing. If I were a Medusa I wouldn't have lice. But I knew I wasn't brave enough to be a Medusa. And I wanted to be pretty. I wondered what I would look like when I was a woman.

Mom asked Nadine to put the radio on and it was smooth and she moaned along. Alan Almond played Sade, Marvin Gaye, that kind of thing. My favourite part was the requests. Someone loves Linda, in Flint, and so the listening audience knows that Linda, of Flint, is loved.

The phone rang. This time my mom just left the comb hanging in my hair while she talked to Papa. After, she asked us about our funeral clothes and we pretended not to feel like funeral clothes are weird and boring to talk about. When they played "My Girl" we all sang along. Mom had the most gusto and Dini had the best voice and all our voices together made a mood.

We didn't talk for a while. I asked Mom how much hair she'd done and she drew a line on my scalp with the comb, way beneath the crown. My sister drew the same two-and-a-half-storey house with a fence that she always drew. The sun and the seagull were there, in each corner of the sky. Looking at her drawing, she asked, "What's for dinner?"

"You're in charge," Mom said. Nadine beamed because she was bossy. Mom knew how to appeal to us. She appealed to everyone, she always said, it's not hard to be nice. There were no more frozen entrees so Nadine said, "Toast," and we said, "Toast." And I was grateful that she put the baguette under the broiler instead of toasting the Weight Watchers bread. I ate slowly, because I was hungry but disgusted. Mom kept pushing my head down and saying, "I've gotta get some light on the subject." But it was hard to eat with my head bowed.

"Shit," Mom said. A louse fell out of my hair onto the dining room table. It scurried onto the napkin and onto my toast and got stuck in the peanut butter. Its posterior, which was most of it, twitched. We all stared at it. Against the rich ochre of the peanut butter you could see that my blood was very dark.

Mom said, "Oh, honey."

The louse twitched still. I didn't want my body anymore. White crumbs fell from my mouth, white louse eggs fell from my hair. Mom said, "Dini, throw away the toast," and Dini whimpered with every breath until she dropped it in the bin.

"Those lice are fuckers," Mom said. Nadine's eyebrows went up. "Call them what you want."

"They're motherfuckers," I said, and Mom grinned.

"Motherfuckers," Mom said. And I wanted to crawl into her grinning mouth.

"Motherfuckers! Motherfuckers! Motherfuckers!" we screamed. We were all looking at the towel that was moist with what my mother had been wiping on it. The bugs and eggs she'd gathered from my damp hair in her comb. Mom touched the small of my back and I was glad she was touching me.

"That feels better," she said. She liked to identify a mood to make sure it was a worthy one. It was an annoying habit, but right then it was right.

Nadine's eyes looked crazed. She didn't even take the Lord's name in vain. If someone said, Oh my god, she would say: God can hear you. Say, I'm sorry God. Mom kept trying to make her stop.

"You said *motherfucker*," I said. She blushed and tore a sheet of paper from her drawing pad.

The phone rang. Mom gasped and said, "Take us off your list of people you call."

"You said *motherfucker*," I said, all smug.

"Mom made me," she said and centred her sheet of paper on the "Map of the World" placemat that Mom had laminated.

"Whatever," I said, and Mom sighed. I hated myself for being small. Mom pushed my head down further and kept combing. Nadine drew two more houses, one was orange and one was purple. There was the sun and there was the seagull in each corner, did they strike a balance?

Mom only had three sections left when Papa called to say Pépé was dead. She hugged my sister and then she hugged me, craning her neck away, and squeezing.

"I'm gonna miss the way he ate," Nadine said. Mémé would be unhappy with nobody to feed. Everybody was always saying how observant Nadine was. I thought of all the things I wouldn't notice if she didn't tell me to.

"He always ate three muskrats," Mom said. They were as big as a rabbit so I never knew how he could eat three at the muskrat boil, and sit there after like it was natural, when Mononcle Vic and Mononcle Zéphir and Papa and the others could only eat one. And I heard my sister and my mother talking the way you talk to someone you love, because their voice makes you feel safe.

Mom finished and said, "We're finished," and put the towel in a garbage bag, and tied it off with a wretched bow. She said no one would want to use it, even after she washed it. I took it out back to the dog shit garbage, so the lice would freeze. I looked at the shed for a while, because I liked the way the slant-ing snow piled on one side and made it slouch. The porch roof collapsing made a very loud noise. A harrowing crack and then there was the whoosh of falling. Seeing the roof pull away from the house, and the sky filling the sky, was shocking.

I remember feeling something spinal and unbearable. Like brain freeze without the freeze. I remember the porch roof covered most of the snowy yard—it looked like a smaller snowy yard. Now the larger yard was liminal.

When Mom and Dini came out I was laughing. Dini stood before the roof and she turned to face us, and to face the roof, and to face us, her little body like a cup without a saucer.

"It's because we said *motherfuckers*," she said.

Mom laughed and I laughed too, and Dini didn't mind for once that we were laughing at her. Mom held on to me, her long arms folded around my neck, her hands bracing my shoulders, the bare edges of me, her breasts a pillow for my brain, which was still in my strange skull, and she shook, and I shook, with laughter, and I felt the weirdness of this orb, how bulbous it felt in the back.

Our faces rose with laughter, until we were all looking at the sky.

After that, I no longer lay awake, afraid of dying in my sleep. I knew that dying would wake me up. This didn't help me sleep. No, I lay awake still, for longer now than before, until the sun rose, sore in the red sky. I wanted to make my dreams, and I did. I dreamt I was the Lady of Shalott, floating along in my rickety rowboat, seated still as it dipped back and forth, pooling with water, finding its level below, until the rowboat was gone, and I was supine, but unsinking, floating still, because my gowns were made of gossamers' wings and weighed nothing. They pulled me along a little, catching the currents, making me look this way and that, like a little girl who's got your fingers in her grip.

I fought sleep still, because I felt like it.

ANNA LING KAYE

RED EGG AND GINGER

Mei answers the phone call, though she knows it will make things worse.

"Baby's full-month party," Mother says. "This weekend. Remember?"

Yes. Worse. Mei scrunches up to the wall next to her bed, mobile phone threatening to slip from between her ear and shoulder. After the silence has gone on for too long, Mei has to fill it with something. "What's the baby's name in the meantime?"

"Little Stinker."

"That's what you called me."

"And the hungry ghosts never came for you, right?"

Maybe not, but Mei remembers being confused as a child about why Mother thought she smelled so bad, no matter how well she washed.

Cousin gets on the line. Every sentence is an exclamation. "The banquet your mother's preparing, Mei! She's candying the ginger herself, dyeing the eggs! God, we're lucky she's here to help out!"

Mei imagines Mother sitting next to Cousin on Big Aunt's lacy couch, shaking her head to deny the compliments. If Mei wasn't so fond of Cousin, she would be jealous of all the attention she is getting. Mother's even moved in to Big Aunt's for the baby's first month, the better to help Cousin with her healing regimen. Papaya soup, wood ear tea, fish maw with black bean sauce. Mei taps a cigarette out of the box. She mouths the word *cousin* to S., who is lying across the bed from her. His combat boots and socks neatly arranged on the floor. Looking at his bare feet, Mei realizes that even after all these months she can be caught off-guard by the near-translucence of his white skin. The first time she'd seen those feet, she had traced the raised blue veins on them, marvelling at the tributaries. Blood tangible where hers is not. Now Mei busies her fingers with the cigarettes, the phone.

S. raises himself on an elbow. He points at Mei's stomach, and points at the phone. Mei shakes her head. She tries to focus on Cousin's happy chatter until Baby cries and Cousin needs to hang up.

S. doesn't understand Cantonese, but he can tell Mei didn't share her news with Cousin. He asks why, forehead wrinkled, pupils widened into marbles of sea-glass green. When Mei asks for a light, he takes the cigarette out of her mouth and throws it out her window. They watch the white paper disappear down the shaft of grimy wall between Mei's building and the office tower ten feet away. Downstairs, the tram to Sheung Wan clatters by, bells warning jaywalkers out of the way.

"I'm sorry," he says. He drags a hand through his hair. Mei watches the brown curls spring back into coils. She used to love when that happened. But today, the hand, the hair, she wants to smack them. "I just want you to have support," S. says. "This is a big decision."

"She just had a baby," Mei says. "I'm a big girl. I can handle this."

The truth is, Mei can't afford to lose any more face to Cousin. "Your English is so good," Mother once said, soon after Mei graduated from university. "Why don't you work in private banking?" The next year, Cousin had done just that, graduating in accounting and landing a steady position at HSBC Finance.

Meanwhile, Mei had spent a few years trying to make it in performance art. Her grandest project was a piece for the anniversary of the 1997 Handover. This involved painting her practically naked body China-red with yellow stars and lying in front of the British Consulate with other fellow artists. It had been a costly statement: the press response was underwhelming, and soon after Father cut off Mei's monthly stipend.

"Get a nice job," Mother had said. "Get settled." By then, Cousin had just married a nice Cantonese bank manager.

"No one changes the world by managing money," Mei had shouted. She had moved out in protest. Soon, tired of the sleeping bags and mildewed towels of her equally destitute friends, Mei took a training position at Hype. She could approach hair as living sculpture, she decided. She would style hair to fund art, use art to fuel change. She always thought she would move to Italy by the time she was twenty-six, study mask-making and shape-shifting from the last inheritors of *commedia dell'arte*. Instead, Mei moved into the staff dormitory above Hype, a room shared with three other trainees. Her bed is an upper bunk with a curtain drawn across it for privacy.

Now, a year later, Cousin has delivered every Chinese grandparent's fondest hope: a healthy boy. Meanwhile, the only global impact Mei's achieved has been seducing Hype's star stylist from Montreal. Mei only ever addresses him by his nickname, "S." It was a tease to catch his attention at first, *s* for *syrup*, as in maple, because that was all she knew about Canada. But now it marks him, sweet and stuck to her, available to no other. This makes the other salon girls cry into their pillows with envy. As for the latest news, only S. and Mei know.

S. gives Mei a brief, brave smile. His hand moves over the rubble of sheets, hesitating in the air between them. Then he rests it on her stomach, gently. The soft pat recalls Mother's hands soothing tummy aches. As a child, Mei used to close her eyes and pretend to still feel bad long after Mother's hands had accomplished their work.

"You're a bit happy, right?" S. asks. "Excited?"

"You're insane."

Still, Mei lets S. pull her close. She folds into the comforting warmth of her usual position in his arms—their first real touch since finding out.

The next day, on the subway train to Family Planning, Mei thinks about the quaintness of full-month parties. Back in the farming days, she could understand why waiting a month to name a child made sense. A baby surviving sickness and death that first crucial month would have been a good reason for all the ritual and celebration. But in modern Hong Kong, only unborn babies really need to be nameless. The shock of this thought thumps in Mei's chest. She turns to S., who is leaning against the glass doors of the train. His jacket is camouflage green, which just makes him more obvious against all the chrome and glass.

"I didn't like the way you threw my cigarette out yesterday," Mei says. "Those cost money, you know?"

Mei watches the apology surface in his clear eyes. It was this contradiction between his sensitivity and guerilla gear that had first gotten her curious about him. She had wanted to know what made him laugh, what made him cry. Even now, riding the train to Family Planning together, she is fascinated with what she is learning about him every day. Charmed, even.

"Sorry," S. says. "I was stressed out. You know what they say about smoking and babies."

This is not what Mei wants to hear. "You think I'm not stressed out? That's why I needed a cigarette, right?"

He shrugs.

"If you can't deal with this, you don't have to come." Mei wishes her voice didn't sound so harsh, but she needs to be clear. "This isn't just a check-up, you know."

"Why isn't it?"

Mei sets her jaw and looks out the train window. What she'd love right now is that cigarette. And an egg-tart, flaky with a sun of gold in the middle.

The counsellor's office is dark and smells like bleach. The narrow-faced woman behind the desk looks too much like Mei's mother: a tight perm crowding her face, her body rigid with efficiency. When the counsellor sees S.'s white skin, her eyes flicker into momentary confusion. She speaks to Mei in Cantonese.

"Is this the father?"

"No," Mei says. "Moral support." In desperation, she adds, "He's gay." Mei's face warms.

The counsellor's mouth makes a tight line as she reads Mei's file. Mei almost expects the counsellor to say something like "your clothes are too tight." Instead, the counsellor asks how she can help. Mei asks, and the counsellor tells her the fetus has to be at least seven-to-nine weeks before there can be a procedure. The counsellor calls it a "termination." They will put a tube into Mei and suck the egg off her uterus wall. It will hurt.

The worst part of the visit is the grainy ultrasound, where the counsellor locates a pulsating pimple in the green shadows that apparently represent Mei's womb. "Baby's heartbeat," says the counsellor.

S.'s face blooms into a startled smile. "Wow."

Mei is surprised to see the counsellor smiling back at him.

Mei, who has to crane her neck from a reclining position to see the image, has a hard time believing it represents what's going on inside her. It is so two-dimensional. Monochrome. She shakes her head at the counsellor's offer to make a printout for home, and is mortified when S. asks for one in English. Mei is hasty wiping the cold goop from her stomach. She feels safer with her shirt pulled down again. The counsellor sees them to the door, presses the printout into S.'s hand.

Back in the bustle of the street, Mei decides to be upbeat. "She said fifty percent of pregnancies don't make it past the first three months. Maybe we should buy a big bag of pot, smoke it out of me."

S. laughs. "Or you could drink four gallons of water, and it will swim out."

"I know. Let's have a really great party, with some good music, and it will just dance out."

S. takes her hand in his, kisses the top of her wrist. "Or we could wait nine months. It'll slip out on its own."

Mei pulls her hand back.

He pulls the sleeve of her jacket, playful. "Come on, Mei. Think about it. I can support us all."

She swats his arm away. "We're not even married."

He drops to one knee with his arms thrown open. "Marry me then, Mei."

"I can't marry you." The indignation in her voice stops both of them. They face each other in the middle of the sidewalk, a pedestrian cursing at the obstacle. *Damn white ghost.*

S.'s face is a mask of goodwill. "So, really, you want to be a good Chinese girl. That's okay." He forces a smile, forces himself up. "I knew that about you."

She tries to be cute, rubs a finger on his forehead. "Let's see, under all this white, maybe you're really a nice Cantonese boy?" But the joke is too weak to make either of them feel better.

On the day of Baby's full-month party, Mei wakes with a sore chest. She takes off her nightshirt in the bathroom and checks her profile in the mirror. It is amazing to think of herself as pregnant. There is nothing different about her soft skin, her smooth stomach. Except her breasts feel different. They are stiff and sensitive in the hand. Mei imagines them swelling with milk, like water balloons, nature's prank on unsuspecting mothers. Mei decides not to consult the literature from Family Planning hidden under her mattress. She walks into the living room to look for her cigarettes.

Her roommate, Ching, is sitting on the couch in a long T-shirt and eating a bowl of ramen noodles. She has the Styrofoam bowl balanced on her bare knees, lifting it occasionally for a slurp of soup. The smell of salty broth fills the tight space, making Mei's empty stomach turn.

"Afternoon, bed-head," Ching says. "No work today?"

"I couldn't open my eyes."

"Romeo called for you. You are so lucky. I need love." Ching flicks a lock of burgundy-dyed hair out of her soup and gives a dramatic sniff. "I'm going to be alone forever. Not like you and Prince Charming."

Mei chews the unlit cigarette in her mouth and notices she doesn't want to smoke. In fact, the thought of smoking right then makes her gag. "You think he's a prince?" she asks. She tries to sound bored, keep the hope out of her voice.

"Of course," Ching says. "He's cute, he's got a good job, he adores you. He's tall, too. He's the pot of gold."

Mei puts the cold cigarette on the table and looks at Ching.

"So your mom would let you marry a white ghost?"

Ching's scandalized laughter is all the answer Mei needs.

To reach Big Aunt's home, Mei descends into the tight air of the downtown subway station, rocking under the harbour with other commuters. She emerges out of the ground in Kowloon, joining the evening shoppers flooding Nathan Road. The crowd forces her steps smaller, belching her into a clothing store where everything is child-sized. She can't show up at Little Stinker's party empty-handed.

The store is full of families: mothers, fathers, daughters, and sons stumbling through a mess of strollers and diaper bags. A woman passes Mei, child strapped to her front like a koala bear on a tree. The child's eyes are shut, its head burrowed into her chest. There is a sour smell on them, like old saliva.

Mei feels lost amongst the aisles. She touches the displays of tiny shirts and miniature socks, trying to envision a half-Chinese child in one of the pink anoraks studded with imitation rhinestones. It's all so wrong, even getting proposed to in the street like that. Mei had always thought there would be more of a story, something she could share at dinner parties. A hot air balloon. A hike to the top of The Peak, Hong Kong's lights below like scattered sparks. Something involving the Mona Lisa. A pair of girls giggle nearby, their laughter tinny and annoying. Mei wonders why the sound also fills her with longing.

Mei is most drawn to the baby shoes. Each one is smaller than a credit card and fits snugly in the palm of her hand. She chooses a tough-looking pair of black hiking boots for Little Stinker. The idea of boots for babies makes Mei smile. Does a baby hike alone? Does a baby carry a tiny backpack and compass too?

Mei's mobile phone begins buzzing in her jacket pocket. It's S.

"I didn't see you on the floor this morning," he says. "Are you okay?" Mei imagines him at Hype, hand cupped over the floor phone for privacy. No one even guessing the tedious ache of their recent conversations. Why Mei can't move to Montreal. Why Mei can't have his child and stay in Hong Kong. Why Mei can't give up the child and stay with him. The thought of S. having to act carefree and witty with Hype's fashionable clientele gives Mei a twinge of guilt. When he asks to meet later, she agrees. It will still be nice to see him after the stress of an afternoon with family. It will be excellent. They arrange to meet at the intersection nearest Big Aunt's building.

As Mei messages him the address, she realizes Cousin might not like the boots as much as she does. Cousin is more practical than that. Mei picks out a red velour jacket with the word *BOSS* stitched across it in big gold lettering. A brand name for Cousin, and ironic humour for Mei. It will complement the boots perfectly. Mei pays for both. She and Little Stinker, the least they can do is look cool.

Big Aunt's door opens very quickly, catching Mei in the middle of fluffing out her hair. Mei's latest do is the faux-fro, a jaunty poof that is all the rage in town. S. says it looks good on her, but declines one for himself, no matter how local it would make him.

"You look beautiful as usual," Cousin says. Her playful hands tease out bigger tufts in Mei's hair. "I can't wait for you to see Baby again. He's started smiling! It's great fun."

"Good thing," Mei says, "or you'd have had to return him to the baby store. You kept the receipt, right?"

Cousin laughs and darts down the hallway, looking behind once to make sure Mei is following. Pregnancy has given Cousin a sheen of health. If she is ever commissioned to make a portrait of Cousin, Mei thinks, she'd represent her as a red-bean bun—a happy pastry puff with a shiny buttered crust. Herself, she'd sculpt as a durian: heavy, spiky, guarding its offensive hidden fruit.

The living room is full of family. Even with the relatives milling about, the cacophony of small talk, Mother spots

Mei's entrance instantly. Her conversation with Small Aunt uninterrupted, Mother glances from the clock to Mei's eyes. Late, late, always late. Mother's message conveyed without a word exchanged.

A sudden feeling of exhaustion overcomes Mei, but as she looks about for somewhere quiet to sit she sees Small Uncle has come up next to her.

"Hello, Uncle," she says, because she has to.

"Hello, Mei," he says. "Still doing art?"

"I work in a salon now." Where, Mei thinks, we could help you with that remarkable comb-over.

"The beauty industry, excellent. Are you in management?"

"Just training."

"Getting married soon?"

"No."

There is a pause before Uncle gives a thoughtless "oh," and moves away. It is a relief when Cousin reappears with a dish of candied ginger. Famished, Mei crams a piece into her mouth.

Mother's candy is wonderfully soft, the sugar crystals big enough to give it some grit, but small enough to melt on the tongue. The candy sweetness gives way to the fiery root beneath, and Mei holds it in her mouth without chewing. Ginger children bouncing up and down on her tongue until she can't take it anymore, and spits them into her palm.

Mother descends on the girls, a platter of red eggs in her hands. The eggs are fresh from the pot, red dye still glistening and steaming.

"Ginger means more children," she teases Cousin. "You need to make a girl next year, a loyal ox to accompany her brother rat!" She turns to Mei. "And you, Ah-Mei. Little

Stinker needs cousins to play with." Mother's eyes focus on Mei. "Why are you wearing so much makeup?"

Mei's hands rise instinctively to cover her face. "I'm not," she says.

Cousin rushes in a comment to cover for Mei. "It must be from the rush of the journey."

Mother thrusts the platter into Mei's hands. "Everyone gets an egg," she instructs. As she walks away, the cousins' eyes meet in mutual relief.

"I don't think I'm ready to have another baby," Cousin says. She gives a short laugh. "The stitches haven't even healed yet."

Mei remembers the scar after Little Stinker's delivery, a small angry mouth stretched above the sallow skin of Cousin's pelvis. Cousin had said an operation was the best way to have the baby, allowing her to get back to the bank at a predictable date. But looking at Cousin's weak body helpless on the hospital bed, Mei couldn't help feeling an incredible violence had been inflicted upon her.

Aunts, uncles, and younger cousins pass by, grabbing eggs and ginger from the girls' plates, each outstretched hand accompanied by a perfunctory greeting. "Congratulations!" "Where's that cute little baby?" "Getting married soon?" The younger children beg for a touch of Mei's hair. "It's like cotton candy," the littlest one sighs.

The girls field the stream of relatives with practised grace, smiling and nodding and giving short answers with just the right amount of information: too much means tedious follow-up questions, too little means painful drawn-out inquiry.

"Eggs and ginger. What you two need to be doing is feeding each other," says Big Aunt. Mother's older sister, Big Aunt is what Mother would look like if she was fatter and happier. Big Aunt takes a piece of ginger and forces it into her daughter's laughing mouth. "The hot ginger gives a weakened new mother energy," she tells Cousin. The jade-ringed hands take an egg from Mei's plate. Big Aunt's quick fingers shuck the vermillion shell, revealing a trembling white meat underneath, streaked red where the dye seeped through. "And for you, Mei, you need the lucky red eggs to make you happy and strong for the future."

As Mei accepts the bite of egg, she looks into Big Aunt's broad face. The wrinkles bunched around her eyes can only have been formed from an excess of smiling. Sometimes, when Mother is deep in a tirade, Mei tries to hear the words in Big Aunt's gentle, supportive style. It helps her resist the urge to argue back. The egg slides slick on her tongue, easing the emptiness she's been feeling all day.

"When you were babies, you were our family's new hope," Big Aunt says. "Now the next generation brings even more joy."

The food in Mei's mouth turns to mush.

Then Big Aunt pulls Mei closer to her, speaks in a whisper. "Mei, I heard there's a magician stylist at your salon, young, from Montreal. Do you think he can help a frizz-head like me?"

Mei catches herself beaming. To be able to think and talk about S. openly in this room. "We're good friends," she says. "Though you're hard to improve, Auntie."

"Flatterer. I heard he's booked months ahead. But *Hong Kong Business Magazine* wants me to do a photo shoot at the new store next week and I thought I'd better get a spruce-up—"

There is a wail from the back of the room, and they all look up, alarmed. Following Cousin's eyes, Mei sees Baby raised in the air above a cluster of fawning relatives. The child's mouth is a black hole of sound, his face purple like he is about to pass out from the effort of screaming. When Cousin rushes over to take the screeching baby in her arms, Mei finds herself following. The three barricade themselves in a quieter room.

Big Aunt has converted Cousin's old room into a nursery, and the familiar walls feel welcoming after the smother of the family room. There is a window that looks down on the main street, and Mei walks over to it, enjoying the sight of ant-sized people scurrying underneath. She can see the intersection where she will be reunited with S., and marks the spot on the glass with her finger. Hopefully they can at least watch a movie or share a meal before resuming the tense conversations of what to do next; if this is their end or new beginning. Maybe even share some wine. Mei had turned S. around on wine when she pointed out that the French seemed to be fine drinking through pregnancy. "Okay," he'd allowed. "In moderation, though, right?"

Mei turns to Cousin, who is sitting on a new couch. The upholstery is covered with cartoon cherubs. The cherubs are cheeky, peeking down at Cousin's breasts, one nipple clamped in the moist circle of Baby's mouth. Between the two of them, Mei had a more impressive bust, it is something they always joked about when they went swimming as teens. Now Cousin has ponderous globes that Baby is vigorously applying himself to. Cousin's breasts are surreal epitomes of fertility, like they're out of some Botticelli painting. Mei can't stop staring. Her newly tender chest chafing under the T-shirt.

Cousin gives a shy smile. "I didn't think it was going to

work, at first. But Baby knew what to do. He started nursing right away." Cousin's voice carries an awed reverence, like someone who has witnessed a miracle.

All of this frightens Mei. Cousin's tone, the sight of her and Baby still fused together, and especially the word *nursing*. Mei lowers herself onto the floor next to them, at eye level with the scrunched face of the baby. His mouth twitches rhythmically; his eyes wide open and fixated on the air near Cousin's heart.

"Well, now we know what breasts are really for," Mei says. The platter of eggs she brought in is on the coffee table. Mei picks up an egg, enjoying the fit of it in her palm. "I'm sorry my mom keeps calling him Stinker," she says. "It is so annoying." Mei raps the egg against the tabletop. Cracks fissure the red shell.

"She's just being protective," Cousin says.

"From made-up ghosts?"

"Maybe they're real to her."

The peeled egg releases from its shell, its oily smell beckoning. Mei has been hungry all day, but nothing seems satisfying except these bland eggs. She sinks her teeth into the soft white mound.

Cousin looks at Mei. "You know what she said to me the other day? She said she hoped I would make a better mother than she is. She said she hoped Baby and I would be good friends."

"What can you say to that?" Mei asks. She is unable to meet Cousin's eyes, staring instead at the bowed baby's head, which has finally slipped free from the breast. His eyelids have lowered into closed flaps, newborn dreams flipping behind them.

"I said every parent is destined for failure. I said I accepted the failure."

"Um." Mei points to Cousin's bare breast, still hanging out of her shirt.

Cousin widens her eyes in horror. They laugh as she re-arranges herself.

Asleep, Baby looks like a beleaguered old man who has fought to be here, cheek smeared against Cousin's chest. Mei closes her eyes too, and in the darkness of her head, she smells them. Cousin and Baby. It is a comfortable smell, of warm skin and baby powder and clean clothes.

For someone who has only ever succeeded, Mei thinks, Cousin seems pretty smart about failure.

Just before the naming ceremony, Mei needs to vomit. With an apologetic smile, she pushes her way through the river of relatives, stumbles into the bathroom.

Hacking coughs force clear bile out of Mei's mouth. Each wave sends her knees digging into the spotless marble of Big Aunt's floor. The family counsellor had spoken about light nausea, but this feels like Mei's guts are trying to jump out of her body. Ginger sandpapers her throat. Her family's joyful cries come muffled through the door.

After Mei flushes away the evidence she feels much better. The purging leaves her almost refreshed. She takes her time washing her hands. Watches the suds build into small mountains of lather. Rinses under scalding water. Her hands come out red and scrubbed. The decisions she made at Family Planning were easy, but now her body's changing.

Mei checks the mirror again. She pinches her cheeks to bring back the colour. She bites her lips. As Mei straightens her T-shirt she passes her hands over the stowaway in her stomach.

It embodies all the stolen kisses she's shared with S. in Hype's cramped storeroom, pressed tight against each other to avoid knocking the silver-pink rows of shampoo bottles from their shelves. All the plans S. and she conjured in their night walks along the churning dark harbour, fantasies of exploring western China by rail, watching the northern lights dance in the Yukon. He could teach the baby things he's tried to educate Mei about: Frisbee, blue cheese, ice-skating. In Montreal, there are even some good art schools to look into.

A knock on the door. Mother's voice calls her name. "What are you doing in there? Hurry up. The ceremony's about to begin." The door jiggles, and then Mother is inside the bathroom. Mei curses herself for forgetting to lock it.

"What's this smell? What's happened?" Mother's nose is wrinkled in judgment, her head tilted back to smell better.

Braced for the reprimand, Mei keeps her face turned to the mirror. "I'm sorry. It's nothing. Maybe food poisoning."

"Poisoning? Now?" Hastily, Mother rubs her hands together to warm them, closes her eyes to concentrate. She puts one palm on Mei's stomach, another supporting her back. Energy courses between the two palms, spreading warmth up and down Mei's body. In the mirror, Mei is surprised to find that over the years she has become the taller of the two, the burr of her hair almost a foot above Mother's sooty perm.

"It can't be food poisoning. Your stomach is warm." Mother's eyes search Mei's in the mirror. Silence hangs between them like a bridge, neither of them finding the words to cross it.

"Well, I feel better now," Mei says. "Thanks."

Mother pushes Mei out the door. "Hurry up, we'll miss the announcement of Stinker's name."

They stand next to each other at the back of the noisy, laughter-filled living room, shoulders almost touching. Cousin's banker husband holds Little Stinker, who stares unblinking at the fan of people around him. Radiant, Cousin stands behind her husband, arms around his waist. With a flash of scissors, Big Aunt lops off a lock of Baby's thick hair and holds it in the air like a winning raffle ticket. The relatives all cheer and clap.

"Long life!"

"Great happiness!"

When Little Stinker's true name is announced, Mei glances over at Mother, and catches the wide smile on her face. Mei has grown up trying to capture these unprotected smiles, nestling them in her memory before the animated joy dies out of Mother's eyes. She leans over to her mother.

"I have something to tell you," Mei says.

Mother turns and meets her eyes, still laughing and clapping.

It is just a moment, but their shared silence is all Mei needs to let in the possibilities. She could quit smoking. She could keep the baby boots. She could go downstairs in a minute and say, "Martin, would you like to come up and meet my family?"

DEIRDRE DORE

THE WISE BABY

I was lying in bed, running a low-grade stress-induced fever, copying passages into my notebook from Heidegger's *Being and Time*, when someone knocked at my door. A tall woman with pale skin stood there with a baby stuffed into a Snugli on her front. Her hair hung down in a thick brown braid that reached her waist, and she wore a pair of baggy jeans, a grey wool Stanfield, and thick-soled worn hiking boots. I recognized her as the woman who had moved into the unit next to mine a few months back. There were six of these units in a row, sharing one long, leaky roof, each with a small yard separated from the others by a rotting wooden fence. The baby's arms were squeezed into the sling against his body and his face was covered in a bright red crusty rash.

Hi. Is Darryl home? she said.

I said, No.

A few nights before, after I got off shift, I had come home and found Darryl lying on the couch, smoking a joint. I took off my shoes and threw my clothes into the washing machine.

I am a philosophy student-slash-server. He is an artist-slash-server and was my boyfriend for four years. He painted large female nudes in oil and hoped to get noticed one day.

Busy? Darryl asked.

Slammed, I said. If I wash my shirt now, do you think you can iron it for me in the morning? I really, really need to sleep in.

Darryl said, Vivian? Listen up.

He had two things to tell me. One, that his art was the most important thing in his life. And two, more important even than his art, he might be gay. I laughed. I said, Oh great, I'm thirty-three years old, ready to start my life, and I'm stuck with a boyfriend who is having a heterosexual meltdown.

Being gay is one thing. Not being gay is another thing. But not knowing, well, that's something else.

I told him, Do me a favour, go sort yourself out somewhere else.

The next morning he moved up the mountain to his parents' condo in Whistler, to paint, wait on tables, snowboard, and sort himself out somewhere else.

I didn't mention any of this to the woman on my doorstep, who introduced herself as Deb and said she had come to return a stamp she had borrowed from Darryl.

She put her hand in her pocket and kept it there. After a moment I said, Anyway, I'm Vivian, nice to finally meet you.

She smiled and said, And this is Caro.

Caro and I made eye contact.

Hi Caro, I said. Caro farted.

Oh, he's having a poo, Deb said.

I started thinking about the root of *ontological* and the root of *ontical* and wondering how long I could let Darryl suffer before I phoned and invited him back. Thing was, I was writing a paper on Heidegger's Dasein for my Ph.D. and having Darryl gone was actually a blessing. I had a lot more time to concentrate, and the deadline for this preliminary paper was coming up quickly. I was desperate to nail a unique perspective, something that hadn't been done before, and it was starting to look like everything had been done before.

Not to mention I was on shift at the Copper House six nights this week.

Deb said her husband, Johnny Rain, was having a caffeine withdrawal fit and could she borrow some coffee. She told me she had met Johnny in Campbell River a couple years before; she was fresh off the fishing boat and he was getting headshots done. Now they were married. With a kid. She told me her husband was the guy in the latest beer commercial and asked me if I'd ever seen it. I told her I didn't have a TV.

She said, He's the guy at the bar who's drinking the wrong beer.

I remembered then that I'd seen the commercial during an après-ski up at the mountain last season with Darryl. In the commercial, Johnny Rain is standing at the bar, holding his beer in the air in a beckoning way, his hair combed down flat, gelled and parted neatly on the side. He looks good but dorky, and when the beautiful blonde walks by, giving him a look, we see that she is actually looking at the man behind him.

I dumped a half-cup of coffee beans into the grinder and pulsed them. The baby jerked.

Drip or French press, I yelled.

Deb yelled, Drip.

I handed her a baggie of freshly ground coffee, and the baby curled his tongue out of his mouth, then pulled it back.

Little boy? I asked. I tried not to notice the raging war zone on his face.

Yep, all boy, Deb said. *Caro* means "dear" in Spanish.

As in expensive? I asked.

That too, she said.

You're not Spanish, I guessed.

Actually, I'm a Newfoundlander, Deb said.

The expensive baby was staring at my hair, which I was absentmindedly twirling.

He loves blondes, Deb said.

I stopped twirling.

Your baby, I said. Ummm, it looks like his arms are trapped.

Yeah I know, she said. I've got his sleeves pinned to his sleeper so he doesn't scratch.

Oh. Cute kid, I said.

Yeah, you should see his little pecker. He's gonna be quite the lady-killer.

When I phoned Darryl later at his parents' condo, a guy answered and I hung up. When I phoned back, there was no answer.

Everyone is the other, and no one is himself. . . . And only that which is unmeaning can be absurd.

The next day Deb phoned. It's on! It's on!

She was talking about the beer commercial. I told her again I had no TV.

Being-alone is a deficient mode of being-with, its possibility is a proof of the latter.

I put Heidegger down. I couldn't concentrate. Out in front

of the units was a communal play area, a few benches, shrubs, a swing set, a slide. As far as I knew, Caro was the only child in the development.

Once I'd looked out and seen Johnny lounging on the bench with his shirt off, leaning back with his arms behind his head, soaking up the sun. The baby was tied into a swing, moving back and forth, a ridiculous grin on his face. Deb was licking Johnny's armpit. Sometimes we could hear them yelling. Asshole, bitch. They really had the hots for each other.

Deb later told me that Johnny insisted that they put Caro in the teepee when they were fighting or loving or doing both. The teepee took up their entire yard. She told me that when she was pregnant she used to lie down in the teepee and listen to Bob Dylan.

I was deep into *One's state-of-mind is therefore based on thrownness* when Deb knocked on the door again.

She had Caro on her hip and his face was buried in her hair, which was braid-free and hanging loose like a wild animal's, almost to her waist. Caro was biting it and twisting it and generally smothering himself in its tangles, sucking at it as if it held the answers to all the questions of life.

Deb: Sorry, sorry to bother you again. I lost my hairbrush. Do you have one? Johnny usually brushes it for me, but he's gone for an audition.

Johnny was trying to break into the film scene. So far he had landed the one commercial. When he wasn't acting, he was window washing. I handed her the brush.

Me: Is Johnny Rain his real name or stage name?

Deb: Real name. He's Native. Can't you tell?

Me: I wasn't sure, I thought he might be Greek or Hawaiian or something. Squamish Nation?

Deb: Yeah. Three-fifths.

Me: Three-fifths? How can he be three-fifths?

Deb: What are you, the fraction police?

Then she shifted gears. Vivian, do you think he's hot?

Me: Well, he's pretty hot. I mean, not my kind of hot, but I can see where Caro gets his looks.

Deb: Oh, really? Well, just so you know, Caro is not his baby.

Me: You kidding me? He's a carbon copy of him.

Deb: Look. If I say he's not Johnny's baby, then he's not Johnny's baby.

Then she said: It's just that, my first kid, I lost him. Me and Iggy just come in from eight days of trolling Seymour Narrows, fighting like cats and dogs and the worst haul we'd had in three years and the weather just sick and Isaac had this nasty diarrhea the whole time and I was bitchin' about the bilge pump and he was bitchin' about the dirty Pampers and throwing them overboard and I smacked him and said he was polluting the harbour and he said I don't need this shit and he picked up Isaac—he was two years old—and got back in the boat and headed north to the Charlottes and I ain't seen him since. Which would have been just right except he took my baby. So I figured out then that the only way to make sure I never lose another is to keep certain factoids to myself. Like who's your daddy, eh? Who's your daddy, Caro? It drives Johnny nuts, but that's the way it is.

Then Deb said, Would you mind brushing it for me?

I began brushing Deb's hair. Starting at the bottom, pulling the tangles. Her hair was stubborn, electric and snarled.

Deb: Don't get the wrong idea, but when Johnny does it, it really turns us on.

Johnny came round the next day to use the phone and sat Caro on the front doorstep. I asked him how Caro was doing.

Johnny: Little better today. I got him smeared up with Vaseline. Deborah's decided not to take him to work anymore, she thinks he's allergic to dog hair.

Two weeks earlier Deb had landed a job at Pet Fabulous in the mall, shearing and brushing dogs while Caro played with a doggie toy in an empty crate.

Caro's face looked like a slice of watermelon, glistening with petroleum jelly. He lit up when Darryl's cat jumped off the couch and pranced up to him. You could tell that Caro really, really, really wanted to touch the cat but he was in his usual straitjacket. His struggle was fruitless and unnerving. He kept crashing over on his side as he reached with his head. Darryl and I had talked about having kids, but we weren't ready. Caro rubbed his bruised forehead on Johnny's pant leg. Outside it was raining like a bastard. In three hours I had to be at work. I had seven days and four thousand words to go. I glanced at my notes. *Anxiety brings Dasein face to face with its own-most being thrown.*

Johnny said there wasn't much window washing now that it was turning cold, and he never got a callback on the Cialis audition. He was holding an apple up to Caro's mouth, letting Caro gnaw away on it. We talked about the strata fees and the roof.

Then he goes, Hey, can I borrow a skirt?

Oh man, I thought, not him too.

He scowled, I mean for Deb. It's our first anniversary and she's got shit for clothes and I want to take her out someplace nice.

The only thing I had that might remotely fit was a stretchy teal blue knit. She was at least thirty pounds heavier than me. Maybe more. I sighed and handed it over.

As they were leaving, Johnny was intoning Skwxwú7mesh-ulh at Caro, encouraging him to repeat it. Ain't this kid something, he said.

I had time for one more chapter. *Dasein is never simply what it presently is, but is "existentially that which it is not yet."*

When the day came, I should have expected that the restaurant they would pick to celebrate in would be mine. They had married on Halloween and this anniversary night the place was packed and half the diners were in costume. My hair was sprayed gold and radiated out in huge rays around my head. I was the Tiger-Sun. I scrambled to find them a table and a high chair.

Johnny was wearing a T-shirt that read *No Olympics on Stolen Native Land*, and he had his hair done in the same way as in the commercial, flat, gelled, and neatly parted to the side. He ordered the boring beer. Deb was in my long teal knit skirt—stretching out the elastic waistband and making lumps in the ass—and a floral blouse that really didn't match. Caro was dressed as a ghoul. His eyes were circled in black and he had long red wounds or tear marks painted on his face. I couldn't tell if the blood was real or fake.

Deb whispered, I know, it scares me too, but it was Caro's own idea, I wanted him to be a baby vampire.

His sleeves were firmly pinned to his tattered ghoul costume.

When he started fussing, squirming in the high chair, the other diners started to notice and muttered amongst themselves. The manager asked me if I knew those people. When I said, Yes, slightly, she said, Deal with it. I took their beers to the table and said, Caro's rash looks a little better.

Deb sighed, Oh, it comes and goes.

Does he still scratch?

Of course not. He can't.

They studied the menu and ordered sweet potato fries, saying they weren't very hungry. I made the kitchen double-size them on my tab and throw in two salads.

Then a party of eight showed up, everybody in costume, including a couple of old white people wearing fake Indian suits, complete with feathers in the headband and beads and faux leather, and Johnny was ready to bust right out of his skin at this point. By the time I got them seated, Deb and Johnny had both gone to the washroom and left the tiny bloody ghoul howling, unable to scratch himself. I couldn't put food down in front of empty seats. When they came back, Johnny's hair look-ing even more like the losing end of a beer commercial than before and Deb with flushed cheeks, the super-sized fries were half cold. Deb sent them back to the kitchen for reheating.

The next morning Deb knocked on my door at eight. Vivian? Do you have any extra Tampax?

I freaked. Don't you ever go shopping?

I told her to look in the bathroom herself because I was going back to bed.

Deb stood stock still for a second, then spun around and left. Caro glared at me from the Snugli on her back.

When I knocked at their door ten minutes later, with a box of Tampax in my hand, Deb slipped out into the hallway. Inside her place were empty Mason jars, a taxidermied pygmy owl, a plastic statue of the Virgin Mary. She picked up Caro and set him on the boot rack. Then she took the Tampax, opened the door, and tossed it inside.

She put her hands over Caro's ears and said, I wish I'd never had this baby. I wish I could go back to the ocean and haul fish.

I said, Come on, Deb, that's crazy.

Deb said, Not so loud, he'll hear you.

I whispered, That's crazy.

She said, It's not crazy, it's true.

I said, Well, why not let Johnny Rain have him, then? Then you could do what you want.

Deb said, I didn't say I wanted to give him up, I said I wish I never had him. There's a difference. You're the philosopher, you should know that.

I asked her if she ever expected to get custody of Isaac again, and she said, Who?

Then she said, Oh, Isaac. A long pause, and in that pause Caro threw up, a volcanic milky eruption.

While she cleaned herself and the baby, she said, Isaac wasn't mine. I lied.

Indeed it is even possible for an entity to show itself in itself as something that it is not.

I went to bed with Heidegger.

Or still, something good which looks like, but "in actuality" is not. Φαινόμενον ἀγαθόν.

It was three o'clock in the morning. A full moon outside.

How the worldly character of the environment announces itself in entities within the world.

I could see the shadow of their teepee in my yard.

The manifest. That which shows itself in itself. Φαινόμενον. *Phenomenon.*

It was so wrong, I mean, nice, but wrong. It was a cliché. The Squamish Natives didn't use teepees, they built longhouses.

And in my dream Deb said, What are you, the teepee police?

I said, But why? Why do you lie to Johnny?

She said, Because I want him to be with me because of how we feel and who we are and not because we feel obliged to love.

The next day Deb needed to borrow five hangers.

Caro was not in her arms. Deb without Caro looked less grounded, less sure of herself. Even I felt unmoored.

Where's the baby? I asked.

With Johnny Rain, Deb said. He took him to the barber's for a haircut.

The barber's? He's eight months old. He doesn't even have hair.

Johnny needed to do some faux father-son bonding. They'll never come back. Or they'll return for the wrong reasons.

I pulled a couple of Darryl's crisp white serving shirts off two hangers and dropped them on the closet floor. I handed Deb five wire hangers.

How's the essay coming? Deb asked.

Slowly.

Read me something.

I started reading. "Appearing is a not-showing-itself—"

Deb interrupted. So did you tell Johnny?

Tell Johnny what?

You know, that Caro really is his baby.

Deb was squinting at me, searching my face.

It's none of my business, I said.

Then she asked if I had a pair of scissors. I found some heavy-duty shears. She was holding her thick braid in her hand.

She said, I want you to cut this off.

But why?

Because I need to know if Johnny loves me only for my hair.

Nobody loves someone because of hair, I said. And even if he does, at least he loves you. You don't test love, Deb, you don't question it.

She let the braid drop. She sighed. I better not. Last time I trimmed my hair Caro was inconsolable.

One day, Deb told me that Caro understood everything. I said, don't be paranoid, he's only a baby. But Caro seemed to be staring out the window, toward the teepee, in such a self-conscious way that I felt a chill run down my neck. Did he understand? I mean, not just phrases like *go potty* or *bad boy*, but concepts, circular concepts of loss and betrayal and identity and love?

We decided to test him.

I said, Dog. Caro didn't react at all.

Deb said, That's insulting, try something harder.

I said, Global warming.

Caro looked at me.

I continued. Is climate change a result of carbon emissions caused by human intervention or a naturally recurring phenomenon based on sunspots and earth tilt?

Caro yawned and closed his eyes.

Deb put her hands over his ears. She whispered, I need to borrow your car.

I handed her my car keys.

She whispered, It's Caro's eight-month birthday, I want to get him a xylophone.

But can he play with it? I asked. I mean with his arms pinned.

Probably not, she said sadly.

He's sleeping, I whispered. Why are we whispering?

He's not sleeping, he's pretending, she whispered.

Caro snored then, a small delicate snore. His mouth dropped open and a bit of dribble slipped down to his chin. Deb swooped it up with her thumb and put it in her mouth. Besides, I have to go to the doctor. I think I might be pregnant.

Caro yelped. His eyes flew open and darted around madly, looking for something to soothe him, and he finally focused on one of Darryl's large oil female nudes, very buxom. He immediately relaxed, closed his eyes, and apparently fell asleep. But he wasn't kidding anybody anymore.

He dreams about things you can't even imagine, Deb said.

What kind of things? I asked.

A lot of times I think he dreams that he's a rabbit.

Sure enough Caro's nose started to twitch, and Deb covered his ears and said, I told you he was faking.

I asked if he always struggled in his restraints and she said, Sometimes he's still, but I know he's only trying to trick me into believing he won't scratch. Regular babies can't feel pain you know, Deb said.

I wasn't so sure.

I mean they feel it, but they don't know where it's coming from. But Caro knows. He knows exactly where it's coming from.

Caro sneezed.

He's coming down with something, Deb said. I gotta get him in bed and put some onions in his socks to draw the fever.

I went to the cupboard. Is one enough? I asked.

Sure, she said and left with my car keys and one onion.

I phoned Darryl. I really needed to unload. The anniversary dinner, the cold fries, the fake blood, Johnny confronting the old people in their Indian suits, Heidegger, the onion. I was gonna tell Darryl I was ready for him to come home. I knew we could work it out. I missed him a lot. A lot, lot. He told me he was going out with Melanie, the bartender at Milestones.

That night I cried my eyes out, and the next and the next. I needed twenty minutes of teabags and ice cubes on my eyes before I could go to work. I thought about suicide. I thought about Europe. I thought about razors and pills and lighthouses in New Brunswick. I thought about climbing up the Angels Crest trail to the top of the Chief and jumping off. I wrote imaginary notes to Darryl: *Dear Darryl, Go fuck yourself.* I thought about all those nights he had stayed up late to cook pad Thai for me because he knew how sick I was of eating fried sweet potatoes at the restaurant.

Deb called to tell me the commercial was on. I hung up on her. I was getting a fever. I called Deb back and left a message, Where's my fucking onion? I felt hot and sweaty. My unit was so damp the walls leaked. A mushroom was growing in the corner of my rug.

I called in sick and the manager said, Oh don't even come back. I emailed my prof for a deadline extension. He emailed back, *R U serious?*

Then one day Johnny Rain phoned and said he needed me to babysit. Deb was running late, grooming a spoiled Shih

Tzu, and he was going to an anti-Olympics demonstration. I told him I was in no condition to babysit. He said he'd wash my windows in payment. I said, for chrissake I wouldn't charge you for it, I'm just saying I can't. I'm not reliable, I'm not safe to be around babies or sharp objects. He hung up.

I soaked in a burning hot bath. I cried and watched myself in the mirror, crying. I looked so good I couldn't figure it out. I hacked my hair off with the shears. I stuffed it all into a manila envelope and addressed it to Darryl. I wrote a note that said, *Here's a souvenir, Asshole. Love, Vivian.* I glanced over at Heidegger lying open on my desk. *Being-alone is a deficient mode of Being-with.* Then the light dimmed. I looked up to see Johnny Rain outside my window, standing on the top rung of an aluminum ladder, smearing sudsy water in a looping pattern on the pane. Caro was strapped on his back in a baby carrier, blinking at me through the smudged wet glass.

When I stepped outside later, on my front step were a box of Tampax with four missing, three quarters of an onion, my can opener, five hangers, my car keys, my skirt, my hairbrush. Even one fifty-nine-cent stamp.

Johnny Rain was sitting on his bike in the street, revving it. When he saw me, he took off. In their apartment Caro was seated on the floor, surrounded by puzzles and hammers, things that popped and whistled and dinged and swung. His arms were pinned to his sleeper and his face looked like a topographical map of Russia in pink. The TV was on, playing a tape of the beer commercial. Caro was staring at the commercial, watching his dad get passed over by the gorgeous babe because he was drinking the boring beer. Caro had a note pinned to his shirt that said, *Vivian, there's mashed avocado in the fridge for when I get hungry.*

I laid *Being and Time* on the floor, next to a pop-up Sesame Street toy thing.

I found the coffee I had lent Deb three weeks before, but no coffee maker. I sat on the floor next to Caro and watched the beer commercial, then rewound it and played it again. And again.

I told Caro about my plans to climb to the top of the Chief. I told him that cliffs were hard and air was thin and gravity was almighty. I explained to Caro that Darryl had semi-sorted out his sexuality and was now dating Melanie the bartender at Milestones. I told Caro how hard it was for me to even say her name out loud. I told Caro that it doesn't matter what beer you drink, it will never help you get the right girl. I told him that his mother was working late at Pet Fabulous and as soon as he was big enough she'd take him fishing on the ocean. I told him he'd outgrow his rash. I told him that the question of the meaning of Being must be formulated. I told him that it was snowing on top of the mountain, and what I wanted more than anything was to climb up the slope with my snowboard on my back and then stand at the top of fifteen hundred vertical metres and look away through the clouds to the Pacific in the distance and then slide and curl and bank down as fast and furious as I could until I was scared to high heaven and drenched in fine snow. I told him that Johnny Rain was his one true father. I told him Dasein always understands itself in terms of its existence, in terms of a possibility of itself: to be itself or not itself. I told him fear has three aspects: what we are afraid of; fearing; why we are afraid.

I unpinned Caro's arms.

When Deb came home she looked at Caro and said, Oh, you told him.

She started kissing Caro's wounded face and his eyes closed in feigned sleep or bliss, and when she lifted her head away from him and turned to me, her lips were bright and vivid with his blood, as if she had smeared them with lipstick, as if she were going somewhere.

ABOUT THE CONTRIBUTORS

Charlotte Bondy is from Toronto and has an M.Phil in Creative Writing from Trinity College Dublin. Her stories have appeared in *PRISM international* and *The Moth Magazine*. She is working on a collection of short fiction.

Emily Bossé completed her Master of Arts in English and Creative Writing at the University of New Brunswick in 2014. "Last Animal Standing on Gentleman's Farm" was her first piece of published fiction when it appeared in *The Fiddlehead*. Her first full-length play, *COCAINE PLANE!* was produced by The Next Folding Theater Company in March 2015. She is currently working on several plays and a collection of short stories entitled *Here Comes Happiness*.

Deirdre Dore writes fiction, poetry, and plays. Her work has appeared on stages and in literary journals, including *Geist*, *Prairie Fire*, and *The Malahat Review*, among others. Her story "Sappers Bridge" won the Western Magazine Award for Fiction. She holds a degree in psychology from Boston University and an M.F.A. in Creative Writing from UBC, where she completed a collection of short fiction. Originally from New York, she now lives in Nakusp, British Columbia, where she is revising her collection of stories and at work on a novella.

Charlie Fiset is a gold-miner's daughter from northern Ontario and a recent graduate of the University of New Brunswick's Creative Writing M.A. program, where she received the David

H. Walker Prize for prose. "Maggie's Farm" is her first print publication, but her story "If I Ever See the Sun" appears in *The Fiddlehead*'s 2015 summer fiction issue. She is currently at work on a Ph.D. in English at the University of New Brunswick.

K'ari Fisher was born in Burns Lake, British Columbia, and now lives in Victoria. She has worked as a Zodiac driver for a killer whale research group off the Pacific coast, and for forestry in the Skeena and Bulkley valleys. She is currently completing her final year of an M.F.A. in Creative Writing at the University of Victoria, where she is at work on a novel. Her short fiction has appeared in *The Malahat Review* and *Prairie Fire*.

Anna Ling Kaye reads and writes in Vancouver, where she is completing a short story collection and working on her first novel. A former prose editor at *PRISM international*, she is co-founder of Hapa-palooza Festival and sits on the board of Project Bookmark Canada. She is the editor of *Ricepaper* magazine.

Andrew MacDonald won a Western Magazine Award for Fiction, is shortlisted for a National Magazine Award for Fiction, and is a three-time finalist for the Journey Prize. He lives in Toronto and New England, where he's finishing a novel.

Lori McNulty's fiction was shortlisted for the 2014 Journey Prize. Her work has appeared in *The Fiddlehead*, *The New Quarterly*, *PRISM international*, *The Dalhousie Review*, *Descant*, and the *Globe and Mail*. She holds an M.F.A. in Creative Writing from the University of British Columbia and an M.A. from McGill University. She's just completed a short fiction collection and is at work on a novel. Please visit www.lorimcnulty.ca.

Madeleine Maillet is a writer and translator living in Montreal. She is also the fiction editor of *Cosmonauts Avenue*. A graduate of the University of Toronto, she is currently an M.A. candidate in English Literature at Concordia University.

Ron Schafrick's short fiction has appeared in *The Dalhousie Review*, *The Prairie Journal*, *The Antigonish Review*, *Asia Literary Review*, *FreeFall*, *The Toronto Quarterly*, *The Nashwaak Review*, *The New Quarterly*, *Plenitude*, and *Southern Humanities Review*. "Lovely Company" was also published in *Best Gay Stories 2015*. He is the author of *Interpreters* (Oberon Press, 2013) and is at work on a second collection of stories. For nine years he taught ESL in South Korea, but he currently lives in Toronto.

Sarah Meehan Sirk's short fiction has appeared in *The New Quarterly*, *PRISM international*, *Joyland*, *Room*, and *Taddle Creek*, where "Moonman" was first published. She studied math and philosophy at the University of Toronto, and was mentored by David Adams Richards at the Humber School for Writers. While not producing national programs for CBC Radio One, she's completing a collection of short stories and working on her first novel. She lives in Toronto with her young family.

Georgia Wilder completed a Ph.D. in seventeenth-century English literature. She teaches poetry and academic writing at the University of Toronto and hosts the monthly "Wild Writers" event at the Poetry Jazz Café in Kensington Market. She has been a feature poet at the Art Bar. "Cocoa Divine and the Lightning Police," first published in *Descant*, is part of a larger cycle of *fin-de-siècle* queer adventures set in disco-era Toronto.

For more information about the publications that submitted to this year's competition, The Journey Prize, and *The Journey Prize Stories*, please visit www.facebook.com/TheJourneyPrize.

For five decades, **Descant** was a quarterly journal publishing poetry, prose, fiction, interviews, travel pieces, letters, literary criticism, and visual art by new and established contemporary writers and artists from Canada and around the world. Editor: Karen Mulhallen. Managing Editor: Vera DeWaard. *Descant* ceased publication in early 2015.

The Fiddlehead, Atlantic Canada's longest-running literary journal, publishes poetry, short fiction, book reviews, and creative non-fiction. It appears four times a year, sponsors a contest for fiction and for poetry that awards a total of $5,000 in prizes, including the $2,000 Ralph Gustafson Poetry Prize and the $2,000 short fiction prize. *The Fiddlehead* welcomes all good writing in English, from anywhere, looking always for that element of freshness and surprise. Editor: Ross Leckie. Submissions and correspondence: *The Fiddlehead*, Campus House, 11 Garland Court, University of New Brunswick, P.O. Box 4400, Fredericton, New Brunswick, E3B 5A3. E-mail (queries only): fiddlehd@unb.ca Website: www.TheFiddlehead.ca Twitter: @TheFiddlehd You can also find *The Fiddlehead* on Facebook.

Geist is the Canadian magazine of ideas and culture—every issue brings together a sumptuous mix of fact and fiction, photography and comix, poetry, essays, and reviews, and the weird and wonderful from the world of words. The *Geist* tone is intelligent, plain-talking, inclusive, and offbeat. At the heart of our enterprise is the imaginary country that some of us inhabit from time to time, and which often has something to do with Canada. Editor-in-Chief: Michal Kozlowski. Submissions and correspondence: *Geist*, #210 – 111 West Hastings Street, Vancouver, British Columbia, V6B 1H4. E-mail: geist@geist.com Website: www.geist.com

The Impressment Gang is very excited to be celebrating its first birthday with its inclusion in this anthology. Our mandate is to be open, critical, and interactive with our community. We are proud of the stimulating and innovative work we publish, and believe that our contributing writers should be compensated deservingly for their art. Inspired by CWILA, we make a conscious effort toward nurturing an inclusive literary community. We welcome impressive new writing. Please find our first issue, in which Charlotte Bondy's "Renaude" is featured, on our website. Fiction Editor: Pearl Chan. Poetry Editor: Cassie Guinan. Submissions: submissions@theimpressmentgang.ca Correspondence: director@theimpressmentgang.ca Website: theimpressmentgang.ca

The Malahat Review is a quarterly journal of contemporary poetry, fiction, and creative non-fiction by both new and celebrated writers. Summer issues feature the winners of *Malahat*'s Novella and Long Poem prizes, held in alternate years; the fall issues feature the winners of the Far Horizons Award for emerging writers, alternating between poetry and fiction each year; the winter issues feature the winners of the Constance Rooke Creative Non-fiction Prize; and the spring issues feature winners of the Open Season Awards in all three genres (poetry, fiction, and creative non-fiction). All issues feature covers by noted Canadian visual artists and include reviews of Canadian books. Editor: John Barton. Assistant Editor: Rhonda Batchelor. Submissions and correspondence: *The Malahat Review*, University of Victoria, P.O. Box 1700, Station CSC, Victoria, British Columbia, V8W 2Y2. E-mail: malahat@uvic.ca Website: www. malahatreview.ca Twitter: @malahatreview

Matrix is a forty-year-old literary journal based in Montreal, Quebec, and housed at Concordia University. Published three times a year, *Matrix* features poetry, fiction, literary non-fiction, book and video game reviews. Editor: Jon Paul Fiorentino. Managing Editor: William Vallieres. Web Editor: Roxanna Bennett. Senior Editor: Jessica Marcotte. Art Director: Tyler Morency. Website: www.matrixmagazine.org

The New Quarterly is an award-winning literary magazine publishing fiction, poetry, personal essays, interviews, and essays on writing. Now in its thirty-fourth year, the magazine prides itself on its independent take on the Canadian literary scene. Recent issues include The War issue and the summer issue on Visual Storytelling, with more exciting projects in the works. Editor: Pamela Mulloy. Submissions and correspondence: *The New Quarterly*, c/o St. Jerome's University, 290 Westmount Road North, Waterloo, Ontario, N2L 3G3. E-mail: pmulloy@tnq.ca, sblom@tnq.ca Website: www.tnq.ca

Plenitude, Canada's queer literary magazine, publishes poetry, creative non-fiction, short fiction, book reviews, interviews, and other articles by both emerging and established LGBTQ writers, including Michael V. Smith, Ashley Little, John Barton, Lydia Kwa, Amber Dawn, and Betsy Warland. Now in its third year, it hosts an annual Emerging Writer Mentorship Award, which pairs one emerging queer Canadian writer with an established writer for one-on-one development of a manuscript. *Plenitude* aims to complicate expressions of queerness through the publication of diverse, sophisticated literary writing, from the very subtle to the brash and unrelenting. Founding Editor: Andrea Routley. Prose Editor: Anna Nobile. Poetry Editor: Matthew Walsh. Reviews Editor: Rachna Contractor. Copy Editor: Kathleen Fraser. E-mail: editor@plenitudemagazine.ca Website: www.plenitudemagazine.ca

Prairie Fire is a quarterly magazine of contemporary Canadian writing that publishes stories, poems, and literary non-fiction by both emerging and established writers. *Prairie Fire*'s editorial mix also occasionally features critical or personal essays. Stories published in *Prairie Fire* have won awards at the National Magazine Awards and the Western Magazine Awards. *Prairie Fire* publishes writing from, and has readers in, all parts of Canada. Editor: Andris Taskans. Fiction Editors: Warren Cariou and Heidi Harms. Submissions and correspondence: *Prairie Fire*, Room 423, 100 Arthur Street, Winnipeg, Manitoba, R3B 1H3. E-mail: prfire@mts.net Website: www.prairiefire.ca

PRISM international, the oldest literary magazine in Western Canada, was established in 1959 by Earle Birney at the University of British Columbia. Published four times a year, *PRISM* features short fiction, poetry, creative non-fiction, and translations. *PRISM* editors select work based on originality and quality, and the magazine showcases work from both new and established writers from Canada and around the world. *PRISM* holds three exemplary annual competitions for short fiction, literary non-fiction, and poetry, and awards the Earle Birney Prize for Poetry to an outstanding poet whose work was featured in *PRISM* in the preceding year. Executive Editors: Sierra Skye Gemma, Jennifer Lori, and Clara Kumagai. Prose Editor: Nicole Boyce. Poetry Editor: Rob Taylor. Submissions and correspondence: *PRISM international*, Creative Writing Program, The University of British Columbia, Buchanan E-462, 1866 Main Mall, Vancouver, British Columbia, V6T 1Z1. Website: www.prismmagazine.ca

Taddle Creek often is asked to define itself and, just as often, it tends to refuse to do so. But it will say this: each issue of the magazine contains a multitude of things between its snazzily illustrated covers, including, but not limited to, fiction, poetry, comics, art, interviews, and feature stories. It's an odd mix, to be sure, which is why *Taddle Creek* refers to itself somewhat oddly as a "general-interest literary magazine." Work presented in *Taddle Creek* is humorous, poignant, ephemeral, urban, and rarely overly earnest, though not usually all at once. *Taddle Creek* takes its mission to be the journal for those who detest everything the literary magazine has become in the twenty-first century very seriously. Editor-in-Chief: Conan Tobias. Correspondence: *Taddle Creek*, P.O. Box 611, Stn. P, Toronto, Ontario M5S 2Y4. E-mail: editor@taddlecreekmag.com. Website: taddlecreekmag.com.

Submissions were also received from the following publications:

The Antigonish Review
(Antigonish, NS)
www.antigonishreview.com

carte blanche
(Montreal, QC)
www.carte-blanche.org

Cosmonauts Avenue
(Montreal, QC)
www.cosmonautsavenue.com

The Dalhousie Review
(Halifax, NS)
www.dalhousiereview.dal.ca

EVENT
(New Westminster, BC)
www.eventmagazine.ca

filling Station
(Calgary, AB)
www.fillingstation.ca

Found Press Quarterly
www.foundpress.com

FreeFall Magazine
(Calgary, AB)
www.freefallmagazine.ca

Glass Buffalo
(Edmonton, AB)
www.glassbuffalo.com

The Humber Literary Review
(Toronto, ON)
www.humberliterary
review.com

Joyland Magazine
www.joylandmagazine.com

Little Brother Magazine
(Toronto, ON)
www.littlebrother
magazine.com

Little Fiction / Big Truths
(Toronto, ON)
www.littlefiction.com

Maple Tree Literary Supplement
(Ottawa, ON)
www.mtls.ca

The New Orphic Review
(Nelson, BC)
www3.telus.net/
neworphicpublishers-
hekkanen

One Throne Magazine
(Dawson City, YT)
www.onethrone.com

On Spec
(Edmonton, AB)
www.onspec.ca

The Overcast
(St. John's, NL)
www.theovercast.ca

*The Prairie Journal of
Canadian Literature*
(Calgary, AB)
www.prairiejournal.org

Pulp Literature
(Vancouver, BC)
www.pulpliterature.com

The Puritan
(Toronto, ON)
www.puritan-magazine.com

Queen's Quarterly
(Kingston, ON)
www.queensu.ca/quarterly

Ricepaper Magazine
(Vancouver, BC)
www.ricepapermagazine.ca

*Riddle Fence: A Journal of
Arts & Culture*
(St. John's, NL)
www.riddlefence.com

Room Magazine
(Vancouver, BC)
www.roommagazine.com

The Rusty Toque
(London, ON)
www.therustytoque.com

subTerrain Magazine
(Vancouver, BC)
www.subTerrain.ca

This Magazine
(Toronto, ON)
www.this.org

PREVIOUS CONTRIBUTING AUTHORS

* Winners of the $10,000 Journey Prize
** Co-winners of the $10,000 Journey Prize

Thomas King, "The Dog I Wish I Had, I Would Call It Helen"
K.D. Miller, "Sunrise Till Dark"
Jennifer Mitton, "Let Them Say"
Lawrence O'Toole, "Goin' to Town with Katie Ann"
Kenneth Radu, "A Change of Heart"
Jenifer Sutherland, "Table Talk"
Wayne Tefs, "Red Rock and After"

3
1991
SELECTED WITH JANE URQUHART

Donald Aker, "The Invitation"
Anton Baer, "Yukon"
Allan Barr, "A Visit from Lloyd"
David Bergen, "The Fall"
Rai Berzins, "Common Sense"
Diana Hartog, "Theories of Grief"
Diane Keating, "The Salem Letters"
Yann Martel, "The Facts Behind the Helsinki Roccamatios"*
Jennifer Mitton, "Polaroid"
Sheldon Oberman, "This Business with Elijah"
Lynn Podgurny, "Till Tomorrow, Maple Leaf Mills"
James Riseborough, "She Is Not His Mother"
Patricia Stone, "Living on the Lake"

4
1992
SELECTED WITH SANDRA BIRDSELL

David Bergen, "The Bottom of the Glass"
Maria A. Billion, "No Miracles Sweet Jesus"
Judith Cowan, "By the Big River"
Steven Heighton, "How Beautiful upon the Mountains"
Steven Heighton, "A Man Away from Home Has No Neighbours"
L. Rex Kay, "Travelling"
Rozena Maart, "No Rosa, No District Six"*
Guy Malet De Carteret, "Rainy Day"
Carmelita McGrath, "Silence"
Michael Mirolla, "A Theory of Discontinuous Existence"
Diane Juttner Perreault, "Bella's Story"
Eden Robinson, "Traplines"

5
1993
SELECTED WITH GUY VANDERHAEGHE

Caroline Adderson, "Oil and Dread"

David Bergen, "La Rue Prevette"

Marina Endicott, "With the Band"

Dayv James-French, "Cervine"

Michael Kenyon, "Durable Tumblers"

K.D. Miller, "A Litany in Time of Plague"

Robert Mullen, "Flotsam"

Gayla Reid, "Sister Doyle's Men"*

Oakland Ross, "Bang-bang"

Robert Sherrin, "Technical Battle for Trial Machine"

Carol Windley, "The Etruscans"

6
1994
SELECTED WITH DOUGLAS GLOVER;
JUDITH CHANT (CHAPTERS)

Anne Carson, "Water Margins: An Essay on Swimming by My Brother"

Richard Cumyn, "The Sound He Made"

Genni Gunn, "Versions"

Melissa Hardy, "Long Man the River"*

Robert Mullen, "Anomie"

Vivian Payne, "Free Falls"

Jim Reil, "Dry"

Robyn Sarah, "Accept My Story"

Joan Skogan, "Landfall"

Dorothy Speak, "Relatives in Florida"

Alison Wearing, "Notes from Under Water"

7
1995
SELECTED WITH M.G. VASSANJI;
RICHARD BACHMANN (A DIFFERENT DRUMMER BOOKS)

Michelle Alfano, "Opera"

Mary Borsky, "Maps of the Known World"

Gabriella Goliger, "Song of Ascent"

Elizabeth Hay, "Hand Games"

Shaena Lambert, "The Falling Woman"

Elise Levine, "Boy"

Roger Burford Mason, "The Rat-Catcher's Kiss"
Antanas Sileika, "Going Native"
Kathryn Woodward, "Of Marranos and Gilded Angels"*

8
1996
SELECTED WITH OLIVE SENIOR;
BEN McNALLY (NICHOLAS HOARE LTD.)

Rick Bowers, "Dental Bytes"
David Elias, "How I Crossed Over"
Elyse Gasco, "Can You Wave Bye Bye, Baby?"*
Danuta Gleed, "Bones"
Elizabeth Hay, "The Friend"
Linda Holeman, "Turning the Worm"
Elaine Littman, "The Winner's Circle"
Murray Logan, "Steam"
Rick Maddocks, "Lessons from the Sputnik Diner"
K.D. Miller, "Egypt Land"
Gregor Robinson, "Monster Gaps"
Alma Subasic, "Dust"

9
1997
SELECTED WITH NINO RICCI; NICHOLAS PASHLEY
(UNIVERSITY OF TORONTO BOOKSTORE)

Brian Bartlett, "Thomas, Naked"
Dennis Bock, "Olympia"
Kristen den Hartog, "Wave"
Gabriella Goliger, "Maladies of the Inner Ear"**
Terry Griggs, "Momma Had a Baby"
Mark Anthony Jarman, "Righteous Speedboat"
Judith Kalman, "Not for Me a Crown of Thorns"
Andrew Mullins, "The World of Science"
Sasenarine Persaud, "Canada Geese and Apple Chatney"
Anne Simpson, "Dreaming Snow"**
Sarah Withrow, "Ollie"
Terence Young, "The Berlin Wall"

10
1998

SELECTED BY PETER BUITENHUIS; HOLLEY RUBINSKY;
CELIA DUTHIE (DUTHIE BOOKS LTD.)

John Brooke, "The Finer Points of Apples"*

Ian Colford, "The Reason for the Dream"

Libby Creelman, "Cruelty"

Michael Crummey, "Serendipity"

Stephen Guppy, "Downwind"

Jane Eaton Hamilton, "Graduation"

Elise Levine, "You Are You Because Your Little Dog Loves You"

Jean McNeil, "Bethlehem"

Liz Moore, "Eight-Day Clock"

Edward O'Connor, "The Beatrice of Victoria College"

Tim Rogers, "Scars and Other Presents"

Denise Ryan, "Marginals, Vivisections, and Dreams"

Madeleine Thien, "Simple Recipes"

Cheryl Tibbetts, "Flowers of Africville"

11
1999

SELECTED BY LESLEY CHOYCE; SHELDON CURRIE;
MARY-JO ANDERSON (FROG HOLLOW BOOKS)

Mike Barnes, "In Florida"

Libby Creelman, "Sunken Island"

Mike Finigan, "Passion Sunday"

Jane Eaton Hamilton, "Territory"

Mark Anthony Jarman, "Travels into Several Remote Nations of the World"

Barbara Lambert, "Where the Bodies Are Kept"

Linda Little, "The Still"

Larry Lynch, "The Sitter"

Sandra Sabatini, "The One With the News"

Sharon Steams, "Brothers"

Mary Walters, "Show Jumping"

Alissa York, "The Back of the Bear's Mouth"*

12

2000

SELECTED BY CATHERINE BUSH; HAL NIEDZVIECKI; MARC GLASSMAN (PAGES BOOKS AND MAGAZINES)

Andrew Gray, "The Heart of the Land"

Lee Henderson, "Sheep Dub"

Jessica Johnson, "We Move Slowly"

John Lavery, "The Premier's New Pyjamas"

J.A. McCormack, "Hearsay"

Nancy Richler, "Your Mouth Is Lovely"

Andrew Smith, "Sightseeing"

Karen Solie, "Onion Calendar"

Timothy Taylor, "Doves of Townsend"*

Timothy Taylor, "Pope's Own"

Timothy Taylor, "Silent Cruise"

R.M. Vaughan, "Swan Street"

13

2001

SELECTED BY ELYSE GASCO; MICHAEL HELM; MICHAEL NICHOLSON (INDIGO BOOKS & MUSIC INC.)

Kevin Armstrong, "The Cane Field"*

Mike Barnes, "Karaoke Mon Amour"

Heather Birrell, "Machaya"

Heather Birrell, "The Present Perfect"

Craig Boyko, "The Gun"

Vivette J. Kady, "Anything That Wiggles"

Billie Livingston, "You're Taking All the Fun Out of It"

Annabel Lyon, "Fishes"

Lisa Moore, "The Way the Light Is"

Heather O'Neill, "Little Suitcase"

Susan Rendell, "In the Chambers of the Sea"

Tim Rogers, "Watch"

Margrith Schraner, "Dream Dig"

Daniel Griffin, "Mercedes Buyer's Guide"
Michael Kissinger, "Invest in the North"
Devin Krukoff, "The Last Spark"*
Elaine McCluskey, "The Watermelon Social"
William Metcalfe, "Nice Big Car, Rap Music Coming Out the Window"
Lesley Millard, "The Uses of the Neckerchief"
Adam Lewis Schroeder, "Burning the Cattle at Both Ends"
Michael V. Smith, "What We Wanted"
Neil Smith, "Isolettes"
Patricia Rose Young, "Up the Clyde on a Bike"

17
2005
SELECTED BY JAMES GRAINGER AND NANCY LEE

Randy Boyagoda, "Rice and Curry Yacht Club"
Krista Bridge, "A Matter of Firsts"
Josh Byer, "Rats, Homosex, Saunas, and Simon"
Craig Davidson, "Failure to Thrive"
McKinley M. Hellenes, "Brighter Thread"
Catherine Kidd, "Green-Eyed Beans"
Pasha Malla, "The Past Composed"
Edward O'Connor, "Heard Melodies Are Sweet"
Barbara Romanik, "Seven Ways into Chandigarh"
Sandra Sabatini, "The Dolphins at Sainte Marie"
Matt Shaw, "Matchbook for a Mother's Hair"*
Richard Simas, "Anthropologies"
Neil Smith, "Scrapbook"
Emily White, "Various Metals"

18
2006
SELECTED BY STEVEN GALLOWAY;
ZSUZSI GARTNER; ANNABEL LYON

Heather Birrell, "BriannaSusannaAlana"*
Craig Boyko, "The Baby"
Craig Boyko, "The Beloved Departed"
Nadia Bozak, "Heavy Metal Housekeeping"
Lee Henderson, "Conjugation"
Melanie Little, "Wrestling"
Matthew Rader, "The Lonesome Death of Joseph Fey"
Scott Randall, "Law School"

Sarah Selecky, "Throwing Cotton"
Damian Tarnopolsky, "Sleepy"
Martin West, "Cretacea"
David Whitton, "The Eclipse"
Clea Young, "Split"

19
2007
SELECTED BY CAROLINE ADDERSON;
DAVID BEZMOZGIS; DIONNE BRAND

Andrew J. Borkowski, "Twelve Versions of Lech"
Craig Boyko, "OZY"*
Grant Buday, "The Curve of the Earth"
Nicole Dixon, "High-Water Mark"
Krista Foss, "Swimming in Zanzibar"
Pasha Malla, "Respite"
Alice Petersen, "After Summer"
Patricia Robertson, "My Hungarian Sister"
Rebecca Rosenblum, "Chilly Girl"
Nicholas Ruddock, "How Eunice Got Her Baby"
Jean Van Loon, "Stardust"

20
2008
SELECTED BY LYNN COADY; HEATHER O'NEILL; NEIL SMITH

Théodora Armstrong, "Whale Stories"
Mike Christie, "Goodbye Porkpie Hat"
Anna Leventhal, "The Polar Bear at the Museum"
Naomi K. Lewis, "The Guiding Light"
Oscar Martens, "Breaking on the Wheel"
Dana Mills, "Steaming for Godthab"
Saleema Nawaz, "My Three Girls"*
Scott Randall, "The Gifted Class"
S. Kennedy Sobol, "Some Light Down"
Sarah Steinberg, "At Last at Sea"
Clea Young, "Chaperone"

21
2009
SELECTED BY CAMILLA GIBB;
LEE HENDERSON; REBECCA ROSENBLUM

Daniel Griffin, "The Last Great Works of Alvin Cale"

Jesus Hardwell, "Easy Living"

Paul Headrick, "Highlife"

Sarah Keevil, "Pyro"

Adrian Michael Kelly, "Lure"

Fran Kimmel, "Picturing God's Ocean"

Lynne Kutsukake, "Away"

Alexander MacLeod, "Miracle Mile"

Dave Margoshes, "The Wisdom of Solomon"

Shawn Syms, "On the Line"

Sarah L. Taggart, "Deaf"

Yasuko Thanh, "Floating Like the Dead"*

22
2010
SELECTED BY PASHA MALLA; JOAN THOMAS; ALISSA YORK

Carolyn Black, "Serial Love"

Andrew Boden, "Confluence of Spoors"

Laura Boudreau, "The Dead Dad Game"

Devon Code, "Uncle Oscar"*

Danielle Egan, "Publicity"

Krista Foss, "The Longitude of Okay"

Lynne Kutsukake, "Mating"

Ben Lof, "When in the Field with Her at His Back"

Andrew MacDonald, "Eat Fist!"

Eliza Robertson, "Ship's Log"

Mike Spry, "Five Pounds Short and Apologies to Nelson Algren"

Damian Tarnopolsky, "Laud We the Gods"

23
2011
SELECTED BY ALEXANDER MACLEOD;
ALISON PICK; SARAH SELECKY

Jay Brown, "The Girl from the War"

Michael Christie, "The Extra"

Seyward Goodhand, "The Fur Trader's Daughter"

Miranda Hill, "Petitions to Saint Chronic"*

Fran Kimmel, "Laundry Day"
Ross Klatte, "First-Calf Heifer"
Michelle Serwatuk, "My Eyes Are Dim"
Jessica Westhead, "What I Would Say"
Michelle Winters, "Toupée"
D.W. Wilson, "The Dead Roads"

24
2012
SELECTED BY MICHAEL CHRISTIE;
KATHRYN KUITENBROUWER; KATHLEEN WINTER

Kris Bertin, "Is Alive and Can Move"
Shashi Bhat, "Why I Read *Beowulf*"
Astrid Blodgett, "Ice Break"
Trevor Corkum, "You Were Loved"
Nancy Jo Cullen, "Ashes"
Kevin Hardcastle, "To Have to Wait"
Andrew Hood, "I'm Sorry and Thank You"
Andrew Hood, "Manning"
Grace O'Connell, "The Many Faces of Montgomery Clift"
Jasmina Odor, "Barcelona"
Alex Pugsley, "Crisis on Earth-X"*
Eliza Robertson, "Sea Drift"
Martin West, "My Daughter of the Dead Reeds"

25
2013
SELECTED BY MIRANDA HILL;
MARK MEDLEY; RUSSELL WANGERSKY

Steven Benstead, "Megan's Bus"
Jay Brown, "The Egyptians"
Andrew Forbes, "In the Foothills"
Philip Huynh, "Gulliver's Wife"
Amy Jones, "Team Ninja"
Marnie Lamb, "Mrs. Fujimoto's Wednesday Afternoons"
Doretta Lau, "How Does a Single Blade of Grass Thank the Sun?"
Laura Legge, "It's Raining in Paris"
Natalie Morrill, "Ossicles"
Zoey Leigh Peterson, "Sleep World"
Eliza Robertson, "My Sister Sang"
Naben Ruthnum, "Cinema Rex"*

26

2014

SELECTED BY STEVEN W. BEATTIE;
CRAIG DAVIDSON; SALEEMA NAWAZ

Rosaria Campbell, "Probabilities"

Nancy Jo Cullen, "Hashtag Maggie Vandermeer"

M.A. Fox, "Piano Boy"

Kevin Hardcastle, "Old Man Marchuk"

Amy Jones, "Wolves, Cigarettes, Gum"

Tyler Keevil, "Sealskin"*

Jeremy Lanaway, "Downturn"

Andrew MacDonald, "Four Minutes"

Lori McNulty, "Monsoon Season"

Shana Myara, "Remainders"

Julie Roorda, "How to Tell if Your Frog Is Dead"

Leona Theis, "High Beams"

Clea Young, "Juvenile"